She stepped from behind a crystal formation in the frozen-food aisle and walked toward him, just as beautiful as she was in his comic books.

"Dad!" Dusty said urgently. "Dad! That's her!"

"That's who?" asked his dad with a sigh.

"The Sun Queen! Isn't she beautiful, Dad?"

"The Sun...?"

Dusty could tell by the way his dad couldn't finish his sentence—and by the way his mouth was hanging open—that he, too, thought the Sun Queen was beautiful.

Dusty knew he needed to act fast...or the Sun Queen might get away! He maneuvered his spacecraft around the bend and raced off in hot pursuit—his dad close on his heels.

The next thing Dusty knew, his spaceship was crashing into a display and the Sun Queen was going down with it...in his dad's arms!

ABOUT THE AUTHOR

A native of Massachusetts, Muriel now lives in Astoria, Oregon, with her husband who is also a writer, two calico cats and a malamute named Deadline. She has three grown children. Muriel loves investigating restaurants and dress shops in the interest of research.

Books by Muriel Jensen

HARLEQUIN AMERICAN ROMANCE

Don't miss any of our special offers. Write to us at the following address for information on our newest releases.

Harlequin Reader Service
U.S.: 3010 Walden Ave., P.O. Box 1325, Buffalo, NY 14269
Canadian: P.O. Box 609, Fort Erie, Ont. L2A 5X3

MURIEL JENSEN

THE COURTSHIP OF DUSTY'S DADDY

Harlequin Books

TORONTO • NEW YORK • LONDON
AMSTERDAM • PARIS • SYDNEY • HAMBURG
STOCKHOLM • ATHENS • TOKYO • MILAN
MADRID • WARSAW • BUDAPEST • AUCKLAND

If you purchased this book without a cover you should be aware that this book is stolen property. It was reported as "unsold and destroyed" to the publisher, and neither the author nor the publisher has received any payment for this "stripped book."

To the bouquet of ladies at Astoria Florist:
Dorothy, Evelyn, Beryl, Dorothy & Carol

ISBN 0-373-16569-2

THE COURTSHIP OF DUSTY'S DADDY

Copyright © 1995 by Muriel Jensen.

All rights reserved. Except for use in any review, the reproduction or utilization of this work in whole or in part in any form by any electronic, mechanical or other means, now known or hereafter invented, including xerography, photocopying and recording, or in any information storage or retrieval system, is forbidden without the written permission of the publisher, Harlequin Enterprises Limited, 225 Duncan Mill Road, Don Mills, Ontario, Canada M3B 3K9.

All characters in this book have no existence outside the imagination of the author and have no relation whatsoever to anyone bearing the same name or names. They are not even distantly inspired by any individual known or unknown to the author, and all incidents are pure invention.

This edition published by arrangement with Harlequin Enterprises B.V.

® and TM are trademarks of the publisher. Trademarks indicated with ® are registered in the United States Patent and Trademark Office, the Canadian Trade Marks Office and in other countries.

Printed in U.S.A.

Chapter One

Burn Starby turned his spacefighter into the narrow canyon and activated his alien locater. The blip roved the monitor, then Alert! flashed, filling the screen with its bright red warning.

Cool as ice, Burn pressed for coordinates and placed his thumb on the nuke trigger.

"Closing fast," the computer warned him. "Twenty miles, fifteen, ten . . ."

Burn looked left, then right. Walls of merciless granite closed him in on both sides.

"Five, four . . ."

Burn stood his space. He had no choice. He had to make the world safe from the Green Menace.

"Three, two . . ."

Nerves of steel steadying his hand, Burn fired. The atmosphere around his craft exploded with flames and sound. Pow! Pow!

"POW! POW!" DUSTY ARCHER cried. "Take that, you ugly Green Menace."

"Dusty." Shane Archer reached down to the floor for the pound of broccoli that had been ejected from his shopping cart. "Knock it off. I don't care how many times you shoot it, we're having broccoli with our chicken tonight, and that's final.''

He smoothed the edges of the edict with a smile. "If you want to grow big and strong to join the space program, you need iron. Broccoli's loaded with it.''

His six-year-old son, sitting in the cart among the groceries, looked up at him with wide brown eyes under shaggy dark hair. In the boy's hands was a homemade weapon Shane had helped him make to resemble the "crud creamer" carried by his idol on Saturday morning cartoons—Burn Starby, Space Ranger.

"Broccoli's gross. Doesn't anything else have iron in it?''

"Yes," Shane replied. "Liver.''

Dusty made an impossible face and leaned an elbow against a ten-pound bag of potatoes. "Fernando was making Spicy Wings and Fried Cheese when I came home from school," he said with a windy sigh. "Can't we eat in the restaurant, or call room service?''

Shane wondered, not for the first time, what growing up in hotels was doing to his son's development. When other children were just gaining their feet in the outside world, his son knew how to order room service, call a cab, check the arrival time of a commuter flight, and charm a housemaid into leaving three mints on his pillow rather than one.

Shane shook his head resolutely. "No. I'm off tonight, and I want to relax over dinner and hear all about what happened at school today.''

"Wouldn't you relax better," Dusty asked hopefully, "if Fernando sent up dinner?''

Shane had to admire the child's determination. "No. I'd relax better if you helped me fix it." He added as a concession, "We'll put cheese on the broccoli.''

Shane was treated to another gusty sigh. Dusty never gave up without theatrics.

BURN CONGRATULATED himself on the last-minute decision to find a peaceful solution to the problem of the Green Menace. Taking them aboard to view his superior weaponry seemed to have calmed them, and he was able to concentrate on the primary purpose of his mission.

He brought the spacefighter into Aisle Six for a landing, and adjusted his breathing apparatus for the unfamiliar environment. He opened the craft's security door and scanned the cold and craggy landscape.

Then he saw her—the Sun Queen. She stepped from behind a crystal formation and walked toward him, as beautiful as he remembered her from their last meeting on Potter-1. Her hair, like Rigel gold, and her midnight-blue garment glistened in the moonglow. She moved gracefully, stopping to study one of Aisle Six's many interesting ice column displays.

She was the one. He was sure. He had to make it clear to the Mission Master.

SHANE JUGGLED the half gallon of cherry-chocolate icecream as Dusty yanked hard on his arm.

"Dad!" the boy said urgently. "Dad! That's her!"

Shane looked up from the refrigerated case and spotted a full-figured woman in a plastic raincoat trying to make a decision between ice milk and yogurt. "Who?" he asked.

Dusty yanked on him again and said in a stage whisper, "Not her. *Her!* The Sun Queen!"

"The Sun...?" Then he saw her, studying the label on a jar of ice-cream topping.

She was beautiful. He could see where Dusty's fertile imagination had cast her in the role of one of his favorite Saturday morning cartoon characters.

Curly, golden hair rioted around her face and skimmed her eyebrows. Raindrops on the shoulders of her dark blue trench coat glistened under the fluorescent lights, making her look like something that had tumbled from a distant galaxy.

The lady in the plastic raincoat looked in her direction, recognized her and called a greeting. The Sun Queen gave her a warm, cheerful smile.

"Isn't she beautiful?" Dusty asked, his eyes wide and lovesick. Then he raised his arm as though to wave.

Shane quickly pushed the cart down a side aisle, past candies and nuts, and turned into cereal and grains, circumventing a tall display of puffed rice in giant bags.

"Da-ad!" Dusty complained, still holding tightly to both sides of the cart.

"I know, I'm sorry," Shane said, leaning into it to excavate his child from the avalanche of groceries. "I just don't want to meet anybody at the moment, okay? She *is* very pretty, and I'm sure she's very nice, but I've had a rough day, and all I want to do is get home."

Dusty looked at him as though he'd grown a third eye, wondering, he was sure, what could be so difficult about meeting a beautiful woman his son obviously considered special.

What Dusty wouldn't remember was that today would have been his mother's thirtieth birthday, and she'd been on Shane's mind—and in his heart—since the moment he awoke. The grief he'd thought he'd finally dealt with and put away had waged a day-long battle to reassert itself.

He'd moved from Hawaii to Merriwether, Oregon, to escape the many matchmaking efforts of his family and friends. And in the six weeks he'd been here, he'd studiously avoided his hotel staff members and patrons who gave him long, suggestive looks.

It wasn't that he didn't want to find someone again. It was that his ability to love and give to a woman had died with Allie. His mother-in-law said that would change with time, but he knew it wouldn't. He adored his son, loved Allie's family and his friends—that was enough. He couldn't stand it when Dusty gave him that downcast look of bitter disappointment. So against all the rules of parenting, he found himself trying to bargain back his approval.

"Why don't we try that monster cereal stuff you were talking about?" He began scouring the shelves for it. "What's it called?"

Dusty sighed. Shane smiled grimly to himself, thinking if he didn't get it together tonight, the kid was going to hyperventilate. "Monster Munchies," Dusty said, as though he didn't care. His arms were now folded, his lip protruding in a pout. It became imperative that Shane find the cereal. He wandered several feet away from the cart in his desperate search.

BURN THREW THE communicator to the ground. He couldn't reach the Mission Master through the ion storm. As the Sun Queen paused to peer inside a cave, Burn realized she was in danger. If he let her explore the cave unattended, she could be lost forever down one of the water channels. Or, worse, she could be found by the Cave Conqueror. He couldn't let that happen.

He freed the Moon Wheel from the side of his craft and raced off in pursuit.

A PIERCING SHRIEK was followed by a loud crash, then the sound of Dusty's voice at high register. "Da-ad!"

Shane turned in the grip of parental dread. The neatly stacked display of puffed cereal now covered the floor several feet deep and had acquired . . . feet? Shane dropped the box of Monster Munchies and covered the short distance in four long strides.

The wheels of his shopping cart protruded from the mess, still spinning. Sticking straight up beside one of them was a small, familiar high-topped tennis shoe. It was wiggling sufficiently to assure him that the child attached to it was fine.

"Dusty!" Shane exclaimed in exasperation as he reached into the pile. He caught a fistful of nylon he presumed to be Dusty's jacket, and pulled. A high-pitched scream then exploded from the mound of cereal bags as the head and torso of a woman emerged, causing a flow of bags in all directions. It was the Sun Queen. And he had her by the front of her silky blouse. A pearly button at her neck parted, and he caught a glimpse of something lacy and pink barely covering small, round ivory breasts.

"Oh, God," he muttered, dropping her instantly. But she clung to him with both hands as she began to sink into the slithering pile of bags. He widened his stance and pulled, applying too much muscle.

She flew out of the pile and into him, colliding with his chest. He was aware of a disturbing sensory impression of those beautiful breasts against his shirtfront. She blinked dark blue eyes and pushed out of his arms. Attached to the tail of her coat was his son.

"Hi, Sonny!" Dusty said, rising up beside her. "It's me. Dusty!"

"Yes," she said, with a quick, embarrassed glance at Shane. "I remember. You're pretty unforgettable."

"Is everyone all right?" a large, stout man in a red apron asked. His badge read "BAILEY, Produce." Shane noticed that they'd collected a small crowd. When Dusty and the Sun Queen nodded, Bailey asked in concern, "What happened? I built that display myself. It was solid."

Dusty studiously avoided Shane's eyes, then opened his mouth, as though prepared to offer an explanation. Shane, who'd had previous experience with Dusty's invisible Martian probes, began to apologize. But he was interrupted by the Sun Queen.

She reached into the pile of bags to right the cart. "I was...um...looking for fat-free granola," she said in the most unconvincing lie he'd ever heard. "And spotted my friend here..." She put a hand on Dusty's dark hair. He leaned into her waist like a love-struck puppy. "And, well, I'm afraid I wasn't watching where I was going."

Bailey wanted to believe her; Shane could see it in his face. But he also seemed to be struggling with the basic laws of physics. "But I had weighted the base. I mean, you'd have had to be doing fifty—"

"I was!" she said, her eyes wide and eager as she warmed to her tale. They were winter-sky blue, he noticed. "I was rushing to get groceries to make it home in time for the news. I'm so sorry about this mess. I'll clean it right up."

She got down on her knees to do just that. Dusty, whose room always looked like this beleaguered aisle, helped her.

"No, please. That won't be necessary." Bailey beckoned two young men in aprons who appeared at the head of the aisle. "We'll take care of it."

Dusty and the Sun Queen were ignoring him, and Bailey turned to Shane for help. "Please, sir. I'll clean up. Just help the lady sort through for your groceries and I'll take care of everything else." Then he added with polite severity, "It might be wiser to push the cart yourself."

One of the stock boys began piling the fallen bags and grinned broadly at Dusty. "That was cool, Dude," he said. "Saw you from the check stand. Too bad these carts don't have brakes or that'd be a good technique for 'The Shopping Challenge.' Next time don't push off so hard."

Dusty accepted his high five, then winced up at Shane.

Shane met his look with one of disapproval, then turned his attention to the Sun Queen.

SONNY WINSLOW thought that Dustin Archer's father looked like an ad for Giorgio Armani. He was tall and lean, shoulders athletically broad in a dark suit. And muscular. She'd just learned that detail firsthand. A gray wool scarf was wrapped around his neck.

He had rich brown hair that was side-parted with just a suggestion of curl, and eyes as deep and dark as his son's.

Despite the lean elegance of his attire, the man's angular cheekbones, strong nose and square jaw suggested Monday night football or sunny afternoons in a hammock.

He was the last thing she had ever expected to see on a Wednesday night in the Merriwether Market.

"You're sure you're all right?" he asked her. He had pulled her along with his son into the side aisle.

"I'm fine," she said, looking down at herself, then quickly buttoned her blouse, pulled her coat around her and belted it. She gave him an embarrassed half smile, but either he hadn't noticed her northern exposure, or he didn't want to discuss it.

"What happened?" he asked. He reached down to turn Dusty from a perusal of the candy bars behind him.

"I'm not sure," she admitted, glad that she'd seen nothing that would get Dusty in trouble—even though she suspected their collision had been deliberate. "I turned around just in time to see your cart come flying toward me. Next thing I knew, Dusty and I were covered in Fruity Puffs."

Dusty grinned. "That was cool."

His father gave him a quick glance that quelled him.

"Did you deliberately aim for the Sun Que—"

Sonny eyed him curiously as he stopped himself, closed his eyes, drew a breath.

"Who?" she asked.

"Her name's Sonny, Dad," Dusty said. "She's a friend of Miss Potter's. She came to school to show us how to put flowers in a pumpkin for Halloween. She owns a flower store."

Sonny offered her hand and a smile, forgetting whatever that was he'd called her. She was anxious to divert the man's parental gravity. *Fathers and mothers should be required to have a sense of humor,* she thought. "Sonnet Winslow," she said, closing her slender fingers around his large, square hand. "My mother was an English teacher who loved Shakespeare, so I have this bizarre name. I've always been grateful she wasn't partial to Falstaff or Macduff.''

He wanted to smile; she could see it in his eyes. But he held back. ''Shane Archer,'' he said, shaking her hand. Apparently determined to handle the immediate problem, he began again. ''I apologize. You could have been . . .''

She tried again to change the topic. ''Don't tell me. *Your* mother was probably a fan of Alan Ladd. My brother is. I've seen *Shane* so many times . . .''

He shook his head and replied politely. ''It was my mother's maiden name.'' His gaze sharpened on her and he asked quietly, ''Are you through trying to take the heat off Dusty, and ready to give me a straight answer?''

Well, she thought, feeling a huff begin to billow inside her. A moment ago she'd looked up at him from the pile of Fruity Puffs, seen those wonderful dark eyes and felt that strong, steady hand and imagined that kismet had touched her cheek. But she'd been wrong.

''The simple truth,'' she replied coolly, ''is that you shouldn't leave a child unattended in a shopping cart.''

Shane's temper flared. Under normal circumstances, it took a lot to make him angry. But his parenting skills had been questioned twice in the space of five minutes. First Bailey, and now her. The single-parent guilt syndrome made him sensitive—particularly since he'd recently moved his child several thousand miles away from the only home he'd ever known.

''He was *not* unattended,'' he replied tightly. ''I was only a few feet away.''

''That was all it took, wasn't it?''

''It wasn't Dad's fault,'' Dusty interrupted staunchly. Shane was thinking he would have to praise him later for his loyalty, when the traitor added ingenuously, "We snuck down this aisle 'cause he didn't want to meet you on account'a he had a bad day and he wants to go home."

She stared at him for a long moment, her cheeks pink, her eyes angry and...hurt. Yes, he saw it just before she lowered her lashes. When she looked up at him again, she was completely composed.

"I understand," she said, with a completely false smile. "Frankly, I enjoyed meeting Dusty in Terri's class, but I wasn't particularly anxious to meet you. I live on the bay and used to have a beautiful view of the herons and the ducks who lived there until the Coast Convention Center parked itself in my front yard and displaced them."

The warmth he'd noticed first about her had changed to a chilling frost. "Yes," he said, "I know all about the Wetland Warriors. My father-in-law was kept apprised of your efforts to stop us from building here."

She shook her head. "I wasn't a warrior. They were a little too militant for me. But I wrote letters to the council, to your father-in-law, and to the State Land Board. Yet," she said with a sigh, "here you are." She smiled at Dusty. "I guess some good came of losing my view. I got to meet your son."

Dusty grinned from ear to ear. Shane truly wished he'd listened to him and called room service. The last thing he needed today was to fight the eternal ecology vs. economy battle with a woman who was now looking at him as though he were pool algae.

Yet he certainly understood how she felt.

"I'm sorry about your view," he said sincerely. "And you know, I'm sure, that the herons and ducks are safely relocated."

They had been—a distance upriver that prevented her from enjoying them on a daily basis. But Dusty was watching her and his father, and hanging on their every word. She decided to end the encounter peacefully.

"It was nice to meet you, Mr. Archer," she said pleasantly, then smiled down at the boy. "Did you get your pumpkin yet, Dusty?"

Dusty gave Shane a forbearing glance that made him feel old. "Dad says if we get it too early it'll die."

"It'll survive beautifully," she said, looking into Shane Archer's deep, dark eyes, "as long as you don't carve it until a few days before Halloween. Then you can enjoy it for weeks."

He knew that. It was just that Allie loved autumn and always had pumpkins everywhere throughout the season. And finding them in Honolulu had not been that easy.

Sonny realized that he'd tuned her out. That was fine; she was more interested in his son, anyway.

"Or," she said cheerfully to Dusty, "you can come to the shop and pick out one of mine. It'll be my present to officially welcome *you* to Merriwether."

Shane knew she purposely left him out of her welcome-to-town speech.

Dusty gave Shane's hand a yank. "Can we, Dad? Can we go to Sonny's shop?"

He wanted to think of an excuse, but Dusty was staring at him, all wide-eyed and eager, and she seemed to be waiting for him to forbid him to go.

"It's right next door to the hotel," she said. "You can send him by himself and watch him from the parking lot if you'd rather not come."

He looked her in the eye. "Thank you, Miss Winslow. *We'll* stop by tomorrow afternoon."

"I'll be expecting you, Mr. Archer." She pinched Dusty's chin and walked away.

Shane went back to the cart and found that Bailey had rebuilt his Fruity Puffs tower.

Chastened and apparently displeased with how his plan to introduce the Sun Queen to his father had gone, Dusty held on to the side of the cart as Shane made his way to the checkout.

BURN WATCHED THE Sun Queen disappear into the cavern. He revved his Moon Wheel, intent on following her inside, but he bounced back from the entrance and fell onto his back, the Wheel crashing beside him.

Damn! A shadow shield! Burn swallowed his disappointment, dusted himself off and dragged his Wheel back to the ship for repairs.

Chapter Two

Sonny loved the excitement of the hotel as much as she disliked its location on the same bay she'd grown up to think of as hers. From her living room window, it was an obstruction and an intrusion, but when she stood in the lobby and people bustled around her coming and going, she felt its energy.

With her shop right next door, she came into the hotel's coffee shop for a quick break every day. She'd never particularly wanted to travel, but from her remote little base on the Oregon coast, it was exciting to glimpse a broader world when she was in the hotel.

She went to the front desk with the fresh pumpkin she'd hollowed out and filled with champagne tea roses, red rover, copper mums, red carnations and Oregonia. She was doing this for Dusty, she told herself. He'd been so fascinated by the pumpkin vases she'd created when she'd visited Terri Potter's class. His father *had* said he'd bring him by the shop to pick one up in response to her offer, but she suspected he hadn't been sincere. And if he had been—she wasn't sure she wanted his tall, dark presence filling her small shop.

"Good afternoon." The desk clerk, a young woman in a brocade vest and frilly white blouse smiled at Sonny over the long highly polished oak desk.

"Hi," Sonny began. "Would you please have this delivered to... ?"

"Oh, God! I've overslept!" A very large man in a three-piece suit elbowed Sonny aside. "Can you get me a cab to the airport, *call* Triangle Air and book me on the next flight to Seattle?"

With an apologetic glance at her, the clerk began punching numbers into the computer for the desperate guest.

Sonny moved to the other end of the desk. A gray-haired male desk clerk, in a brocade vest over a white shirt, was dealing with a very frazzled middle-aged woman. Clustered around her, looking worried, were a dozen teenage girls in the plaid uniforms of a private school.

"What do you mean, we aren't in the computer?" the woman was asking.

Clutching the pumpkin to her, Sonny turned away from the counter in search of a bellman. One was coming toward her pushing a wheelchair.

"Excuse me," she said. "I know you're busy, but I have something for Mr. Archer. Is there someone who... ?"

He smiled and pointed behind him to the elevators. "Suite B, top floor."

"But, I..."

He was gone, racing toward the door to the parking lot, riding the back of the wheelchair as if it were a scooter.

The elevator doors parted. Sonny stared at the empty car. The last thing she had wanted to do was make a

personal delivery to Shane Archer's suite. But she did
want Dusty to have the pumpkin she'd specially prepared for him with its pop-up ghost wearing a space
helmet and pointing a laser gun. Terri had told her he
loved anything to do with outer space.

Sonny stepped onto the elevator and stabbed the
button for the top floor. Undoubtedly, Dusty's father
would be on duty in the middle of the afternoon, closed
in the rarefied atmosphere of the hotel's administrative
office. She would find someone from Housekeeping,
and ask them to put the pumpkin in his suite.

She followed the blue-and-silver carpeting around a
bend in the hallway to an abrupt curve that concealed
suites A and B, which sat across from each other, in a
private little pocket of the floor. A Housekeeping cart
stood in the middle of the hall, and the sound of vacuuming came from the slightly open door of Shane
Archer's suite. Good. She would put the pumpkin in the
capable hands of the housekeeper and get back to the
shop where Denise was probably wondering what had
happened to her.

She rapped on the door. There was no answer.

She knocked again and peered around it. "Hello?
Hello?"

Still no answer. But the sound of vacuuming was
coming from beyond the tidy living area. She followed
it cautiously, the sound growing louder as she passed a
child's room that was knee-deep in toys.

She rounded a corner, a smile of greeting ready for
the housekeeper, who probably wouldn't hear her approach over the noise.

She made two discoveries simultaneously. The hum-
ming sound of rushing air was not a vacuum at all, but
a blow-dryer. And her tracking had not produced the

housekeeper but Shane Archer himself—wrapped in a towel and standing before his bathroom mirror.

She had only a moment to stare in openmouthed shock—combined with a tingling fascination. Last night, the Armani suit had been impressive, but what lived under it was *much* more pleasurable to view. She saw only the back of him, but it was enough to make her heart stall.

His shoulders were thick and strong. Deeply tanned skin covered muscles that rippled as he moved the blow-dryer in a careless sweep with one hand while ruffling his thick crop of glistening dark hair with the other.

His back tapered to a neat waist around which was wrapped a stark white hotel towel. She saw the outline of slim, taut buttocks on which the royal blue "CCC" monogram rested like a brand. Then below the towel, two long, slender and gracefully muscled legs were firmly planted several feet apart.

The trickle of water over her arm made her realize that she was tipping the pumpkin in her wide-eyed perusal of Shane Archer's body. She tried to right it at the same moment that he discovered her reflection and spun around. Startled, she lost her grip on the arrangement and juggled it as it slipped from her grasp.

SHANE WAS NOT surprised to see the Sun Queen's face reflected in his mirror. He'd tossed restlessly most of the night, and had finally fallen asleep just before dawn. But Dusty had awakened him when room service arrived with breakfast and had talked about Sonnet Winslow nonstop until he'd dropped him off at school.

He supposed that was why she was on his mind throughout the morning while he'd dealt with various problems that were part of his job as hotel manager. But that didn't explain what she was doing in his bath-room!

He turned and found a pumpkin coming at him. He dodged it just as Sonny lunged forward to intercept it. Her chin collided with his shoulder, her heel slipped in the spilled water and she screamed as she felt herself lose traction.

Shane caught the pumpkin in one hand, and Sonny in the other, and was about to congratulate himself on his dexterity when he, too, slipped in the spilled water.

The three of them went down in an awkward tum-ble—with Sonny sprawled across Shane and the pump-kin landing miraculously upright and sound.

Then unbelievably—before there was even a mo-ment to regain breath and composure—the sound of a female voice floated toward the bathroom. "Shane? Shane, darling?"

He let his head fall against the tile floor with a thud. "No," he groaned in a whisper. "Oh, no."

It all began to click for Sonny. The reason Shane Archer had showered in the middle of the afternoon—the honeyed voice calling "darling." He and the woman she'd yet to meet had planned an assignation. She closed her eyes at her own naïveté. And *she'd* thought an autumn arrangement in a pumpkin would make his afternoon.

Red-faced, she began to scramble off him as the voice drew closer. "Shane? Where are you?"

He caught Sonny's shoulders in an iron grip and pulled her back down to him. "You are my lover, do you understand?" he whispered urgently. *"My lover."*

She stared at him, her confusion growing more acute. "I'm not—"

"My lover," he repeated in a low, desperate voice. "I'll explain later."

Then before she could tell him she had no idea what he was talking about—he showed her very clearly what he wanted. He took a fistful of her hair and turned her so that he cradled her in his arms, his upper body blocking her escape, and his leg across hers making it difficult to move.

He opened his mouth on hers and kissed her. To a woman who hadn't been seriously kissed in two years, the experience shocked her to her toes.

She felt warm lips that tasted of toothpaste touch hers in gentle exploration. As her lips parted with interest, as well as alarm, his mouth roamed over hers—his teeth nipped lightly at her bottom lip, then his tongue teased her with a stroke across it before it delved into her mouth and blurred her awareness of everything but him.

She kissed him back—it would have been impossible not to. She didn't care that she didn't know what was going on. She only knew that on this very physical level, she understood everything. This was how a kiss was supposed to be.

Shane put his heart and soul into the kiss, showing his sister-in-law that he was not now, nor would he ever be, interested in her romantically.

He had to discourage Charmaine, or he'd be right back where he'd started when he left Hawaii. Thank God Dusty's Sun Queen had been here.

This kiss had begun as a desperate measure, but when Sonny Winslow combed her fingers through his hair and opened her mouth under his, he felt desperate in an entirely different way.

He'd closed the door on romantic involvement, pushed it so far within himself even he couldn't find it. But now feelings surfaced cautiously, like one bubble on the surface of the water indicating life underneath.

Surprise held him immobile for a moment. But now Sonny had both arms wrapped around him, and she was responding in a way that fanned his dormant feelings back to flaming life.

"Well," a low, smoldering voice said from several feet away. "And I was sure you were languishing in this godforsaken rustic little place, and came to your rescue."

The sultry voice brought Sonny back to reality with a jolt. *His lover.* She was supposed to pretend to be his lover.

"Char!" Shane said with convincing surprise. He eased Sonny off him onto the carpet and propped up on an elbow. "What's up? The folks okay?"

Her sharp green gaze went from him to Sonny with a knowing expression, then she reached a long, silk-clad arm down to give Shane a hand up. He pulled Sonny up beside him.

Sonny saw a tall, full-figured woman with clouds of dark hair and a stunningly strong and beautiful face. She wore a red silk suit that lent drama to her flamboyant good looks.

"Everyone's fine," she said, folding her arms and continuing to study them. "So, apparently, are you."

Shane's voice held mild censure. "I told you I was fine when you called last week."

She nodded. "But you always play the stoic hero. I was sure you were hurting inside."

Sonny saw a subtle change in her expression when she said those words, as though under the seductive front was serious concern. Maybe something more.

"That's what you get for second-guessing me. Charmaine Prelotsky, I'd like you to meet Sonny Winslow. Sonny, this is my sister-in-law, the Countess Charmaine Bedford Delgado Prelotsky." He pushed both women through the door into the hall. "Sonny, why don't you take Char into the living room and get acquainted while I put some clothes on?"

Sonny looked at him in alarm as Charmaine preceded her. He caught the back of her neck in his hand and leaned down to kiss her, whispering quickly, "Make it good. She's a barracuda."

Charmaine seated herself in a Bentwood rocker, elegant stocking-clad legs crossed, hiking her skirt to midthigh.

Contrary to the peace-loving, nonaggressive behavior Sonny had always fostered in herself, she now found herself feeling challenged, pushed. She made herself appear confident and comfortable.

"Would you like a cup of coffee?" she asked hospitably.

Charmaine shook her head. "I didn't come thousands of miles for a drink, Cindy," she said.

"Sonny," Sonny corrected.

Charmaine sighed and glanced out the living room window. Large, leaden clouds were moving in from the Washington side of the river.

"Strange name for a woman who lives in a place where the sun seldom shines."

"That's an exaggeration," Sonny said, sitting on the sofa. She leaned an elbow on the cushions, trying to appear as though she belonged there. "But, if you don't like stormy weather, shouldn't you have stayed in Hawaii?''

Charmaine gave her a bold smile. "I like Shane more than I like sunshine." She heaved another deep sigh. "You're very pretty and I imagine you're probably sweet, but what *does* he see in you, I wonder?"

Sonny smiled back. "My working knowledge of the *Kamasutra,* I imagine."

Charmaine laughed aloud. "I like you, Sunshine, but you look too angelic to have carnal knowledge." She frowned suddenly. "Although you did seem to know what you were doing a moment ago. Do you often come up here to take him away from his work in the middle of the afternoon? My father would not be pleased to know that."

"Your father?"

"Joshua Bedford, who owns the Bedford chain of hotels to which the Coast Convention Center belongs."

"Ah," Sonny said, her expression stiffening slightly. "Yes. We've corresponded."

"Oh?" Charmaine seemed genuinely surprised.

"Over the building of the center where a large colony of herons nested."

"You were against it, I take it?"

"Strongly."

Charmaine tucked a leg under her in the chair. "Then how do you reconcile an intimate relationship with the man who represents the Bedford Hotel Corporation in this little burg?"

Sonny opened her mouth to reply, when Shane appeared in the doorway, gorgeous in a blindingly white shirt tucked into the pants of a dark suit. The ends of a subdued tie lay around his neck. He warned her with a

look not to let feelings of ecological guilt ruin the charade.

It wasn't a plea as much as a demand, but she was
beyond being annoyed. Her life had been filled with
strong and serious men and because of that, drama and
humor had been virtually absent. This was as close to
excitement and fun as she'd been since she and Polly
Dugan had run away from home in the sixth grade.

She replied with a careless shrug, "Consummate lack
of character, I suppose."

Shane dropped the jacket over his arm on the back of
a chair, and placed the pumpkin arrangement with his
other hand on the coffee table. Then he pulled Sonny
off the sofa, took her place, then drew her into his lap.
He squeezed her affectionately. "That's how I like my
women. Without character."

Charmaine propped an elbow on the arm of her chair
and rested her chin on her fist. Her smile held disbelief. "I suppose that's why you married my churchgo-
ing, fund-raising sister, rather than fun-loving, hard-
living me."

He smiled fondly with the memory. "She had a wild
side only I knew about."

Charmaine accepted that with a nod and a curious
expression that coupled jealousy and affection. Sonny
wondered about it.

"You know," Charmaine said with sudden gravity,
"Daddy would not be pleased to know that his favorite
VP and the manager of his newest venture is having
quickies in the middle of his shift. As his head of quality control, I'd have to report that, you know."

Shane nodded with equal gravity. "Of course you
would. But if you're interested in telling him the truth,
you might explain that you found me freshly showered

and in a towel because the night manager called in sick, so I'm on duty until midnight. I took a break to shower and change."

She studied him doubtfully. "And Sonny scrubbed your back?"

He pinched the fabric on the arm of Sonny's sweater. "You'll notice that she was dressed when you arrived."

Sonny was surprised to see Charmaine momentarily without argument. "Where is my nephew?" she asked finally.

"We have a day-care center downstairs," Shane replied. "He goes there after school until I'm off duty. How long are you planning to stay, Char?"

She shrugged an elegant shoulder. "As long as it takes."

He didn't have to ask what she meant. As a clone of her hard-driving father, she went after what she wanted with single-minded determination—and unfortunately she wanted him.

He molded a hand over Sonny's knee and rubbed gently. "You don't have that kind of time, Char. I love Sonny."

Charmaine studied them again, shrewd mossy green eyes appraising their cozy pose on the sofa. Sonny felt weirdly adrift in an unfamiliar world, yet curiously possessive of this little bit of fantasy.

She leaned an elbow on Shane's shoulder and rested her weight against him, trying to create an impression of belonging in his arms.

He held her closer and shook his head at his sister-in-law. "I'm out of the running, but the hotel gets a very interesting clientele. If you're going to be around a while, I'm sure you'll find one of them worthy of your attentions."

Charmaine gave him a long-suffering sigh. Sonny got the impression they'd had similar discussions before.

"I didn't just come to the mainland on a manhunt, Shane. I came for you." She let that sink in a moment, then got to her feet. She smiled sweetly from one to the other as Shane eased Sonny to her feet and stood. "But it seems it's going to be a little more complicated than I anticipated. Fortunately I have patience—and more tricks up my sleeve than Sunshine, here."

"I'll get you a suite," Shane said, moving toward the kitchen phone.

"No need." She stopped him by dangling a key. "I told the clerk at the desk who I am, and guess where they put me?"

He didn't have to. He'd been the target of her tactics before. "Suite A?"

She pinched his chin. "Your nimble brain is one of the things I love about you." Then she went to the door and paused in the opening to look over her shoulder. "What are you going to do about Dusty tonight while you're working?"

"One of the ladies in Housekeeping sits for me."

"Couldn't I pick him up for dinner? I've been looking forward to seeing him." The seductive woman was now replaced by a loving aunt, Sonny noted.

"Of course," Shane agreed. "He'd love that."

"Good." That issue settled, Charmaine focused on Sonny. "Looks like you and I are about to fight it out, Sunshine. I hope you're going to be a worthy adversary. I hate easy victories."

Sonny leaned into Shane, returning Charmaine's smile. "How do you feel about easy defeats?"

Charmaine laughed and closed the door behind her. Sonny closed her eyes and let the back of her head fall against Shane's shoulder. "My God," she said. "I feel like I've been fed into a leaf shredder!"

Shane wrapped both arms around her waist and squeezed. "You were brilliant!" His praise came with an easy laugh.

Then he straightened away from her, as surprised as she was by the spontaneous gesture. "Sit down," he said, his manner suddenly brisk. "We have to talk about this."

The telephone rang and he pressed a button on the speakerphone in the kitchen. He knotted his tie while listening to the frantic voice on the other end.

It was the desk clerk with the private school girls whose reservations weren't on the computer.

"We have two rooms close together on three where we can put them, and a third room on four, but their chaperon is concerned about having four of the girls that far away from her."

"Of course she is." He made an expert loop as he talked. "See if you can find a guest on either side or across the hall from the two rooms, who would be willing to move to four. Offer tonight's lodging free as incentive."

The voice sounded relieved with the solution. "Yes, sir."

"Send the girls and their chaperon to the coffee shop to wait, with cokes or shakes or whatever they want—on us."

The voice now sounded reverent. "Yes, sir. Thank you."

Quick thinking and a thoughtful, generous solution. Sonny was impressed.

"About tonight," Shane said as he came to sit beside her on the sofa.

"Tonight?"

He braced a hand on the sofa's back, blocking her into the corner. She wryly accepted that she'd felt cornered from the moment she'd discovered him in a towel in his bathroom.

"Tonight," he said firmly. "I'll have a dinner break at eight. I'd like you to join me, preferably in something that'll threaten Charmaine's confidence in her seductive supremacy."

Sonny frowned. "But she's going to be watching your son."

He shook his head at her naïveté. "She's going to be watching *us*. She's probably calling the desk right now to ask them to alert her when I take my break. Then she'll come down, armed with my son, probably on the excuse of having dessert. You have to be there with me. And you have to stay here until she's gone."

Sonny asked flatly, "What?"

"You have to stay *here*. I've told her we're in love. She knows me, Sonny. I was engaged to my wife three weeks before I married her. I don't dawdle over decisions, and what belongs to me is never very far away. With her staying right across the hall, she'll use every excuse to be over here. She'll have to see you here."

Sonny shuffled mentally through a variety of excuses. "I can't...just...I mean, it isn't..."

"Your shop is right next door," he said reasonably. "And you told me last night that your home is by the bay. You can get to your shop in a minute, and watch your house from my window. Meanwhile, you'll be on hand to decorate the hotel for the fall season, and the dining room for Halloween. The hospital auxiliary is having a fund-raiser on the thirtieth."

"Decorate?" she asked, interest sparked despite the fantastical quality of the rest of his proposal.

"The lobby, the dining room, the coffee shop, the suites."

Sonny's mind began to calculate. Even giving the hotel a price break, she could make her rent for the next few months. Added to the financial bonus was the opportunity to undertake a big decorating challenge. Excitement lit her eyes.

Shane saw that and pressed. "Charmaine's been after me for a year," he explained. "She'd be the perfect wife for a combat general or a heavyweight boxer, but I prefer a quieter life-style and less confrontation. She likes things stirred up and preferably airborne."

Sonny asked gently, "She loved you when you were married to her sister, didn't she?"

He raised an eyebrow, surprised that she'd seen that.

"It was in her eyes," Sonny said, "when the two of you were remembering your wife. She loved her, too, but she's always wanted you, hasn't she?"

That observation put Shane slightly off guard. He found it strange that she'd seen in a matter of minutes what Allie had finally had to explain to him after several years of marriage.

"I used to wonder," he admitted, "why she always went into high gear around me. She's usually aggressive and forceful, but with me, she was always pushing, as though she wanted some reaction I was unaware of. Allie explained it to me after a particularly difficult family dinner."

Sonny felt sympathy for Charmaine. She was obviously a strong, competent woman who needed an even stronger man. In this age of living freely and equally, Shane was becoming a rare breed.

"I keep hoping," he said with a tolerant smile, "that one day a Chicago Bulls quarterback will come along and toss her over the goalpost." His expression firmed. "But until that happens, and for as long as she's here, you and I are lovers."

She smiled wryly. "I suppose 'but I hardly know you' makes me sound like some yokel out of *The Perils of Pauline*."

He grinned as he stood and crossed the room for his jacket. "And not at all like a woman with a working knowledge of the *Kamasutra*."

She groaned and closed her eyes as color inched up her face. "You heard that?"

"I did," he said, shrugging into the jacket. He tugged on the cuffs of his shirt and magically became the dangerously elegant man in the Armani suit. "And I was glad to hear it. It's going to take that kind of determined quick thinking to discourage Charmaine."

Then he extended a hand and drew her to her feet. "But you do have a good point. What would you like to know about me?" He glanced at his watch. "I've got five minutes."

She gave him a fatalistic smile and led the way to the door. "The things a woman needs to know about a man before agreeing to move in with him can't be discovered in five minutes. But I'll take it on trust that a wonderful little boy like Dusty couldn't come from a less-than-kind-and-honorable man."

She might be taking an awful lot on trust, he thought, but he wasn't going to be the one to tell her that.

"So, you'll be here for dinner at eight," he reminded. "Bring a few changes of clothes in a small bag, and I'll have someone bring them up to the suite while Charmaine's out."

She winced, remembering his requirement for her dinner attire. "I don't own a dress that would threaten Charmaine's seductive supremacy." She added on a doubtful note. "Do you think there's anything in this world that would?"

"The dress shop in the lobby has a lot of glittery things," he said. "Charge it to me."

Sonny sighed. "At the risk of speaking another melodramatic line, 'I can't accept expensive clothes from a gentleman.'"

He hesitated patiently, a hand on the doorknob. "I'll deduct it from your decorating fee. Anything else?"

"Yes," she said, folding her arms. She knew she should sound more reluctant than she felt. "This is crazy. I just came by to deliver a pumpkin."

He glanced to the table where he'd placed the arrangement. Then he looked into her eyes. "Why *did* you do that?"

"So that Dusty could have it," she replied. And while she was at it, she explained why she'd walked into his bathroom.

He nodded. "I had called day-care to tell Dusty I'd be home for half an hour, showering and getting ready to work tonight. He came up, we had cocoa, then he went back down. He often forgets to close the door. Anyway, it was a thoughtful gesture. Thank you. And your arrival on the scene was perfect timing."

Sonny didn't see it in such a positive light. "And this is what resulted—you and I . . . joined at the hip." She groaned. "It's like something out of a horror movie."

He laughed and opened the door. "Two weeks until Halloween. Mystical things happen when ghosts and goblins abound."

Chapter Three

"Is that the slip or the dress?" Denise Potter, who worked for Sonny part-time, stood back in her Say It With A Sonnet smock, and studied her boss over the rim of her glasses. She was Sonny's best friend's mother and felt called upon to offer advice and pass judgment on most aspects of Sonny's life.

"This is it." Sonny pulled up on the low-cut top with thin rolled straps, then tugged down on the skirt slit to midthigh, and still felt naked.

Denise suddenly smiled. "It's time you stopped looking like a celestial painting and remembered what being a woman is all about." She shook her head wryly. "If Terri paid more attention to being a woman, she might find a man. But she worries more about her schoolchildren than she does about herself."

Sonny leaned her weight on one hip and placed her hand on it. "You, who wouldn't even let Terri date until she was seventeen, are telling me being a woman is about showing skin?"

Denise pushed her glasses up and placed a stem of yellow statice into a dried arrangement she created for the display window. "It's about showing softness," she corrected. "Men forget it's there, unless we remind them. We have to show them that a peaceful attitude is just as effective as shouts and muscle. When we've proved *that*, we can go for universal disarmament and world peace.''

''Ah,'' Sonny said with a grin, scooping up the tiny purse she'd bought to go with the silk outfit. ''So dressing this way is really a political statement. I had no idea.''

''In a man's world—'' Denise pointed a star flower at her ''— you could be elected president in that dress.''

Sonny rolled her eyes and dismissed the praise with a wave of her hand. ''I just want a solvent flower shop. You're sure you won't mind helping full-time for a week, so I can do the hotel job?''

''For the third time,'' Denise said emphatically, ''no. And I don't mind staying tonight to replenish the window. Now, get going if you're going to save young Tyrone Power from the femme fatale.''

Sonny pulled on a short velvet jacket patterned in subtle purple and burgundy flowers. She blinked at Denise. ''Tyrone Power?''

Denise fluttered a hand over her heart. ''I was madly in love with him at seventeen, and Shane Archer looks just like him. Terri pointed him out to me at the school's open house.''

Sonny wondered if Tyrone Power had had a sense of humor. She picked up her small bag with its two changes of clothes and let herself out of the shop. She stood in the shelter of the storefront for a moment and drew a deep breath. She was insane to agree to this, she thought. Seductively, she was no match for Charmaine Bedford. She had a feeling this charade wouldn't last very long.

Yet something inside her leapt with excitement as she watched a long black limo pull into the hotel's semicircular driveway. For a woman raised in an extremely sedate military family, this would be a very special adventure.

This curious liaison with Shane Archer was a great opportunity to grow professionally and personally. And he was interesting although a typical male. She could put up with him in order to get a little taste of drama.

She buttoned the large single button on her short jacket and started toward the hotel—then stopped abruptly. She spotted Charmaine and Dusty about a block away, walking hand in hand and talking animatedly.

SHANE STOOD BEHIND the front desk, running down the next day's reservations. It was two minutes after eight, and he was torn between disappointment that Sonny hadn't arrived yet, and the fervent wish that she'd decided to break their deal by staying away.

But his ambivalence disappeared the moment Regis, the doorman, pushed open one of the double-glass doors and the Sun Queen walked in.

She glanced around as heads turned in her direction, then she spotted Shane behind the desk and came toward him like a vision-come-to-life.

At first, his eyes focused on her smile. It was warm and bright, and touched something deep inside him. Then he gazed at her hair. The loose ringlets that usually gave her an angelic look had been tamed into a smooth swirl that swept over her left eyebrow and curled at her chin. The other side was tucked behind her ear where something golden sparkled.

The jacket was pretty, but her long elegant legs in dark stockings and very high heels made the air rush out of his lungs as though he'd been tackled and brought down.

He was still staring when she reached across the desk to put her hand behind his head and pull him to her. "You'd better look happy to see me," she whispered, her mouth flirting a breath away from his. "Charmaine and Dusty are right behind me."

He needed little encouragement to close the small gap between their lips and kiss her with all the wonder and gratitude he felt that she'd decided to keep her part of the bargain. That had to be what this clamoring of his senses was, he told himself as her mouth moved on his. Gratitude.

BURN STARBY'S spacefighter hovered over Hearth Base II as he stared at his research data. The Mission Master had received his communication after all? He'd rescued the Sun Queen? Burn couldn't quite believe it.

He was inclined not to trust this sudden turn of events, but experience had taught him that he could count on the Mission Master with every detail of their assignments, including even his personal safety.

The MM, he decided, probably had a plan.

"Well . . . !" An exclamation of disgust and several words of the language banned in all Hearth Base communications came from the lips of the Dragon Dame Burn had been sent to ferry back to Eos.

"DON'T LET DAD hear you say that, Aunt Char," Dusty said gravely. "You'll get a swat."

"Something is going to be swatted," Charmaine said, marching him toward the desk, "and it's not going to be me. Well, good evening, darlings. Let up, Sunshine, before we have to have his teeth reenameled.''

Sonny drew back and let her eyes drift open. She focused on Shane's dark gaze and saw pleasant surprise. She experienced a mild annoyance. What she felt was closer to cardiac arrest. She'd known him all of twenty-four hours, and what she'd thought she'd known about men and passion had been shaken and rearranged. And *he* was simply pleased.

But she had other things to think about at the moment. Charmaine and Dusty stood right beside her. She released Shane and turned to spare Charmaine an acknowledging glance before squatting down beside his son.

''Hi, Dusty,'' she said. ''Did you have a great dinner?''

He nodded eagerly, smiling up at his aunt. ''We went to the Pancake Palace. I had chocolate-chip pancakes, and Aunt Char had them with chili. You look beautiful!''

''Thank you.'' She stood up and smoothed his hair. ''Your dad's taking me to dinner.''

Dusty looked slyly from one to the other. It reminded Sonny of Charmaine's suspicious looks. Then it occurred to her—the playacting between her and Shane would very likely confuse the child. That could prompt him into saying something that would undermine the entire deception.

But Shane, apparently, had it handled.

He came around the desk to lift the boy into his arms and hug him. ''Be good for Aunt Char and don't tell her all our secrets, okay?''

Charmaine made a scornful sound and shook her head. ''I deny once again that I *asked* Dusty for infor-

mation about the young heiress on Kona that you took
to the beach.''

With Dusty resting easily on his hip, Shane leveled a
stare of disbelief on his sister-in-law. "Do you deny that
you harassed us while we were trying to picnic?''

Charmaine folded her arms and looked away. "I fell
off the roof of your cabana. That's not the same thing.''

"Unless one considers what you were doing there.''

She met his gaze blandly. "There'd been tsunami
warnings....''

"Of course.'' Shane took his son several feet away
and engaged him in earnest conversation, while Charmaine fidgeted and Sonny pretended disinterest. She
guessed he was explaining quickly about her sudden intrusion into their lives.

"He's probably coaching him not to answer my
questions,'' Charmaine said.

Sonny smiled. "He isn't coaching *me*. Ask me anything you'd like to know.''

"Do you love him?''

Charmaine's question came so quickly, so unexpectedly, that Sonny hesitated. "Yes, I love him,'' she finally replied, with what she hoped sounded like honesty. But Charmaine didn't appear convinced.

She frowned at Sonny. "I like to think I still have a
chance.''

Sonny spread her hands, palms up. "It's a free
country, Charmaine.'' Then she pretended to fan her
cheeks and removed the concealing jacket. She placed
it over her arm and grinned into her adversary's flatteringly annoyed expression and offered her hand.
"Luck to the better woman.''

Charmaine took her hand without hesitation and said
pityingly, "Sunshine, I've been competing for men since

Mother walked me in my stroller and I ogled all the little boy babies.''

Sonny patted her hand. "So you have experience with little boys. I'm not sure that poses a threat to me." She looped an arm in Shane's as he came to stand beside her. "You'll notice I have a man."

Charmaine looked more depressed than angry. "Not for long," she said, then took her nephew's hand. "Not for long." She smiled graciously. "Have a wonderful dinner."

Shane handed her a key. "Why don't you watch him in the suite since all his toys are there? Sonny will be up in a little while. Did you get settled in all right across the hall?"

She nodded. "Thank you. Everything was perfect and I was shown every courtesy. You run a tight ship."

Shane accepted the compliment with a nod. "Of course I do. If you need anything at all, call the desk and they'll find me."

"I'm sure Dusty and I will be fine. Have fun...while it lasts." She headed for the elevators with a wave, Dusty skipping along beside her.

Sonny drew a deep breath as Shane turned her toward the dining room. "I always feel as though I need to be put on life support after talking to her."

"Well, you can relax now," he said with an appreciative glance down at her dress. "As far as I'm concerned, you don't have to say another word. I'm just going to stare at my beautiful companion all through dinner."

"MAYBE WE'LL GET LUCKY, and she'll leave tomorrow." Sonny spoke the words lazily as she spooned the last bite of amaretto flan into her mouth. It dissolved on her tongue like cream. "Of course, if I get to eat like this every night, I'll try not to be too convincing so I can take advantage of this as long as possible."

Shane could find nothing wrong with her plan. He had passed on dessert and leaned back in his chair, one elbow propped on the back of it, his other arm stretched out so that he could toy with his coffee cup. The casual attitude he'd adopted when they'd sat down to eat was beginning to wear on him.

Her smile was relaxed, and her eyes looked a little tired, though they settled on him with the most intriguing speculation. It pleased him and concerned him at the same time. She was doing what he'd asked—and very well. He could only applaud her for that. But he didn't want her *really* interested—and *he* didn't want to be taken with *her*.

Still, his eyes kept wandering to the soft swell of breast just above her dress every time she moved or sighed. Her smile kept making him smile.

"I was married for eight years," he said abruptly, thinking that the width of the table seemed to have shrunk during dinner. She leaned toward him when he spoke, and he felt her invading his space, crowding the shadowy corner in which he'd lived the last two years.

Sonny heard the message in those words as clearly as though he'd added the postscript aloud. "And you'll never know how much I loved her, how much I still love her."

But she did. Dusty had told Terri Potter that sometimes he and his father cried together over his mother.

She patted his hand like a sister. "It's all right," she said. "I'm in this for the adventure, not the romance. And the work for my shop, of course."

He couldn't have explained why that simple reassurance irritated him. But he pretended otherwise. "Why not the romance?" he asked.

She smiled and poured tea into her cup from a white china pot. Her glance up at him was apologetic and just a little superior. "Because, generally, you're all incapable of it. Not that I'm unaware that men have other sterling qualities that serve women well. Romance just isn't one of them."

Shane, who'd always prided himself on having a romantic turn of mind, leaned toward her over the table. She gave him her full attention, her cup in her slender hands, "I challenge that," he said, smilingly defensive. "I am very romantic."

She gave him an even look, then sipped her tea. "Wasn't it you who displaced nesting birds to put up a hotel? Kissed me on the bathroom floor? Told me in dulcet tones that I'd get the hotel job if I moved into your suite and pretended to be your lover?"

Before he could reply, she added, "Ecologically, stylistically and moralistically, I'd say you're romantically challenged."

Shane leaned back in his chair, one eyebrow raised, his mouth open to protest. All that came from it was a gasp of abused male pride.

Sonny knew she'd carried that a little far. But it annoyed her that he could bamboozle her into this situation, then hold her at arm's distance with the mention of his marriage.

"I have a father and brother just like you," she continued, enjoying his speechlessness. "Military through and through. My father's retired and living in Virginia with my mother, and my brother's in Somalia."

He waited for her to make the connection.

She didn't waste a moment. "Very responsible, protective, and take-charge kind of men. Fine if you like the type. But I'm not military at heart. I'm living for the moment."

He winced in confusion. "That doesn't make sense. You have a business, show schoolchildren how to put flower arrangements in pumpkins, and probably even belong to Kiwanis. That doesn't sound like your average adventuress to me."

She nodded and leaned her chin in her hand. "That's the old me. This little escapade has turned me in the direction I've always wanted to go. I'll always have my flower shop, and make time for first graders, but from now on I'm on the lookout for some wild times."

The wince became a frown. "I hope you're kidding."

She waved a hand airily. "Why? Because I'd be asking for trouble? That's what my family would say, but why should someone else's adventure be any more of a threat to me than yours is?"

"I'm honorable, remember?"

She disregarded that with a shrug. "True. But I'll wager for every ten women in this world with a broken heart, eight of them were fractured by an honorable man."

"I'd like to see your source for those stats, Sonnet," he said.

It took her a heartbeat to recover from the sound of her full name on his lips. Then she went on to make her point. "Admit it," she said. "We could have met several nights ago in a very middle-American romantic moment, but you'd had a rough day and tried to escape me. I have that information firsthand from your son."

He felt a spark of relief that that was at the bottom of her attitude. He grinned.

"So, that's it. A woman scorned—or in this case simply eluded. How female, trying to blame your own pique on me."

She chose to be regal rather than embarrassed. "*I* would never have run away to avoid meeting you."

He grinned again. "Really. You find me that appealing?"

A laugh erupted, vanquishing the royal pose.

Shane caught her hand and pulled her to her feet. "Come on," he said. "We're going to settle this once and for all."

"Settle what? How?"

She would have preferred to have an answer to those questions before she was tugged through the dining room and across the lobby. She insisted on one as they waited for the express elevator.

"Settle the question of whether or not I'm romantic," Shane replied. The light flashed and the bell rang as the elevator arrived. The doors parted and he reached out to hold them back for her.

She remained where she stood. "Settle it how?" she asked.

He took a step into the elevator to hold the doors open with his body. "Come and see," he challenged quietly. "It's my understanding that suspense is an important element in romance."

She eyed him suspiciously. "Not to me, it isn't."

"I thought you were becoming an adventuress." he challenged.

He was right, of course. This was a lark. She had to stop thinking of it in terms of consequences. She stepped onto the elevator.

"Did you bring a bag?" he asked as they stood on opposite sides of the small car while it ascended.

"I left it in the shop. I saw Dusty and Charmaine coming up the street when I stepped out, so I put it back. I'll go down for it when we . . . after . . . when it's time to . . ."

He folded his arms and grinned at her. "Now, I don't think an adventuress would stutter over the words *bed*, or *sleep.*"

"Yes, well . . ." She struggled to retain her aplomb. "Those words don't happen to be what this particular adventure is about."

"Charmaine has to think so," he corrected.

"She will," she assured him, "as long as you don't."

The doors parted on the sixth floor. She studied Shane another moment as he held them open, then decided that this was nothing more than they'd planned she would do. She would spend the night in his suite. If he tried to narrow that plan to his bed, he'd find out that as adventuresses went, she could put Sheena, queen of the jungle, to shame when provoked.

She stepped out into the hallway. Shane led her around the corner to his suite. But instead of stopping there, he led her through a door to a stairway that went up.

She stood in the doorway in confusion. "The roof?"

His outstretched hand was his only answer.

She took it and was led up the stairs and through a narrow doorway onto the darkened rooftop. The chilling autumn air bit into her instantly. Shane stopped her, pulled his jacket off and slipped it over her shoulders.

The silk lining retained the warmth of his body and decimated the chill as though she'd been placed near a fire.

He laughed softly. "You look like a freshman quarterback."

She didn't understand for a moment, then looked down at herself—the shoulders of the jacket stuck out emptily and the hem fell to her knees. She, too, laughed.

"I guess I haven't been an adventuress long enough to have shoulders."

He anchored the overlarge jacket to her by placing an arm around her.

"Come on," he said. "I want you to see your view."

He took her to a waist-high railing lit at thirty-foot intervals with globular lights.

Sonny gasped at the nightscape spread out before her.

A freighter coming into port from the mouth of the river glided over the invisible water, running lights and every porthole sparkling like a jewel in the darkness. In the distance automobile headlights crawled along the shoreline of Candle Bay and the glass gazebo of the Candle Bay Inn's ballroom stood out like a beacon.

Shane pointed into the shadows below them. "The herons are gone, but somewhere down there, mallards and cormorants are asleep in the reeds, and this week we've noticed canvasbacks and a pair of Canada geese."

"Ohh." Sonny stood on tiptoe to lean over the railing. "I wish I could see them."

Shane lowered his arm to her waist and held firm. "You'll be able to see them in the morning. Dusty has to check on them every day before he goes to school. In the summer I want to put a table and chairs up here so we can have our meals out when it's nice."

Sonny didn't want to tell him that he'd have five or six weeks maximum when the sun shone hot enough for outdoor eating. He'd discover that on his own. And the northwest had so many other attributes to recommend it.

"That'll be nice," she said.

Shane pointed overhead to a sky aglitter with stars. He indicated the brightest one. "The North Star. Shall we make a wish?"

His arms came around her as she tilted her head back to look up and she suddenly felt surrounded by him, breathless, cornered again. Curiously this time, the feeling had more to do with comfort than confinement. She was afraid to give it too much thought.

"Is there such a thing as a tandem wish?" she asked, her voice soft and a little high. "I mean, aren't you supposed to make wishes individually?"

"Sonny," he said with an air of exasperation, "you must have gotten your romance degree through the mail." He tightened his grip on her, then reached one hand up to tilt her chin up higher. She felt his touch down to her kneecaps.

"What could be more powerful," he asked quietly, earnestly, "than the single wish of two people all wrapped up together and yearning for the same thing?"

The thought was intriguing—and sent ripples of sensation up her spine.

"What are you wishing for?" he asked.

"You're not supposed to tell," she admonished.

"That's birthday candles," he corrected. "This is God's very own megawatt candle power."

She wasn't convinced that that had anything to do with it, but on the chance that it did... "I'm wishing that this all works out for you, that you convince Charmaine to leave you alone, and that some wonderful macho man with patience comes along to take Charmaine away."

He thought Charmaine's needs would be better met by a man who had very little patience. But their wishes were close enough for him to believe there was something mystical at work here.

"What do you want for you?" he asked.

"Oh . . . far horizons, new adventures. And you?"

"Just to be left alone," he replied, "to watch Dusty grow up into a strong, caring man, and to be able to do my job without everyone else meddling in my life." He widened his stance, and looked up at the stars. "Ready?"

"Yes," she whispered.

"All right. Now."

Sonny swore she felt the energy course between them, the wish in its slightly divergent forms circling them, then shooting heavenward with the propulsion of their common concentration.

Its power rocked her. She reached up to the arms wrapped around her and caught one of his hands. His fingers tightened around hers and held.

Shane had felt this jolt of energy only twice before in his lifetime—the day Allie Bedford walked into his life, and the day Dusty was born. From the instant each had appeared, his life had been irrevocably changed.

As Sonny relaxed in his arms, he told himself it was just the romance of the moment. After all, wasn't that precisely what he was trying to prove? That he *was* a romantic?

It meant no more than that. And just to prove it to himself, he took it a step further.

Sonny turned in his arms, eyes wide.

"Tandem wishes," he said softly, putting a hand to the back of her head, "are always sealed with a kiss."

At that moment, she didn't care if that was legend or not. It was precisely what she wanted.

As he drew her to him, she wrapped her arms around his neck and met his lips. They were warm and sure and tasted of the windy, salty night. His free hand wandered over her body, touching lightly at her wings and her fragile rib cage, boldly shaping her hip in his hand and pressing her closer.

Shane experienced a drowning sensation. He felt as though he'd somehow vaulted the protective railing and gotten lost in the darkness below.

Sonny clung to him, mouth drinking from his as well as slaking his thirst, taking his air, pulling him down.

It never occurred to him to struggle for the surface. He wanted to go where she led, abandon what he knew, be hers, make her his.

The loud blast of the freighter's horn split the silence and broke them apart. They stared at each other, breathing hard.

"It'll work," Sonny whispered, thinking privately that there was more to that statement than met the eye— or the ear.

"Yes," Shane said, glancing up at the star in mild concern. "I think it will."

Chapter Four

Shane's bedroom was painted a soft white, and filled with bleached oak furniture. Mallard green paisley covered the bed and matched the long draperies. Colorful, dimensional collages hung on the walls, and Sonny went to inspect one while Shane pulled an extra blanket off the closet shelf.

"These are lovely," she said, putting her fingertip to a paper heart woven in many shades of pink. Red ribbon bled from the bottom of it. It rested behind glass in a shadow-box frame. Above it was a colorfully plumed bird done in the same style. And on either side, a butterfly, and a star that radiated gold threads.

The work was so gently done, Sonny knew this was no hotel art bought in large quantities.

"That's Allie's work," he said, crossing to the foot of the bed with an armful of plump, white thermal blanket. "She was an officer in the Bedford chain, and she enjoyed the work, but she had an artistic side that never really got the time and attention it deserved."

Sonny saw flair, humor and tenderness in the collages, and suddenly felt very intrusive. Charmaine had left politely after Shane thanked her for spending the evening with Dusty, but not before she gave Sonny a backward glance that said "you don't belong here."

And she didn't—at least not in this room with Allie Archer's art work.

"I'd be perfectly comfortable on the sofa," Sonny said, taking the blanket from the foot of the bed. "All I need is a pillow and an alarm clock set for seven."

"You'll be even more comfortable in the bed," Shane insisted, taking the blanket from her and putting it back on the bed. "And with Dusty around, you won't need an alarm clock. He seldom sleeps past six. I'll be fine on the sofa. I have to go back to work for a few hours anyway, and I won't disturb you when I come in."

She nodded agreeably, deeming it pointless to argue. Then she asked with a shade of concern, "You don't think Charmaine will break in in the middle of the night to make sure we're in...you know...the same bed?"

Shane focused for a moment on the image her words painted in his mind—the two of them curled together in warm intimacy in the middle of the flannel sheets. He expected guilt to stab him but it didn't. And that was somehow alarming. But it reminded him of a practical detail.

He shook his head. "That would be going too far—even for her." He pointed to the telephone as he pulled a pair of blue cotton pajamas from the dresser. "Red button is the desk. They can reach me anywhere, anytime. Dusty shouldn't stir until morning, but if there's a problem of any kind, or if you need something, don't hesitate to call."

He placed the pajamas in her hands.

She accepted them a little nervously. "Thank you. As I told you before, I packed a bag, but had to leave it at the shop when I saw Charmaine and Dusty coming up the street."

He nodded. "You can get it tomorrow when Charmaine's out. Anything I haven't covered?"

She guessed not, but it was difficult to imagine what could come up in this bizarre situation. She shrugged a shoulder. "I'm sure we'll be fine."

He smiled. "Good. See you in the morning." He started out the door, then turned back as though suddenly remembering something. "We always call room service for breakfast. What would you like?"

"I'm partial to the coffee shop's scones," she admitted. "And coffee."

"You got it. Good night."

It wasn't until Sonny had showered and sat in the middle of the bed that she allowed herself to think.

She was in a strange man's bed—in his pajamas! She'd jumped into this situation with both feet, but that didn't mean she wouldn't be extremely careful with the other parts of her body.

It would be best not to let him kiss her again. Strange things happened to her when he did. Reality dissolved, and all she knew was the magical ignition that took place inside her. At this point in time, she didn't want to know where that could lead.

She leaned over a nightstand that held a leather portfolio and a gold pen, and turned off the copper-shaded light. She pulled up the sheet and quilt, snuggled into the fresh-smelling pillows, and felt herself relax. It was no big deal. She could convince Charmaine that she was Shane's lover without having to let him kiss her. So much could be said with a look or a touch.

She heaved a deep sigh and closed her eyes. It was all right. Hadn't they both agreed on the roof that this would work?

BURN STARBY patrolled the Mission Master's chamber, prepared to lay down his life for the booty the master had placed under his protection. The Sun Queen lay asleep in the middle of the large bed, a beautiful vision against the dark green pillow covers.

She stirred, muttered a quiet little sound, and Burn readied his weapon and drew closer, certain the Cave Conqueror had left his lair, determined to win her back from his archenemy. His overlarge ears could detect the smallest sound, even through ionic interference.

Burn smirked, unafraid. Let him come. He and his crud creamer were ready.

SONNY WOKE to the sight of Dusty sitting squarely in the middle of the foot of her bed. He wore a bath towel around his shoulders like a cape, tinfoil had been shaped to his head like a helmet and in his right hand was a plunger with a potato masher protruding from the suction cup.

"Ah...hi," she said, trying to remember if she'd consumed anything alcoholic last night.

The masculine surroundings confused her for a moment, then she remembered that she'd spent the night in Shane's suite; that they were pretending to be lovers to deceive Charmaine.

That situation came back to her with equal parts of trepidation and excitement. Then her adventuress persona asserted itself, and she felt in control. She smiled at Dusty.

"Good morning," she said sitting up and pushing her hair back from her face. One long sleeve of Shane's pajama top had unrolled during the night and now hung past her fingertips. She folded it back. "Are you my bodyguard?"

"Yes, Your Highness," he replied.

She blinked. "Your Highness?"

He began to explain, then suddenly turned toward the door—the plunger-potato masher aimed at it—as it pushed inward.

Shane appeared in the opening, frowning. "Dusty, I asked you not to wake her," he scolded.

"I didn't," Dusty insisted. "I was just making sure she was okay."

Shane shook his head. "I don't think anything could happen to her in our suite."

Dusty returned his father's even look, then glanced at Sonny as though to tell her only *he* knew the dangers she faced, but that he was perfectly capable of handling them for her.

Shane turned his gaze on Sonny. She smiled a good morning, then realized he wasn't looking at her face. His dark eyes roamed her upper body in his pajama top, visible above the quilt.

Instinctively she put a hand to the open collar, expecting to find that a button had opened, or the wide neck had slipped to reveal a bare shoulder. But that wasn't the case. Whatever caused the boldly appreciative look when his eyes finally met hers was apparently all in his imagination.

That was fine with her. She knew the reality to be far less impressive than whatever his mind had conjured.

"Good morning," he said. "Would you like to have breakfast with us? Yours will keep if you'd rather shower first."

She'd been about to choose the shower, thinking she needed a little fortification before sitting across the table from him this morning, but Dusty changed her mind.

"We have orange juice with treasure kabobs in it!" he said excitedly. "Fernando only makes those when something special's happening."

"Treasure kabobs?"

"Well, there's this stick thing, and he puts pieces of the really yummy fruits on it." He grimaced. "Not just melon, you know? Pineapple, papaya and mandarin oranges. And for *you*—" in his excitement, Dusty jabbed the plunger at her and she couldn't help but raise an arm in defense "—he stuck on a bite of chocolate truffle!"

Shane took the child by one hand and his weapon in the other. "Our chef spoils him abominably," he explained to Sonny. "So does everyone else around here. Dusty likes to place our breakfast order, and when he did it this morning, he told the kitchen we had someone very special staying with us, and asked for the treasure kabobs. I'm afraid you do have a square of chocolate in your orange juice."

Sonny smiled, deciding to set the precedent that every adventuress begin her day with orange juice and chocolate.

"Wonderful," she said. "I'll be out in a minute."

SHANE SETTLED DUSTY at the table, placing the crud creamer under his chair. "Do not point that at Sonny," he said firmly, going to the sofa to fold the blanket he'd used the night before. "Even make-believe guns should never be pointed at anyone."

Dusty looked at him pityingly while pulling a plump maraschino cherry off the bottom of his kabob. "It was on stun, Dad."

Of course. He should have noticed that. But his brain had been occupied with the sight of Sonny in his bed.

This was beginning to concern him. When he'd finally stretched out on the sofa at one this morning, he'd managed to convince himself that Sonny Winslow was not reactivating his emotions. He'd imagined that. He'd worked very hard since arriving in Merriwether. Trying to keep Dusty out of harm's way took every spare moment he had and many he didn't. He'd been burning the candle at both ends in his attempt to be the consummate father and the perfect hotelier.

When he'd walked into his room and seen the tousled vision in the middle of his bed, in his pajamas, all his careful reassurances flew apart. His heart had seemed to pound out of control and reminded him sharply that his romantic nature might be buried, but his sexual attraction certainly wasn't.

Aggravated with himself, Shane stacked pillow and blanket and headed for the bedroom to put them away.

Charmaine's sultry voice stopped him halfway across the carpet. "Good morning," she said, her eyes going to the bedclothes in his arms, then giving him a look of wide-eyed and completely artificial concern. "Did we get thrown out of the nest by Little Mary Sunshine?"

Shane closed his eyes, his effort to concoct an explanation hampered by the knowledge that *he'd* been the one who'd neglected to lock the door behind the waiter.

Rescue came from a source he hadn't suspected was even aware of the problem.

"Good morning, Charmaine," Sonny said with a bright, welcoming smile as she belted his robe over the baggy pajamas. Everything hung on her in a charmingly seductive fashion. Then she took the blanket and pillow from Shane with a long, languid glance.

"I keep telling you," she scolded softly, "when you have insomnia, I have cures that don't require you to leave the bed." She shook her head at Charmaine with a long-suffering expression. "Men. They never listen." Then she gave him another heavy-lidded glance before disappearing into the bedroom with her burden.

Charmaine stared after her. "Whatever made me think that girl was an innocent?" she asked.

Shane had to concentrate on keeping his actions normal as he guided her to the table and pulled out a chair for her. "You just like to think you're worse than everybody, Char. Something to eat?"

"Just coffee, please." She leaned sideways to kiss Dusty's cheek. "What are you eating, sweetie? I didn't know our chefs made anything like that."

"It's just for me," Dusty replied proudly. Then he pointed to the second orange juice across the table with its opulent kabob of chunked fruit topped by an elegant truffle. "And Sonny. Fernando made them."

Her mouth took on a wry twist as she settled into her place and picked up the steaming cup Shane filled for her.

"Of course. Princess Sunny."

Dusty turned to her with a grave expression. "She's a queen, not a princess."

"Oh, sorry. And ready to ascend the throne, no doubt. Well." Charmaine sipped her coffee, then replaced the cup in its saucer, propped her elbow on the table, and rested her chin on her hand. "I had breakfast in the dining room," she said to Shane, who poured coffee into his cup, then went to the cupboard to get one for Sonny. "To look over the field, so to speak. I mean, you *are* hosting a convention of plastic surgeons. They make buckets of money and could be a real help to me when everything begins to fall or wrinkle."

"Somehow, I doubt that'll happen to you," Sonny said, breezing into the kitchen to take her place beside Shane. He gave her a quick, proprietary smile. She forced herself to remain unaffected.

"Have one of my scones," she invited Charmaine, looking around for an extra plate. "If you keep an extra few pounds on, it takes longer to wrinkle."

Charmaine cast an interested glance at the scone, then a doubtful glance at her. "This theory is proven?"

Sonny went to the cupboard, praying she'd remember from yesterday where the plates were. "Not yet, but I'm working on it. It's my theory, and I'm my own test case."

Charmaine rolled her eyes. "Oh, good," she said flatly. "I'm...a few...a year older than you are. By the time we know for certain, I'll either be the most seductive woman in the islands, or backup for the Sumo Wrestling Federation."

"But you'll have been an adventuress." Mercifully Sonny opened the right door and carried a small plate back to the table. "So, were there any interesting plastic surgeons having breakfast?"

Charmaine wrinkled her elegant nose. "Not one. There were a few handsome ones, but that's not the same."

"Amen," Sonny said feelingly.

"I'm sorry, Sonny," Charmaine said, leaning toward her on folded arms, "but it's Shane and Dusty for me, or nothing. Why don't you just bow out grace-fully?''

Sonny gave her a sympathetic smile as she trans-ferred a scone onto the empty plate.

"Because I'm a tigress where my men are con-cerned," she said, imagining that was what a bold ad-venturing woman would say. She handed the plate across the table. "You'll just have to make do with a scone for now. I'll give you full recognition for re-search assistance when I write my final 'Wrinkle-proof Weight' report."

Charmaine considered her suspiciously for a mo-ment, frowned at Shane, then propped an elbow on the table and became serious. "You don't understand, Sunshine," she said reasonably. "We're fighting over the same man. We're not supposed to be pals. Now, you either have to take this more seriously, or I'm going to make mincemeat out of you."

Dusty, who'd been busy creating patterns with his fork on an abandoned pancake, looked up with sud-den interest.

"Time to brush your teeth and get your jacket, Dus," Shane said, while the women measured each other over their scones.

Dusty frowned, well aware, Shane was sure, that he was being removed from his front-row seat. He leaned toward his father to whisper, "Are they gonna fight?"

"No," Shane assured him, giving him a gentle push toward the bedroom door. "Light your booster rock-ets, buddy. I'm leaving in five minutes."

Dusty went, watching over his shoulder as he walked into the hallway to the bedrooms.

"No, *you* don't understand," Sonny said amiably the moment the boy was out of earshot. She buttered her scone, then passed the dish of butter curls to Charmaine. "I don't *have* to fight for Shane because I already have him."

Charmaine shook her elegant head at her adversary's innocence. "Don't tell me you've never heard of a man being taken away from the woman who loves him?"

Sonny nodded, now fully into the fantasy. "Oh, yes. But I doubt that any man, particularly this one..." She gave him another one of those sultry looks that made him feel as though he were under her spell. "Could be taken away from the woman *he loved.*"

She turned her attention back to Charmaine as she placed subtle emphasis on the last two words.

The important difference they made registered in Charmaine's eyes, and for the first time since he'd known her, Shane saw his sister-in-law at a loss for words.

Sonny also saw the effect of her words—and thought that she'd caught a glimpse of heartbreak. She suddenly felt off-balance in this charade and struggled to right herself.

She patted Charmaine's hand and poured her more coffee. "But we shouldn't waste this beautiful morning on arguments." She indicated the bright sun coming in from the patio windows. "Tell me about your work. It must be very exciting to travel, seeing the world and meeting new people. I think I'd love that."

Her brow wrinkled in genuine puzzlement, Charmaine stared at her plate as she began to stutter a response.

Sonny gave Shane an accusatory glare.

THE SUITE WAS EMPTY when Shane returned from taking Dusty to school. The women's witty and pointed exchange still hung in the air, creating a curious atmosphere of change he didn't precisely understand. Except that he knew Sonny had made Charmaine really suspect for the first time that she couldn't have him.

And Sonny, he knew, had mistaken Charmaine's injured pride for feelings of unrequited love. He had to set her straight.

He told the desk where to find him and headed for the flower shop.

The bell over the door rang cheerfully as he let himself in. The perfume of a dozen different fragrances hit him immediately, along with the warm, bright palette of fall colors.

The familiar old pang that fall decor always gave him struck for a moment, then Sonny walked out of the back room with her arms filled with a dozen fat-faced, sunny yellow mums, and he forgot suddenly that there was anything about the season to sadden him.

Her golden blond hair was tousled, probably by the denim cobbler apron she'd pulled on. Her cheeks were pink, her eyes mysteriously moody, and she looked like another flower in the bouquet she held. He had half expected to find her still in his pajamas.

She stopped abruptly when she saw him, obviously unhappy. He was surprised by the instant distress that caused him.

"Hi," he said quietly, coming toward her. "Did you walk here in my pj's? I'd have liked to see that."

She moved sideways until she'd placed the counter between them. She clutched the mums to her like a shield.

She angled her chin. "I asked the dress shop to send up jeans and a sweatshirt," she replied. Then she added gravely, "I'm glad you're here. We have to talk."

He leaned an elbow on the counter, collecting his thoughts. He had the feeling she intended to back out of their agreement.

"I'm here," he said, "to thank you for your quick thinking with Charmaine this morning."

She smiled thinly and nodded. "I was good, wasn't I? It's a little scary to know I can lie that smoothly."

He smiled, too, a little concerned by the unhappiness in her usually cheerful face. "All in a good cause."

She dropped the bouquet of flowers on the counter, and fiddled with one long, slender leaf before finally looking up at him.

"Shane," she said with a gusty sigh, "I think Charmaine loves you. I mean, really loves you. Maybe you should give this a chance. Maybe you could be happy with her."

He was shaking his head before she stopped. "She doesn't love me, Sonny. This is simply a case of a spoiled woman, who's always had everything she's wanted, making a crusade out of getting something she's discovered she can't have."

Sonny turned to open the floor-to-ceiling, refrigerated glass case behind her and placed the bouquet of mums in a utilitarian white vase filled with water. The case contained a dozen varieties of flowers in a rainbow of colors. She slid the door closed and turned to face him with a frown.

"I don't think so. I was looking into her eyes today when I told her you'd never be lured away from a woman you loved. She looked...heartbroken at the thought that she couldn't have you."

"She probably was heartbroken," he admitted, "but because she couldn't have what she wanted, not because she couldn't have *me.*"

"I don't know..."

"In a relationship, Charmaine and I would kill each other inside of twenty-four hours. Trust me."

She fussed with the red-silk maple leaves in the pumpkin display on the corner of the counter. "Well, I think you're missing a bet by not giving her a chance. All you do is work. Maybe your life could use her kind of tumult."

Shane caught her hand as she played with the leaf.

Sonny's eyes, wide and startled, settled on him.

"Is there another reason behind this?" he asked, his thumb running gently over her palm. "Do you want out of the deal?"

"Yes," she replied, deciding it was best to be honest. "I awoke this morning feeling frisky and full of myself, certain I was embarking on a great adventure. Then I found myself alone in the hotel suite with your clothes, Dusty's toys, your wife's artwork and the memory of Charmaine's heartbroken expression and I felt very... out of place."

"Sonny," he said gently. "Adventures seldom happen at home. I imagine you'll often find yourself having to adjust to strange surroundings. What can I do to make you more comfortable? Shall we bring some of your things over, pick up a few..."

He didn't seem to get the point.

"It isn't *things,*" she said. "It's... it's that the three of you are... connected. I'm just somebody who slipped on your bathroom floor at the right moment. A few minutes either way and you'd have been saved from Charmaine's attentions by someone else."

He had no idea how to explain to her—or himself, for that matter—how wrong she was. So he didn't try—at least not directly.

"Dusty's delighted that it was you."

She smiled wryly. "Dusty lives on an alien planet." She grew serious suddenly and squared her shoulders. She pulled her hand from his grasp. He continued to feel the soft silky touch of her skin. "I mean, who are we trying to kid, Shane?"

She *was* changing her mind. And though he didn't entirely understand what prompted her, he suspected it had something to do with the way they reacted to each other. He couldn't blame her. It worried him, too.

But he knew how to solve the problem—temporarily. Simply remind her and himself what it was all about.

"We're trying," he said evenly, "to kid Charmaine. And you're doing remarkably well. Don't panic now."

Of course, Sonny thought. That was all it was. A performance to keep his predatory sister-in-law at bay.

"Look," he said with a quick glance at his watch. "I've got to get back to the hotel. Promise me you'll think this through before you decide to back out."

She sighed. "If I do, will I lose the account?"

Shane gave that serious thought, annoyed with himself for not having seen that as an advantage before she'd brought it up. He smiled at her heartlessly. "If you decide not to help me, and Charmaine discovers it was all a plot, then it'd be pointless to have you around, wouldn't it? It'd be awkward for all of us."

Sonny wasn't sure why she was surprised and hurt. In the brief amount of time she'd spent with him, she'd found him autocratic, but kind. This threat seemed out of character.

She looked into his eyes and knew he was hiding something when he glanced downward. When he looked up at her again, his expression was free of innuendo.

"Just try to take it all a little less seriously. You're an adventuress, remember? And Charmaine doesn't need your sympathy, believe me. She does not love me, and I do not love her, except as a sister-in-law. But her amorous advances complicate my life, and we're hosting the hotel's first big dinner dance on Halloween. I don't need her in my way." He put a hand to her cheek, his touch light and insidiously affecting. "Think about how much we need each other."

She broke contact by walking to the door and opening it for him. "I'll think about it."

"Good."

She watched him walk away, hands in the pockets of his slacks, the hem of his jacket tugged tightly across his lean, muscular hips. She groaned, remembering the sight of them covered by nothing but a towel.

She turned briskly and went back into her workroom. Speaking of towels, she was throwing hers in. This was just too nerve-racking. She'd never been a coward, but she'd never been a fool, either, and that's what she'd have to be to subject herself to any more of Shane Archer.

It was time to make a clean break.

She was not going back.

Chapter Five

Burn couldn't find the Sun Queen. When he returned from his Federation duties, he checked Hearth Base 1 and saw no sign of her. He hadn't been alarmed until he checked her personal locker and found that her kit bag was gone.

He ran to inform the MM, but he was in diplomatic negotiations with the Federation's chief of security and couldn't be disturbed.

He tried Hearth Base 2.

"I HAVEN'T SEEN HER this afternoon, Dusty," Julian said, passing him one of the butterscotch candies he always kept at the desk. He glanced at his watch. "She has that flower shop next door, doesn't she? She's probably still there."

He shook his head. "Her shop's closed now. And she's supposed to be staying *here*. Remember? Dad told everybody."

Julian nodded, looking surreptitiously left, then right. "I know. To keep the Hawaiian barracuda off his back. But, you know, maybe they changed their minds."

"But it's only been one day."

"Sometimes that's all it takes to realize that you can't live in a pretend situation."

Burn didn't like the sound of that at all. He headed for Transportation, thinking they'd better have his Moon Wheel repaired.

Someone called his name, but he ignored it. He was heading for the Flowership.

SONNY IGNORED the knocking. The sign on the door clearly read that she closed at six. And she was busy with the terrariums. They were enjoying a resurgence in popularity, and required time and care to assemble. She also needed a chore that would keep her mind off Shane.

She wasn't going back to the hotel. She'd retrieved her bag at lunchtime when she'd seen Shane leave in a cab with several other people. She wanted to go to *her* home on the bay where no one kissed her unexpectedly, then reminded her that it was all a game.

The knocking at the door became urgent and moved to the side window. She peered out from the back, wondering if it was some poor out-of-favor husband needing a peace offering to take home to an angry wife.

She saw Dusty's face pressed up against the window just above her leaning stack of copper pots and buckets. With a groan that spoke more of her reluctance to let him further into her heart than simply into her shop, she went to open the door.

So this was the Flowership. Burn Starby was impressed. It was built more for comfort than for speed, but he liked the sensory detail of color and fragrance. The Sun Queen had a contingent of Pumpkin People aboard, and he went to present himself.

That protocol accomplished, he scolded her gently for not heeding the MM's instructions to stay put.

"Your father and I," she said, snapping a bright yellow flower from a bouquet on the counter, "have kind of agreed that maybe this wasn't such a good idea after all."

He doubted that. The MM would have told him. He had his complete confidence.

"He told me," Dusty said, "that we were all going out for Chinese food tonight."

"Well..." She leaned over him to tuck the flower into the eyelet on the front of his sweatshirt. "We talked about it and...you know, I have lots to do at home, and your aunt's here and wants to spend time with you. I really shouldn't be in the way."

He wondered if she were from Mars, rather than the Flower Planet. "*You'd* never be in the way. And he doesn't like her. I mean, he *likes* her, but not the way he likes you. You have to come back."

She stopped smiling, and gave him a look the MM sometimes wore. It usually came before he told him he couldn't have something he really wanted.

"That wouldn't be a good idea," she said, and straightened again. Then she smiled and touched his head. "Wait a minute. I just got something in today that I think you'll really like, but they're not unpacked yet. You sit right here—" she pushed him gently into a chair at a worktable in the back "—and I'll get one for you."

She disappeared behind a stack of boxes at the far end of the Flowership's freight bay.

He wasn't getting through to her, Burn thought, as he studied the various armaments around the room. There was a single red rose in a bud vase, and he leaned over to sniff it.

Alien environments, he knew, could garble communication. Perhaps she hadn't understood him.

Her voice continued to reach his ears from behind the boxes as his eyes fell on a Flowership helmet. That was it! Surely if he said the words again through a Flowership speaker, she would understand. Then he would take her back to the Master.

"Dusty!" Sonny shrieked from across the back room as she emerged from the stack of boxes, a ceramic rocket ship planter in her hands.

Dusty smiled at her, his head *inside* one of the terrarium globes she'd placed on the worktable to fill. She dropped the planter on the edge of the table and ran to him, reaching for the globe and pulling upward. Her heart thudded when it stopped firmly at his chin.

"Dusty!" she cried again, staring in horror at the slight curve the glass gave his beautiful little face. "How did you get in it?"

He shrugged, the action raising the globe up a few inches—but just until it reached his chin. Then it fell back again.

"I just put it on," he said, sounding as though he stood inside a bottle—an almost apt description she thought, trying desperately not to succumb to hysteria. "You have to come back to Hearth Base 1," he said. "The Mission Master wants you there."

"Dusty..." Sonny searched frantically through the old wooden box of tools she kept on the counter for assembling displays. Hammer. She needed a hammer.

She dug through every other tool she owned, wondering how much oxygen was contained within that small space. It wasn't airtight, of course, but still. If he panicked and began to hyperventilate...

She glanced at him. That didn't seem to be happening. She was the one who felt as though she were gasping for air.

Her fingers fell on the cool, rounded head of the hammer, and she raised it triumphantly out of the box.

Dusty's faintly fish-eyed expression grew a little concerned, and he took a step backward.

She couldn't use the hammer. Of course not. It would break the glass globe, certainly, but it might cut his face, and she wasn't sure what the blow required would do to his head.

The fire department! No, his father. With trembling fingers, she picked up the phone. Then she put it down again as she scrambled through the phone book for the number.

"It's 555..." Dusty said from his glass prison, reading her mind. "And, um... 7622. Extension 11."

But before she'd stabbed out the number, she heard a knocking at the door.

"Not now!" she shouted in the direction of the door, misdialing in her distraction and pressing the disconnect button to begin again. Then she straightened, waiting for the ring, and saw Shane's face peering through the glass door into the shop. He knocked again.

"Shane!" she called, slamming the receiver down and running to let him in. "Shane, I'm so sorry," she babbled, grabbing his arm and pulling him with her to the back room. "I left him for just a minute to find the rocket ship, and when I looked up, he had one of the terrariums on his head!"

For an instant, Shane feared Sonny had become part of his son's fantasy world herself. Then he spotted Dusty, looking a little like a Jules Verne character.

Shane took his son's arms and knelt on one knee in front of him. He frowned, reached his fingers inside the globe, testing, Sonny guessed, for air space.

"Can you breathe, Starby?" he asked.

Dusty nodded, the heavy glass wobbling against his head. He winced and put a hand up to it.

"Okay." Shane steadied the globe and smiled into the faintly distorted little face. "Just stand still. I'm going to call hotel maintenance."

Sonny handed Shane the receiver and stabbed the redial button. He cradled the receiver on his shoulder and began to pull off his jacket. Sonny helped him.

"Maintenance, please," Shane said into the receiver. He focused on Sonny as he waited to be connected, and pushed her gently into the chair at the worktable. "He's going to be fine. He's done worse than this and come out without a scratch. Mr. Busby? Hi. Archer. I need you to come to the flower shop next door to the hotel with your glass cutter. Yeah, right away. No. You'll see when you get here."

Shane cradled the receiver, then knelt in front of his son again. "So, what was the mission today, Starby?"

Dusty pointed to Sonny. "To bring her back to Hearth Base," he said in his eerily contained voice. "You left instructions she was to stay put."

"Mmm," Shane replied quietly. "But haven't I also left instructions that you're not to leave the hotel alone? Julian called me when you walked out."

Dusty managed to strike a dignified pose despite the globe on his head. "The mission is more important than my personal safety."

Sonny saw Shane's lips twitch, but he agreed gravely. "Of course."

Busby was a short, wiry little man with a thick shock of gray hair and an air of experience with this sort of crisis. He began at the side of the globe, cutting it up the middle with a careful, even stroke, talking all the while about an episode several weeks earlier when he'd helped extract Dusty from the laundry chute.

Shane grinned over the boy's head at Busby. "It was a wormhole," he corrected.

Busby chuckled, his hand still steadily cutting the glass. As he reached the top, Shane held the globe still with both hands. "Don't move, Dus," he said calmly. "Unless you want a sideways Mohawk."

"A what?" The boy's puzzled voice came faintly through the glass.

"Never mind. Just stand still."

Busby made it over the top of Dusty's head and started down the other side.

"Second day we were in residence here," Shane said with a smiling glance at Sonny, "he tried to slide down the awning over the coffee shop and into the pool."

"Really?" Sonny didn't want to hear the story, but it served as a distraction as the knife worked within a fraction of an inch of Dusty's ear and cheek.

"Got caught in the sag," Busby said with a laugh. "Had to haul out the fifteen-foot ladder. Kids. Make you crazy."

Busby reached the thick rim that was the top of the bowl, and Shane wedged his fingers into the opening to protect the boy's neck from the last stroke of the knife.

"Close your eyes tight," Busby said. Dusty complied.

Busby made his last stroke, missing Shane's fingers by a hairbreadth, and caught one side of the globe as it split apart and Shane caught the other.

Dusty emerged from his glass helmet with a big sigh. He smiled at Sonny, then glanced up at his father, his expression uncertain. "Am I in trouble?"

Shane dropped his half of the globe into the wastebasket Sonny held up. "I'd like to hear your explanation before I decide. And try to do it from planet Earth, okay?"

Dusty frowned. "But we're on the Flowership. The Sun Queen speaks only Flower. That's why I put on one of her helmets. I thought its communicator would help her understand me. Because she didn't before."

Sonny took Busby's half of the globe and put the basket down before giving the boy her full attention. She tried to ignore his father. She was only vaguely aware that Busby let himself out after a handshake from Shane.

"I did understand you, Dusty," she said, sitting in the chair and pulling him to her. "You wanted me to come back to the hotel, but I..."

Dusty put his arms around her and rested his head on her small bosom. "Please? I like having breakfast with you. We could have treasure kabobs every day."

Sonny looked up at Shane for support, but he merely looked back at her, challenging her to handle this in her own way.

She told herself it would be wiser, and more gentle in the end, to make Dusty understand that she was not a *real* part of his life. But he raised his head to look up at her with soulful dark eyes—and she took the coward's way out.

"All right, but only until your aunt leaves."

She hugged him fiercely and set him on his feet. She stood to challenge his father. "Until Charmaine leaves."

"Of course," he said. "That was the original plan, after all."

She looked shaken and a little confused. Shane resisted the urge to touch her.

She nodded vaguely. "I'll get my coat." She disappeared through a door at the back.

Dusty turned to him, palm raised for a high five. "Mission accomplished," he said with a broad grin.

Shane allowed him the momentary success, then caught the hand Dusty slapped against his, and held it as he leaned down to say firmly, "You are not to leave the hotel by yourself again for *any* reason. Is that clear?"

"But, Dad." Victory was eclipsed by concern. "Sonny wasn't going to come—"

"I know," Shane interrupted. "But that was between her and me."

Dusty opened his mouth to complain. Shane shook his head. "This is one of those things you don't have a say in. You do not leave the hotel alone. Do you understand me?"

Dusty heaved a deep sigh. He'd encountered these situations before and hadn't liked them then, either.

"Yes. I understand."

"Good. And you have to pay Sonny for the terrarium—" At the boy's puzzled look, he amended the name. "The helmet—out of your allowance."

Dusty nodded. "Okay."

"And don't push her."

"Push her?"

"Don't make her feel like we're going to die if she isn't there."

Dusty thought that over for a moment before asking with a look of puzzlement, "You mean... don't love her?"

Shane closed his eyes for a moment and decided to retreat while he could still consider this a partial victory.

SHANE TOOK SONNY and Dusty to the Golden Star for Chinese food. Sonny marveled at the boy's dexterity with chopsticks.

Shane, opting to use a fork as she did, smiled fondly at his son, expertly collecting a bite of chow yuk. "The chef at our hotel on Honolulu was Chinese, so Dusty was coached by the best."

Sonny studied the child. His beautiful, pink-cheeked face was set as he gave the task his complete attention, and it was impossible to tell that less than an hour before, he'd been trapped in an overturned fishbowl.

"He certainly looks none the worse for his experience," she noted, her eyes revealing her own less-than-relaxed reaction. "I was about to hyperventilate myself when you arrived. It's a good thing I'm just pretending motherhood. I don't think I have the nerves for it."

He shrugged a shoulder and dipped a shrimp in hot mustard. "Parenthood is half terror and half joy. I guess you just learn to cope with one to experience the other. He's probably going to be the next Indiana Jones, or something equally hazardous to his health."

"Indiana Jones in space," she mused with a little laugh. "Or Indiana Starby? Is that what you called him?"

Shane bit the shrimp in half, then nodded as he popped the last bite into his mouth. "Burn Starby," he said after he swallowed. "A sort of troubleshooter in space on Saturday morning television. He's Dusty's full-blown fantasy life."

Dusty put his chopsticks down and reached for his water. He took a long gulp, then wiped his mouth on his shirtsleeve.

"Hey," Shane said, handing him the linen napkin ignored on his lap. "Handling your napkin is as important as handling your chopsticks."

"Forgot," Dusty said. He dutifully dabbed at his mouth, then told Sonny seriously, "Dad's the Mission Master. He's the boss of the Federation in our quadrant."

Shane gave her a teasingly superior look as he reached for his teacup. "Show a little respect, please. Or I can have you exiled to one of the moons of Jupiter."

"A cold and barren place, I suppose?"

"Right. No flowers. You'd be out of a job."

Dusty pulled on his father's arm. "No she wouldn't. She's the Sun Queen. They can't fire you from that, can they?"

Sonny blinked. "The sun who?"

"The Sun Queen," Dusty repeated, leaning earnestly toward her. "You're important to the future of our planet."

Sonny's eyes went to Shane's. He put his now empty cup down and nodded gravely. "It's true."

"Why?" She looked from Dusty to Shane, willing to play along just to enjoy the bright sparkle of imagination in the boy's eyes. "Does my kingdom have the water you need, or something? Or, I know! We mine a crystal that provides your fuel? Is that it?"

"Got me," Shane admitted, reaching to the edge of her plate for the red pepper she'd removed from her kung pow chicken. "It's his scenario. Why do we need the Sun Queen, Starby?"

"She has the babies," Dusty said matter-of-factly. "So our planet will be strong and powerful."

"Babies?" Sonny and Shane exchanged a wary look. "How many babies?"

"Well, you don't have any *yet,*" Dusty explained, as though surprised she didn't already understand. "You'll have them with the Mission Master because he's the strongest and the bravest man on the planet, and you're the kindest and the most beautiful woman in the galaxy."

"I . . . see." She tried to avoid Shane's eyes, but they drew her as though he truly did have great power.

He held a hand casually over his mouth, but his eyes were alight with humor.

Laughter finally bubbled out of her. "I didn't know cartoons dealt with interplanetary propagation."

He shook his head. "And to think all I was worried about was Beavis and Butt-Head."

Dusty shifted into his father's lap. "Dad, I'm getting full," he complained on a yawn.

Shane leaned back in the booth and pushed his plate out of the way. Dusty settled into the crook of his arm, his eyelids drooping. "Should I fall asleep?" he asked practically. "Or are we going to have dessert?"

"There's no dessert here," Shane replied. "But we can get that praline torte you like from Fernando when we get home."

Dusty sat up, eyes big and heavy. He smiled sleepily at Sonny. "It has nuts and brown sugar. I'm going to stay awake."

He tried valiantly, but was asleep before Shane turned the red Audi into the hotel's parking garage. He sat buckled into the back seat, his body slumped sideways, and Sonny reached in to protect his head as Shane pulled his limp body out.

His eyelashes fluttered and he muttered something before settling against Shane's shoulder and falling sound asleep again.

"He'll be disappointed that he missed the torte," Sonny said, as she waited in the bedroom doorway while Shane placed him in the middle of the twin bed and pulled his shoes off.

"He can have it for breakfast." Shane pointed to the bright blue dresser that matched the campaign-style furniture. "Pj's are in the second drawer."

"Torte for breakfast?" Sonny whispered in surprise as she looked through the tidy drawer and found white flannel pajamas imprinted to look like a space suit. She held them up. "These?"

"Yes." Shane took them from her as he held the child against him while removing his jacket and shirt. "Dessert for breakfast isn't generally accepted," he admitted with a smiling glance up at her as he skillfully managed limp arms and legs and a lolling head. "But I bend the rules to keep him smiling. He's been through a lot for a little guy, and much of it without complaint."

Sonny reevaluated her earlier assessment of him. Maybe he wasn't *just* like her father and her brother.

She remembered a similar incident with her father when she'd been nine, and too excited to eat lunch before her birthday party. Her father had stuck to the 'no clean plate, no dessert' rule, and she'd been unable to

have a piece of her own birthday cake. She'd never forgotten it.

Shane stood to pull the blankets over Dusty, and noticed her frowning study of him. "What?" he asked
softly.

She straightened away from the molding and shook
her head. "Nothing. If you'll excuse me, I'll say good-
night."

He leaned down to place a kiss on Dusty's forehead,
then came to the doorway. "Without praline torte?"

She smiled faintly, feeling a desperate need to put
space between herself and him. "Maybe I can have mine
for breakfast, too. Good night."

He caught her arm as she turned away. She felt every
one of his fingertips in contact with the sensitive flesh
of her inner arm, was aware of both the gentle but in-
escapable grip and the pulse at the bend of her elbow
that reacted like a hovering hummingbird.

She raised an eyebrow in question, pretending calm.

The pose lasted all of three seconds. He backed her
gently against the wall and braced an arm above her
head. The hand that held her arm stroked gently where
her pulse beat.

He could feel it racing, she was sure. And he could
probably tell that his nearness had pinched off her air.
Only willpower prevented her from gasping for breath.

"Thank you for coming back," he said, his voice just
above a whisper. Dusty's door remained half open. "I
know you didn't want to."

There were a dozen reasons why she did and why she
didn't, but her mind couldn't organize them. The narrow corridor seemed to be shrinking, closing her and
Shane into a smaller and smaller space. She struggled
to retain control of her senses.

"I . . . don't want to hurt Charmaine," she said.

She felt Shane's hand toy with a strand of her hair. Gooseflesh rose on her scalp and followed the line of her spine. She shifted her weight to disguise the little shudder of sensation.

"Neither do I," Shane said. While he spoke, his head dipped lower until his mouth was just inches from hers and the concentration in his dark eyes roving her face had her paralyzed with anticipation. "That's why it's important for her to understand I'm not available. Please. Just settle in and help me convince her."

His mouth was a centimeter from hers when she wedged a hand between them and flattened it against his chest.

"I will," she said, her voice high and breathless. "If you'll stop kissing me. Kisses . . . should mean something."

His heart pumped firmly against her hand. "Who says they don't mean anything?"

"You did." She pointed a finger at his chest. "I asked who I was trying to kid, and you said 'Charmaine.' We're trying to fool someone, so it doesn't mean anything. It's not that hard to figure out."

He considered that while his eyes continued to rove her face with a fascination he seemed to find endless. She found it torturous.

"It *shouldn't* be hard to figure out." That hand above her head dipped into her hair again. It felt as though he wrapped a curl around his finger. "But it is. I kissed you the first time to shock Charmaine, but actually . . . it shocked me." A line of concern formed between his neat dark brows. "I felt your lips against mine all afternoon."

The hand that had held her arm now moved so that his knuckles stroked gently along her jaw. "Then you walked into the hotel and kissed me." He shook his head, giving her a smile that reflected genuine wonder. "It threw me for a loop, Sonny."

It seemed urgent to struggle against the seductive net slipping over her. "I came back," she said, forcing a steady tone of voice. "For Dusty."

"Really." His bland expression somehow communicated disbelief. "What happened to the adventuress?"

"Got some sense," she whispered.

He leaned down and kissed her very lightly. "Don't let that happen," he said, raising his head to let those dark eyes rove over her face again. They settled on her trembling lips for a moment, then looked into her eyes with gleaming satisfaction. "Adventurers thrive on impulse, don't they? On living for the moment and going for the outside limits of what's possible."

She should pull away, but she couldn't. "I don't know," she said against his lips. "Do they? This is my first adventure."

He proceeded to test his theory. He took the hand she held between them and curled it into his as he pulled her into his free arm . . . and opened his mouth on hers.

She kissed him back, Sonny told herself, because it was like being resuscitated and she desperately needed the oxygen. It filled her lungs, rayed out to speed her blood and feed her brain, to intoxicate her.

Shane felt her hand at the nape of his neck, her fingertips reaching up into his hair, activating every nerve ending in his body.

He didn't know what possessed him. Kissing her had begun as an act to show Charmaine that she couldn't have him. But now, at this moment, with his sister-in-law safely behind her locked door across the hall, he concluded that he was trying not only to prove something to Sonny—but to himself, as well. He realized that meant he was putting the past behind him.

Part of him wanted to reach back for it, afraid to let it go. But another part, the one that was holding Sonny, didn't want to free either hand. Some psychiatrist would probably understand his reaction, but it confused the hell out of him.

So he chose not to think about it. He just went a little deeper into the kiss and was rewarded with her soft lips.

Sonny felt his hand, splayed against her back, begin a downward movement. It caressed her spine, measured her waist, slipped over her hip. As it cupped her bottom, she felt a delicious shudder, and she pushed out of his arms, afraid all the oxygen she'd stolen from him would cause her to combust.

"Even an adventuress," she said, drawing a shaky breath, "has to have some sense of self-preservation."

He guessed she was right. He felt a little threatened himself. But it was a risk that drew rather than repelled him. But he honored her need to break away.

"Right," he said. He put a hand to the back of her neck and walked her the few feet to the bedroom doorway. "We're having a staff meeting in the morning about the Halloween ball. Can someone watch the shop so you can be there?"

The sudden invasion of practical matters left her momentarily disoriented. But she pulled herself together, and recalled that Denise had promised to be on hand for a while.

"Yes. What time?"

"Ten-thirty. I'd like you to tell the staff what you're planning to do. And Fernando wants to talk to you about centerpieces."

"Yes, of course." She blinked at him, marveling that he could be the consummate lover one moment and the quintessential businessman the next. "I made some sketches in bed the other night. I could copy those."

He gave her a suddenly wicked smile, reverting without warning to the lover of a second ago. She struggled to maintain her equilibrium. "You work in bed?" he asked.

She dared him with a look. "Don't you? I saw a leather portfolio on your bedside table."

He gave her a rueful smile. "I guess that's the lot of the single capitalist. Sad, isn't it?"

She had to admit that it was. One should be either too exhausted by a full day to lie awake a single moment, or have some wildly passionate lover to fill the time until sleep.

She, unfortunately, had enormous reserves of energy and no one on whom to expend them.

He read the thought in her eyes, felt the uncomfortable pressure of aroused and unfulfilled desire and said with a sigh, "Yeah." It was a simple sound of frustrated understanding that locked their gazes, and made them even more in tune than the kiss had.

"Good night," he said, and turned and walked away.

Chapter Six

"Pastry?"

Sonny turned to her right to accept the silver tray of pastries presented on a fussy paper doily. Jenny Biggs, short, plump and the kindhearted but authoritarian head of Housekeeping, pointed to a fresh round bun dusted with powdered sugar. "Try that one," she said. "It's filled with cream cheese and strawberry. Fernando makes them himself."

Across the table, a stout middle-aged man wearing a pristine chef's hat and kitchen whites—and a pencil-thin mustache—inclined his head in a regal bow.

Sonny transferred the treat to her plate, unwilling to admit that she'd had Fernando's praline torte for breakfast. She would wrap it in a napkin and take it back to the shop for lunch. The chef had every right to that confident, royal air—and if she was going to stay at the hotel for any length of time, she was going to have to find a way to put distance between herself and his irresistible food.

As the tray passed among the seven gathered around the table in Shane's office, he reviewed the basic points they'd discussed for the past hour.

"I'm sure I don't have to tell you how important it is that we make a good impression with a memorable menu . . ." Shane inclined his head in Fernando's direction as though to indicate his confidence in that direction. "Perfect appearance . . ." Jenny got the nod. "Flawless service . . ."

Jason Culbert, the head waiter, shifted in his chair and said with a quiet, cultured accent, "Of course."

Shane turned to Sonny. "And dynamite decor."

His attention surprised her for a moment. She'd arrived an hour ago, convinced Shane had invited her merely to give her something to do to until Charmaine left.

But Shane had a wonderful staff who were willing to help convince Charmaine that their boss and Sonny had a loving relationship.

And when he'd introduced her around, the small group had pored over her sketches with all-apparent interest and approval, and eased her into their professional but comfortable circle. For someone who usually struggled alone on a daily basis, the acceptance was a bonus she hadn't expected.

She nodded regally in an imitation of Jason and Fernando. "You'll have your dynamite decor."

Shane created an impression of relaxed, but complete, control—yet there was something in his smile for her alone. "Good." He turned to the desk manager, a tall, elegant blonde Sonny guessed was probably ten years older than she looked. "We'll be well staffed, I'm sure, Brenda?"

"Already scheduled, with two clerks on call, just in case."

"Excellent." He looked around the group. "Anything we haven't covered?"

"Costumes." Alice Falkner, the banquet manager, spoke from the far end of the table. "The mayor has decreed that we *all* appear in costume—in fact he's pledged a considerable personal donation to the hospital's geriatric unit if he doesn't find one person in street dress. There are definite advantages to having a wealthy mayor."

Sonny saw Shane hesitate a moment. "The serving staff can't wait on tables in costume."

Jason, apparently not as stuffy as he looked, cleared his throat and considered the matter. "We could think of something that would permit us to comply. Mardi Gras masks, or something." He turned to Alice. "Would that do?"

"I think so." She grinned. "But the rest of you will have to come through in full costume. Some of us have been to this annual ball in the past when it was held at the fairgrounds or in the armory. The charitable spirit was there, of course, but both places are cold as a barn and about as stylish.

"Because we're hosting it this year, the hospital auxiliary is expecting to double attendance and also make an impressive contribution to the geriatric center. Come on. What do you say?"

Fernando indicated his hat. "I am already in costume. Therefore I am exempted."

Alice shook her head. "Sorry, Ferd. You'll be expected to come out of the kitchen after dinner and take your applause. The guests will expect to see you in costume."

He seemed to be caught between the impossibility of moving around a busy kitchen in costume, and the tempting thought of accepting praise.

"You can dress after dessert is served," Jason suggested.

Fernando gave him a lethal glance for finding a plausible solution. It changed eventually to a sunny smile. "Very well. I will appear in costume."

Alice challenged Shane with a direct gaze. "And you, boss?"

"I," he said with a disarmingly embarrassed grin, "have to be visible as the manager in case there's..."

Teasing catcalls from the staff halted his excuse.

"If Fernando has to dress," the chef said with a broad Latin gesture of his magic hand, "El Jefe—the chief," he translated for his non-Spanish-speaking companions, "has to dress as well."

Shane looked grimly from face to face. "What is this? Mutiny?"

"Yes!" they replied in chorus.

He raised his hands in defeat. "Fine. I was just asking."

"I think you'd better simply agree to appear in costume," Sonny said, barely suppressing a smile, "or resign yourself to walking the plank."

"There!" Alice said. "You could be a pirate."

"Or a Gypsy king," Jenny suggested. "All that takes is colorful old clothes and beads."

Shane grimaced at the thought. "All right, all right! I'll be in costume. But you'll all pay for this." He grinned as he threatened, "I'll solicit the next Bigfoot Watcher's convention."

"Can't scare us," Brenda said. "We hosted the Mosquito Abatement District meeting and survived the boredom to talk about it. We're invincible."

Shane gave her a dark glance and closed his calendar. "Back to work, you scurvy lot. Back here same time next week for an update."

When the office had cleared, Shane and Sonny remained at the table. He groaned as he rubbed a hand over his face.

"I'll make your costume," Sonny said, patting his shoulder comfortingly. Watching his employees tease him had been enlightening. The boss had a soft side. "You don't have to give it another thought."

He studied her suspiciously. "What kind of costume?"

She smiled. "It'll be a surprise."

"Oh, no," he said, moving to take the chair beside her. "I want to know what you have in mind."

She shook her head. "It's going to take a little research."

"Uh-oh."

"Relax," she said. "You can approve the sketches. I minored in Fashion Design in college, so I know what I'm doing. Trust me."

He leaned toward her on an elbow, his eyes dark and suddenly lazy. "I'm not sure that's safe," he said softly.

"*I* trust *you,*" she reminded him, resisting the snare of his seductive teasing.

"That might not be safe either."

"Now you tell me," she whispered, slipping into his trap.

The office door burst open. "Well. I was told there was an important meeting in progress." Charmaine walked into the room, Shane's sputtering secretary behind her.

"It's all right, Millie," he said to the gray-haired woman staring indignantly at the back of Charmaine's head. She pulled the door closed with a burning glare at the intruder.

Charmaine tilted her head toward the door as she approached the table. She wore a simple purple suit that dramatized her vivid coloring and clung lovingly to her generous proportions. "Witch. She wasn't going to let me see you, even after I threatened her job."

"My staff is fearlessly loyal," Shane said, an ironic tone in his voice. "What's up?"

She sat on the edge of the conference table and crossed one knee over the other, revealing a flawlessly shaped limb covered in purple hose with a subtle pattern running down the side. She smiled into Shane's eyes. "I came to see if I could take you to lunch?"

"Thanks." He shook his head. "But Sonny and I—"

Sonny stood and interrupted him with a pleasant smile at Charmaine. "Of course you can. I have a shipment of cornstalks coming into the flower shop in fifteen minutes."

Charmaine raised an eyebrow. "Cornstalks?" She shuddered. "We're not having a hoedown, or something equally vulgar, are we?"

"Close enough," Shane said. "A Halloween costume ball." He gave Sonny a warning look and made a grab for her wrist. She stepped beyond his reach with a teasing smile calculated to make Charmaine think this was all just play between lovers.

Sonny stuffed her notes and sketches into a flowered briefcase. "But I have to give you a few ground rules," she told Charmaine. "You have to sit across the table from Shane, not beside him, you *cannot* order oysters, and if you leave fingerprints on him, I'll know about t." Then she smiled. "And there'll be hell to pay. Otherwise, have fun."

Sonny waved and left the room, aware of Charmaine's look of surprise, and Shane's silent promise of retribution.

SHANE INSERTED HIS CARD in the lock, then pushed the door open with his shoulder, a gray cloud over his customary positive outlook. Two hours sitting across the table from Charmaine had drained him of the last vestige of social finesse. A scene in the elevator—where she'd tried to kiss him and he'd been forced to give her an attention-getting shake—had probably ruined their relationship forever.

He needed an hour on a racquet ball court, he thought, or a couple of rounds with Joe Frazier to rid himself of temper and frustration.

He wasn't sure why it annoyed him to find Sonny lying on the carpet on her stomach in front of the television watching one of the films from the *Star Wars* trilogy. Maybe, he reflected, because he was presented with the appealing sight of shapely calves in black tights, bent at the knee and tipped backward toward a round little derriere. And because all the while Charmaine had been giving him seductive looks, tracing his calf with her stockinged toe under the restaurant table, and wrapping her arms around his neck in the elevator—all he'd been able to think about had been Sonny...who'd left him to Charmaine's mercy.

"Hard at work, I see," he said quietly, a mild snap to his voice as he tossed his briefcase on the sofa and headed for the bathroom and a long, hot shower.

He pushed the door open and stopped on the threshold with a gasp of surprise. The bathroom was full of cornstalks tied together in fat bundles and leaning on one another like dominoes in the act of falling.

A voice in his brain rang in a strong soprano "...the corn is as high as an elephant's eye..."

A trail had been cleared to the tub, to the commode and to the sink. He turned, prepared to shout at Sonny, and found her standing right behind him. She wore a long red-and-black flannel shirt over the tights. He made a point of not looking at her legs.

He leaned a shoulder against the molding and folded his arms. "Why," he demanded, "does the bathroom look like the opening sequence of *Oklahoma?*"

"You wanted fall decor," she replied evenly, "and this is a big place. My shop is small and rather full. I'm putting it up tomorrow, so it'll be out of your way in the morning."

Sonny thought he seemed unimpressed with her explanation. His ill temper was obvious, and she guessed it had something to do with the way she had abandoned him to Charmaine at lunchtime.

"I wish you'd put as much enthusiasm into the part of the bargain that was to benefit *me*..." He indicated himself with a thumb jabbed at the white shirt visible under his dark suit jacket. He'd shed his tie somewhere along the way. "As you are into the part that's to benefit you."

She pretended to misunderstand. "You'll be pleased with my work, I assure you."

He leaned down several inches until they were eye-to-eye. He was impressive in a temper, she thought. Eyes dark and sparking fire, jaw taut, and that usually smiling mouth in a stark, straight line. Her eyes lingered there a moment.

"I'm talking," he said with strained patience, "about this morning when you abandoned me to Charmaine."

Considering his stature and the almost pathetic sound of the words, she had to exert all her self-control not to smile.

"I thought a man with those shoulders," she said, her eyes running quickly over their considerable proportions, "could protect himself from a much smaller woman."

"Inside that much smaller woman," Shane said lightly, "is the spirit of an armored tank. Handling her would require everything I learned in boot camp about hand-to-hand combat. And I'm simply not willing to knock her unconscious."

Sonny asked interestedly, "So she *did* leave fingerprints?"

"She tried valiantly, but I escaped, no thanks to you." Deciding to forget the shower, Shane headed for the bedroom door, planning instead to change his clothes and go down to the sauna.

He tripped over a pumpkin before he realized the entire floor was littered with them. There must have been over one hundred. He turned again, prepared to shout, and found her standing in the doorway.

Before he could ask, she said, "I called an order in right after you asked me to decorate. The shipment arrived more quickly than I expected, so I wasn't really prepared. They, too, will be gone in the morning."

"There are enough pumpkins in here to feed the entire Plymouth Colony!"

She sighed patiently. "The trucker had an uncommitted stock of pumpkins, and since this morning's meeting when both day care and Fernando asked for them, I got more."

He struggled for patience. "Anything else I should know? Where is my son, incidentally?"

"In the kitchen peeling carrots." On cue, Dusty's voice called from the kitchen, "Hi, Dad!"

"Hi, Dusty!" Shane called back. To Sonny he said moodily, "I remember when he used to come to the door to welcome me home."

She gave him an innocent smile. "You were probably nicer then. You should know that there are wheat bundles and gourds and dried corn in Dusty's room, and a meat loaf in the oven. If you think you can be civil, dinner's in half an hour. The steam won't hurt the cornstalks if you want to take a shower."

She marched off in a haughty huff that somehow sapped his anger and restored his equanimity, if not his sense of humor.

Dusty had seconds on meat loaf and ate his carrots without complaint. He molded his mashed potatoes into a lunarlike landscape, then ate them.

"Dinner was delicious," Shane said, catching Sonny's wrist and standing beside her when she tried to take his plate. "Dusty and I will clean up. I'd forgotten how delicious meat loaf can be."

The return of his good humor brought back her own. "I suppose chefs like Fernando can spoil your palate for simple food."

"Sonny should show Fernando how to make this!" Dusty said, his eyes wide with enthusiasm as he picked up his empty glass and his father's coffee cup. "I'll bet everybody who comes to the restaurant would like it, too."

Shane wrapped an arm around Sonny and laughed as he walked her to the hallway. "Now, there's an idea. Have a long, slow soak while we fill the dishwasher."

He stopped in the doorway to smile down at her. "Thank you for cooking. I've missed that most of all, I think."

Sonny nodded. "I enjoyed it. Living alone, I seldom spend time in the kitchen."

His arm still rested lightly around her shoulder as he leaned distractedly against the door frame.

"I don't mean that I just miss Allie cooking for me," he said quietly, "because by the nature of our work, we ate out so much of the time. But when we were home, I loved the aroma of something cooking, the comfort of sitting around a table, even with Dusty banging his high-chair tray with a spoon." His smile widened at that thought. "Of lingering over second and third cups of coffee while we talked over the current crisis or big decision. Getting up in the middle of the night to have leftovers."

He came out of the **past** with a shake of his head and, curiously, a quick hug for her. "Take your time," he said. "We don't have perfumed bubble bath, but Dusty loves that stuff in the turtle bottle. A capful makes enough bubbles to hit the ceiling, so be careful."

Sonny sat in the hot tub, completely confused. She'd used only half a cap of the turtle stuff and had bubbles up to her chin—and lovesickness up to her brain.

This was no good, she knew. This was trouble. But there didn't seem to be much she wanted to do about it. He'd come back, she'd fixed dinner—she was falling in love.

Laughter reached her ears even through the closed door—high-pitched childish giggles, and deep, rich male notes of happiness. A little thrill of satisfaction filled her at the thought that she was partially responsible for

It was curious, she thought, that Shane had seemed so at ease talking to her about those cozy times with Allie, and that she hadn't been uncomfortable hearing about them.

Maybe something was developing between them. That would be nice. What this situation needed was the stability of mutual appreciation and respect. Yes. That would get them through until Charmaine left.

Judging by Shane's report on his lunch with Charmaine, she had no intention of abandoning her pursuit anytime soon.

So the question became—Sonny inspected a handful of bubbles and saw her face reflected in the tiny spheres—did she have the courage and ingenuity to convince Charmaine that Shane was hers?

She remembered his gentle hug, then saw her smile reflected over and over in the bubbles.

She laughed softly and blew the bubbles away. She intended to do her damnedest.

WHILE DUSTY placed plates in the dish rack, Shane checked the living room for the coffee mug he usually left there, or the pop can Dusty often forgot. Finding nothing, he began to turn back to the kitchen when his eyes fell on the sketch pad on the floor in front of the television.

He went toward it, wondering what it was doing there. Then he remembered Sonny lying on the floor when he'd come home, a pencil poised over the pad as she watched television.

What she was doing with it was none of his business, but he chose not to let that stop him. He reached down for the pad, then perched on the arm of a chair and looked through it.

The first page was a fairly competent sketch of a young boy in a costume resembling Burn Starby's. Attached to the page with a clip was the cartoon character himself cut out of the newspaper. She'd noted colors, and had done a few detail sketches of costume accessories.

At the top of the page in block letters were the words, Dusty's Costume.

He smiled and turned the page. Then he grimaced at the words, Shane's Costume. The frown turned to a surprised tilt of his eyebrow at the sketch of a tall man in tight-fitting, military-looking jacket and pants. He wore epaulets, knee-high boots, a sword and an insignia of a flower crossed with a crescent moon and the monogram MM.

SONNY WALKED into the bedroom wrapped in a towel, and found Shane sitting on a corner of her bed. He squared one knee on the other, and concentrated on the sketch pad balanced on it. She stopped just inside the door with a little gasp of surprise and a quick backward step.

He looked up and stopped any thought she may have had of retreating unseen with a softly threatening, "Oh, no, you don't."

Sonny clutched her clothes in one hand, and the top of her towel in the other while she debated nervously what to do.

She could put the clothes on, but that would require removing the towel. She could remain in the towel, but he was already surveying everything visible above and below it as he unfolded slowly to his feet. And when he looked at her in that way, she became dangerously impulsive and downright reckless.

When his roving gaze met her eyes, she replied coolly, "Oh, yes, I do. Or you have to turn around while I get dressed."

"I'm more interested," he said, coming toward her, "in your thoughts on dressing *me*."

She took two steps backward. "You mean the costume thing?"

He kept coming. "I mean the costume thing. I want modifications, or I'm not wearing it."

"But..." She stood her ground and angled her chin. "Dusty's thrilled with it."

"I'm not," he said simply. He stopped with barely a hairbreadth between them, not touching her but close enough that the expansion of his chest—or her nervous breath—would put them in contact. She remained still.

He folded his arms and looked down at her. It was only then that she saw the smallest betrayal of humor in his eyes.

"I refuse," he said, "to look like some Spandex Buck Rogers."

He reached out and she ducked sideways, intent on avoiding contact at all cost. But he caught her with his free arm, an eyebrow raised in gentle mockery.

"A queen should have steadier nerves," he observed as he held up the plush robe he'd reached for off the chair.

"A queen," she countered, trying to keep the quiver out of her voice, "should have privacy in her chambers."

He grinned as he placed the robe around her shoulders. "But you're going to have my babies, remember?" He held the sides out until she found the sleeves. "Seems silly to stand on ceremony."

She moved carefully, mindful of the towel, then closed the robe and belted it. "I thought ceremony and being royal went hand in hand."

"In this case," Shane corrected, "at least according to Dusty, it's about allying our tribes to save our planet. And I can't imagine any serious stud wearing tights and a Nehru jacket." Then without warning, he reached into her robe at about thigh level and grabbed the end of her towel. "Untie it," he directed.

"I'll do it when I'm—"

With a deft yank, he relieved her of it and balled it in his hands.

She uttered a strangled little scream and held the robe more tightly around her. "What do you think you're doing?"

"Preventing you from catching pneumonia. Tell me that isn't more comfortable." He leaned into the hallway and tossed the towel into the bathroom with a hook shot. Then he turned back to confront her, hands loosely on his hips. "Lighten up. You're still wearing a robe."

"Shane Archer," she threatened, "the moment you start taking liberties I—"

She wasn't sure what it was about Shane's expression that alerted her to another presence in the room. He barely moved a muscle, and his calm, even gaze barely wandered. But she saw his focus sharpen at the same moment that she caught a whiff of Charmaine's cologne. Dusty, watching TV in the living room, must have let her in.

Without betraying knowledge of the woman's appearance, Sonny mustered self-control with considerable effort and crossed the space that separated her from Shane. His expression changed with dramatic subtlety from vague annoyance to masculine satisfaction.

"The first time you take liberties," she repeated, but in a low, seductive tone as she looped her arms around his waist, "I'll follow you to the ends of the earth."

"Mmm," he said, wrapping his arms around her and lowering his head to taste her lips. "I love you when you act wanton. Why don't we ... ?" He made as though to slip the robe off her shoulders, then pretended to notice his sister-in-law.

"Charmaine," he said, turning Sonny in his arm and holding her to him. "Something wrong?"

Charmaine, dressed in silky red-and-black sweats Sonny was certain had never been exercised in, lounged in the doorway. She smiled blandly from one to the other, her expression void of emotion.

"Sorry to intrude," she said politely, "but since tomorrow's Saturday and you're working, I was wondering if I could have Dusty for the day. I thought I'd take him to Portland to the zoo and do some touristy things."

He frowned. "Do you know where you're going?"

She raised an eyebrow. "I've hired a car and driver. Merriwether has only one, but he does seem competent."

"Then, sure," Shane replied. "I imagine Dusty will be thrilled."

Charmaine shifted her weight and smiled wryly. "Actually, he wanted to stay with Sonny, until I showed him the newspaper ad about the "Star Trek" cast visiting the museum of science and industry right across the road. Then he was putty in my hands." She focused significantly on Sonny in his arms. "You ought to know all about that."

Before either of them could comment on that remark, Dusty appeared at Charmaine's side in blue sleepers. "Can I go, Dad? Can I?"

"Of course you can." Shane freed Sonny to catch the boy as he ran into his arms. "As long as you promise all the usual."

"Right. No wandering off, no talking to strangers, no turning knobs and flipping switches."

"Then it's a deal."

Dusty ran off whooping.

"I'll pick him up at eight," Charmaine said with a smile. "I have a big day planned." She turned away, then turned back as though suddenly remembering something. "Do go back to whatever it was you were arguing about," she said quietly, emphasizing her words with a waggle of one eyebrow. "It appeared to be headed toward an interesting outcome. But don't grow complacent. I haven't given up. I'm just regrouping while you two work this weekend. 'Night."

The moment the outer door closed behind her, Sonny turned to Shane as though their conversation had never been interrupted.

"The moment you take liberties with the situation, I..." she threatened, shaking her finger at him.

He caught it and used it to pull her toward him. He kissed her quickly. "You'll follow me to the ends of the earth," he reminded her with a final little nibble to her bottom lip. "That promise is imprinted on my mind."

Sonny opened her mouth to protest, but Dusty called from his bedroom, "Da-ad!"

Shane acknowledged the untimely interruption with a rueful groan.

"Coming!" he called back over his shoulder. "Gotta tuck him in," he said to Sonny. "Want to come?"

She wanted to say no because it didn't seem fair to Dusty to deepen his belief in the fantasy of the Sun Queen and the Mission Master. Then the boy's voice rang out again, "Sonny! I need you to come, too!"

Sonny shared the parental duty with Shane, then excused herself the moment the boy's bedroom door was closed.

"Getting angry isn't going to help, you know," Shane said matter-of-factly as she headed for her bedroom. "Anger only seems to feed what I'm feeling, so I let it go."

She frowned at him worriedly. "What are you feeling?"

"Lust," he admitted honestly. "And strong feelings of any kind just seems to fuel it. So the best thing to do is just not get excited—about anything."

She gave him a scornful roll of her eyes. "Spoken like a man." She mocked a deep voice saying, "*Just keep cool, darlin'.* Well, that doesn't work for me. I feel deeply about a lot of things. And one of them is that this is just so much thornier than I expected it to be."

He opened his mouth to comment, but she interrupted him with a raised hand. "Not that I intend to back out. I won't. But *you* have to find a way for us to deal with this."

"Me?"

"Why not? It was all your idea in the first place."

"Fine," he said, a little annoyed that she tried so hard to keep a neutral distance, when he was finding it next to impossible. "Let's just stop dancing around each other and *really* deal with it."

She folded her arms. "You mean you're ready to fall in love again?"

That wasn't precisely the direction his libido was taking.

Sonny caught the hesitation and answered her own question with a knowing intonation. "Then, you mean you're ready to have sex."

Because she was more on the mark than he cared to admit, it seemed only fair to blame her for it. He, too, folded his arms and asked wearily, "You're going to make it even thornier, aren't you?"

She shook her head and put a hand to his chest. "No," she replied. "I always keep it simple. I never have sex with a man who isn't ready to fall in love." She applied pressure with the flat of her hand and pushed him toward the door. "Relationships are difficult enough. It's better to know going in that you have a chance."

He braced his hands on his hips and frowned down at her, stopping at the door. "I was married for a long time," he said, feeling an urgency in himself as he tried to explain. It was important that she understand. "I'm sort of learning my way back."

"I know." She nodded with a gentle smile. She did understand. Then the smile altered subtly and he knew he was in trouble. "And I sympathize," she said. "But you can't practice on me. Good night, Shane."

She closed the door.

Shane ran a hand over his face, realizing that he'd been cast out in the cold by the Sun Queen. Not that he blamed her. He hadn't handled that with Mission Master style.

He turned and headed for the kitchen, taking heart in the words of a beauty from the home planet—Scarlett O'Hara. "Tomorrow is another day."

Chapter Seven

Shane closed the door behind Charmaine and Dusty as the living room clock chimed eight a.m. He wandered back toward the sofa, which he'd tidied of bedclothes before Charmaine arrived, and thought it looked particularly uninviting. What he would give, he thought, to be able to climb back into his own bed. He smiled wryly at the thought that Sonny was still in it. After their discussion last night, he wasn't betting on his chances of that happening.

The next moment the bedroom door closed quietly and she emerged from the shadowy hallway in full stride, wearing black sweat bottoms and a gray hooded sweatshirt with a heron screen-printed on the front.

She stopped at the sight of him. He wished she would stop doing that. Just once he would like her to look pleased to see him rather than startled and uncertain.

"Good morning," he said, remaining a nonthreatening distance from her. "Morning run?"

"'Morning," she replied, putting both hands into the pouch in the front of her shirt. She wore no makeup and looked good enough to eat. "No. I want to get some oak and maple leaves for my arrangements. Do you have a big plastic bag? Garbage-can liner, or something like that?''

He shook his head. ''Housekeeping does all that for us. Where are you going for the leaves?''

''City park.''

''Give me ten minutes to shower and dress and I'll come with you.'' He headed for the bathroom as he spoke, trying to deprive her of the opportunity to refuse his company.

''Well...'' Sonny trailed him as he pulled off the white T-shirt he wore over a pair of silky blue pajama bottoms. ''I thought you were working today.''

He tossed the shirt onto the hamper in the bathroom and detoured to the bedroom to collect jeans and a sweater. ''I usually do work Saturday mornings, but this week I traded with the night manager who was ill...remember...?'' How could she have forgotten what the man's bout with the flu had brought about in her life? ''He's already used all his paid sick days and wanted to make up the time, so he's working for me today.''

''But you let Charmaine think...''

He grinned as he crossed to the bathroom. ''I know. It seemed like a good way to have her out of our hair for a whole day.''

She leaned a shoulder against the doorway as he dropped his clothes onto the closed commode and leaned into the stall to turn on the shower. ''You're missing something here, Archer. If Charmaine isn't here, we aren't required to spend time together.''

He came to stand over her as steam began to billow behind him. She looked determinedly away from his well-shaped pecs and shoulders, but discovered that looking into his eyes was no easier on her composure.

They were still a little heavy with sleep, but his gaze was familiar enough to remind her of the suggestion he'd made last night about how to handle their attraction.

"If you think I'm coming along because I think it's where I'm *required* to be," he said quietly, emphasizing the word she'd used with a pinch to her chin, "then you're the one who's missing something. Excuse me." He began to close the door, then held it partially open as she continued to stand there. "Unless you'd like to join me?" he asked.

Resisting the urge to laugh, she pushed a hand gently against his face and pulled the door closed from her side.

"I'LL BET THIS kind of a morning makes you miss Hawaii," Sonny said with a shiver. They stood in the middle of a hilly forty acres right in the center of Merriwether. The lush green grass was strewn with colorful leaves from the old oaks and maples that once forested a large estate.

The sky was a gemlike blue this morning, but the wind whistled down the hill from the north with enough force to scatter the carpet of leaves and make Sonny pull up her hood and tie it closed.

Shane shrugged a shoulder against the suggestion that he missed the sunny climate. "I loved the balmy weather while I was there," he admitted. Then he looked around him at the flamboyant display of nature, then down at her with a significant smile. "Now I think I'm ready to be here. Sun is wonderful, but it isn't everything. There's something to be said for wind and color and..." He sniffed the air filled with the smells of woodsmoke, healthy grass, a river that mingled with the salty sea and the taunting aroma of a bakery. He closed his eyes a moment and made a sound of approval. "God, that air. Even perfumed Hawaii doesn't quite match it."

Sonny hooked her arm in his and led him up the hill. "I know." She squeezed his arm unconsciously. "I think this is the most wonderful place in the whole world. And this time of the year is magic. Many flowers are going to sleep, but we have fat pods with the promise of a next generation, exotic and colorful gourds and pumpkins, a grain harvest that's beautiful as well as sustaining..." She stopped and drew a cold breath, overwhelmed with the splendor of the morning.

She was even able to acknowledge to herself that its particular sparkle had a lot to do with the man beside her. He might not be ready to fall in love, but she might be ready to wait until he was.

Shane was pleased to see that she wasn't angry about the night before, and that she wasn't a woman who pouted. He liked the feel of her arm in his and the laughter in her eyes when she looked up at him. It made him feel warm and alive in a way he hadn't experienced for far too long.

He squatted down beside her holding open the large white trash bag they'd liberated from a housekeeping cart on their way out of the hotel. She crawled around the pungent underside of a wizened oak, carefully studying each leaf. She tossed some into the bag and replaced the others where she'd found them, performing both tasks with careful concentration.

They moved to a maple with hubcap-size leaves and she was thrilled to find one fat, perfect, crimson leaf after another.

"Look at this one!" she exclaimed, holding it up for his inspection. One starry lobe of the leaf was bright yellow while the rest had turned scarlet. He admired it dutifully, but had difficulty concentrating on the leaf when her smile commanded his full attention.

He followed her at a crouch to the underside of a mountain ash. "I'm beginning to feel as though I'm part of a terrorist raid or something," he said, settling on his knees beside her. "I imagine half the people in the houses across the street have called the police to tell them there are two disreputable characters, one of them in a hood, creeping around in the park."

Sonny laughed as she inspected a cluster of small red berries. "The police chief's wife is one of my best customers," she said absently. "I'll be in the clear." She gave him an innocent side-glance. "I don't know what you'll do, though. And once I tell the mayor you're not planning to wear a costume to the Halloween ball, they'll probably put you away for a long, long—ah!"

It was easy to yank her sideways into his arms and ease her to the soft carpet of leaves. She giggled as he leaned over her threateningly.

"You're saying you wouldn't come to my defense?" he demanded with mock ferocity. "When I came along so you didn't have to do this backbreaking work by yourself?"

She rolled her eyes, one hand clutching the front of his sweater. "Backbreaking? Spoken like a man who's always been an administrator. A little gardening, Mr. Archer, would teach you about backbreaking. When I—"

"Please." He cut her off with a finger to her lips. "Don't give me a long story about how you picked strawberries or something equally low to the ground to pay your way through college. I worked in a cold, smelly fish cannery, so I'm not likely to have a lot of sympathy. I didn't become a capitalist until later."

"I waitressed my way through college," she corrected with a "so there" tilt of her eyebrow. "And anyway, you invited yourself along. This is all your fault."

He rolled his eyes. "Why am I surprised? Gathering leaves was your idea."

"Because *you* hired me to decorate the hotel. So this is still your fault."

"I did that as a bargaining chip so you'd help me with Charmaine."

"Whose love for you..."

"Infatuation with," he corrected.

"Infatuation with," she amended, "is also all your fault."

He frowned in genuine puzzlement. "How so?"

The truth bubbled right up out of her to the tip of her tongue. She barely held it back, looking deeply into his eyes, wondering what it would do to their tenuous truce if she spoke it aloud.

"What?" he asked finally, a crease forming between his eyes as he studied her complex expression.

She opened her mouth to speak, but no sound emerged. She couldn't quite force it out.

"Sonny," he warned softly, the arm still cradling her on the ground tightening around her as he lowered his body more closely over hers. "If you don't tell me what you're thinking, I'm going to kiss you."

At the moment, she hardly considered that a deterrent, but she'd lose her nerve to tell him what she thought if he kissed her, and this was an important crossroads. She had to take action.

"It's your fault," she said finally, softly, "because you're so damned cute."

Shane stared at her for a full moment, unable to form a coherent thought. That admission was so much more than he'd expected from her, but so much less than any man wanted to hear.

"Cute?" he asked flatly, moving his arm out from under her and letting her head and back hit the soft pile of leaves and berries. "I'm guilty of...being *cute?*" He struck his heart in a theatrical gesture of unspeakable pain and rose to his feet.

"Wait!" Sonny rose beside him, catching his arm as he leaned down to snatch up the plastic bag. "Cute isn't bad, Shane."

"No," he said, "cute is insipid and ineffective." He extended his hand. "Goodbye, Sonny. It's been fun knowing you. I'll just let Charmaine have her way with me."

"Shane..." Sonny said his name on a little laugh as he shook her off and struck out across the park. She ran after him, uncertain if he were truly offended or merely teasing. In either case, she felt obliged to explain.

"As soon as Charmaine gets me—" he said as she danced along beside him, trying to keep up "—she'll try to push me around. I'll then have to do away with her, and I'll end up on death row."

"Shane!" She caught up with him at a small wooden bridge that crossed a little creek. He was forced to shorten his stride on the narrow, rickety structure and she caught the back of his sweater in a fist. "Will you stop?"

"Why?" he asked, trying to pull away. "You wouldn't want to be seen with *cute*, would you? You wouldn't—"

She turned him around, took hold of his arms and shook him.

"Shut up and listen," she said firmly, "or you will become *bruised* instead of cute!"

"Really." A slightly dangerous edge came into his voice, completely unrelated to the ambiguous expression in his eyes. "You don't want to find out the hard way that even cute men have their limits."

"Shane." Sonny held him still with one hand while running a hand over her face with the other. She missed the quick smile that came and went on his lips. "May I explain?"

He sighed and leaned a hip on the bridge railing as he lowered the sack to the planks. The action brought them eye to eye. "You're welcome to try," he said.

"Okay." Sonny placed her hands on his shoulders and thought carefully. "Cute," she said at last, "has a different meaning to a woman than it does to a man."

She looked into his eyes to see if that statement had any effect. He seemed unmoved and waited for her to go on.

"A woman's life," she said reasonably, "is filled with many things that are cute and wonderful at the same time. Her children, her pets, her favorite dress. Cute describes her feelings toward them, rather than their physical appearance or attributes. You see what I mean?"

She smiled at him, hoping that he was getting the picture.

He was mercilessly unresponsive. He knew what she meant, of course. Had known from the very beginning. He'd once been married to a woman with an extensive vocabulary to whom many things remained "cute."

But this pretended obtuseness was a way to keep her hands on his shoulders, her hip leaning unconsciously against the inside of his thigh, her floral perfume scenting his space, her eyes looking beseechingly into his. He was going to milk this for all it was worth without remorse.

"No," he said flatly. "I don't."

His actions earned a bonus when she took his face in her hands, apparently intent on assuring herself of his attention. He remained impassive only because it seemed to draw her nearer.

"I'm sure," she said, her eyes dark with the determination to make him understand, "there are many women out there who would never use the word, and that's fine. But for those of us who cherish the small, sweet stuff, many of life's finer things are *cute*. And many things that touch us deeply we consider cute because they make us feel warm and snugly enclosed and content."

She shifted her weight and he was forced to incline his body slightly toward her to avoid pitching both of them into the creek. That placed them loosely in each other's arms, their lips mere inches apart.

"I think that feeling of...contentment," she went on softly, every particle of her being focused on him "...of security, can't be bought with *handsome,* or *cool,* or even *buff.* It's a connection some men make with a woman's heart that no other quality can form but...*cute.* Understand?"

Afraid he'd already overplayed, he made a small concession. "Faintly. You're saying a cute guy makes you feel protected? Does that even make sense?"

She closed her eyes to summon patience and he took the opportunity to devour her features with his eyes, thinking he'd give her one more minute to make a move on her own, then he was going to devour her with his lips.

"Men," she said with a groan as she opened her eyes. She dropped her hands from his shoulders, pushed up her shirtsleeves, firmed her stance and framed his face in her hands once more. "You're all so literal. Maybe if I show you how a cute man can make a woman feel, you'll understand."

That held definite promise. He pretended innocence.

"Please be gentle," he said. "Cute guys probably aren't as tough and controlled as—"

Her lips on his stopped him midsentence. When her tongue invaded his mouth, he held her to him and straightened to his feet, afraid he might lose track of his precarious perch and land them in the creek after all.

Sonny didn't give him any slack. Her hands moved to the back of his neck and she held on as her mouth did insidious things to his, pushing aside inhibitions he hadn't even been aware he held, calling up a response from deep inside him that seemed to fill his being with fire.

He felt her hands in his hair, her fingertips in his ear, the beaded tips of her breasts even through his sweater. And more than that, he felt a need in her that belied her rejection of his plan last night.

Sonny judged by Shane's hands roving over her that she was making a very effective point. And given a moment free of his touch to think about it, she might remember what it was. Now all she was aware of was how broad and possessive his hands were, how ardent and artful his lips—and how paradoxical it was to feel physically safe and emotionally endangered at the same moment.

She pushed at his shoulders, needing desperately to take one deep breath that wasn't mingled with his. She was supposed to be proving something to him after all.

The smoldering quality in his eyes suggested that she'd done that. He allowed her to lean away from him, but locked his fingers behind her waist to keep her close.

"So that's what *cute* makes a woman feel?" he asked lazily. That kiss had definitely made him feel something.

She nodded. "Being considered cute isn't such a bad thing after all, is it?"

He studied her, a gust of cold wind ruddying his cheeks and narrowing his eyes. His arms, she noted, protected her from the chill. She resisted the impulse to snuggle closer.

"What I'm more interested in," he observed almost clinically, "is that the demonstration seemed to show that *you* must consider me pretty cute, too."

Trouble. Truth, in this kind of situation, was not wise. Particularly when he'd admitted interest but nothing more.

"Of course I do," she said with openhanded honesty. "But I've learned to require more in a man. We talked about this, remember?"

The clinical expression slipped into something deeply personal. "You mean the sex versus love thing."

She puffed out a breath, more impatient with herself than with him for bringing the whole thing up in the first place. "I mean the sex that *requires* love thing."

She glanced at her watch. "I have an entire hotel to decorate this weekend. Do you think we could have this conversation another time?"

"No," he replied simply, locking his wrists behind her and bringing her that much closer. She felt his knees against her, his thighs, the forward jut of his pelvis against her abdomen. She had to swallow to remain calm.

He studied her frowningly for a moment, then swept her up into his arms and strode off the bridge with her toward a bench that stood in a cluster of trees. He placed her on it and sat beside her, crossing a knee over hers to hold her in place when she tried to escape him.

"Women," he said, holding her firmly in his arms, "are all so metaphorical. You find a man who makes you feel what it really means to be a woman and you call that appeal about him *cute?* Then you talk grandly about love, because it allows you to maintain a ladylike distance from your basic, raw feelings like desire."

He threaded his fingers in her hair and held her still as he lowered his head.

"Let me show you," he said, his mouth hovering over hers, "how a man reacts to desire in a woman."

His kiss was hot and demanding, and drew all those qualities in her to the surface. As his mobile mouth swept over her face, the moment took on the colors of the vibrant leaves.

His hand slipped up between her sweatshirt and her slender back and it felt like a red hot flame against her sensitive skin.

Then his hand touched her face, held her chin still as he studied her sensuous eyes before kissing her again. The heat his fingertips left there made her spill a tear.

When the passion in his eyes changed to concern and he kissed each tear away with a groan of dismay, she dissolved against him and gave up the struggle to find sense and reason in his arms. She couldn't. And at the moment, she didn't care.

Her arms wrapped around his neck, she pressed her face into the hollow of his throat and uttered a broken little sigh. "Oh, Shane."

He wondered what that sound meant. It seemed to contain equal parts of contentment and distress. But he didn't intend to analyze it. The moment was too important.

He held a sensual and fascinating woman in his arms, in the middle of a park that looked as though it had been painted by an artist, on a morning when nothing could be wrong with the world.

Each had learned something from the other, and neither had run from the intoxicating result.

Sonny raised her head suddenly and looked into his eyes; her own were gravely serious, her cheeks pinched and pale.

"If I don't get sugar in the next five minutes," she said feebly, "I will expire."

He leaned down to nip at her lip. "Sugar?" he asked suggestively.

She slapped at his shoulder and held him away with both hands pressed against his chest. "Funny. I mean the kind of sugar you find in a Bismark."

He studied her in confusion. "You find sugar in a German battleship somewhere at the bottom of the English Channel?"

She scolded him with a look. "It's like a jelly doughnut only it's filled with custard and frosted with chocolate. How did you get to be vice president of a hotel chain without ever experiencing a Bismark?"

"Nepotism," he replied. "I married the boss's daughter. Lead me to the bakery."

"I CAN'T BELIEVE you ate two of those," Shane said an hour later as he helped her drag bundled cornstalks onto the freight elevator. He leaned back against the wall of the car with them while she pushed the button for the main floor. "And I understand why they call them Bismarks." He placed a hand to the mild distress in the pit of his stomach. "They do sort of land like depth charges."

She, on the other hand, apparently had metabolized the pastry like some godly nectar. She glowed with good health and the excitement of decorating the lobby.

"I told you you'd feel better if you had two," she said airily, grinning at him as she relieved him of two of the stalk bundles. "They fight each other for supremacy and before you know it there's nothing but sugar fuel in your stomach and you feel great. You eat just one, and it settles there and dies of inactivity. It's all very scientific."

"Is this part of your wrinkle-free weight theory?"

"The cornerstone. Here we are."

The elevator doors parted and Jenny stood there waiting to board with her cart. She studied the tall, dried bundles they carried and asked with malicious interest, "Are we burning someone at the stake? Mrs. Prelotsky, maybe?"

Sonny exchanged a knowing smile with the housekeeper. Rumor had it Charmaine demanded silk sheets, doubled the towel allotment, and wanted a different brand of chocolate mint on her pillow.

"'Fraid not, Jenny," Shane replied. "Mr. Bedford would come down hard on both of us. He happens to love his daughter and wouldn't take kindly to our roasting her."

"We're going to decorate the lobby." Sonny took one of the smaller dried maple leaves she'd piled on a tea cart they'd borrowed from the kitchen, and tucked it into the buttonhole on Jenny's collar. The cart also held pumpkins, gourds, berries and ears of dried corn. "I'll try not to make too much of a mess, but dried arrangements tend to scatter their dust."

Jenny shrugged. "No problem. Call me when you're finished. Have Dustbuster, will travel."

The doors closed behind her, and Shane and Sonny went about their task.

Shane admired the economy of movement with which Sonny arranged her pieces. She studied the corner of the lobby near the stone fireplace and the simple oak table at the beginning of the corridor that led to the elevators. He knew both spots were on her list.

Once she decided what to do, the arrangement went together with a minimum of fuss. The corner of the lobby required three bundles of cornstalks tied together and given an artful, fanlike twist at the top and bottom. Around the base she placed pumpkins and gourds with a precision that gave the whole a look of casual abandon. Slightly to the right, she balanced an old wooden crate on its side. And across from it, a pot of bright yellow chrysanthemums brought sunshine to the corner from atop a bale of hay.

She stepped back to survey her work, then turned to Shane with a hopeful smile. "What do you think?"

"I think you'll get to do Christmas, too," he replied, frankly amazed at the warmth she'd managed to build with what he'd considered awkward elements.

She pushed her cart of goodies toward the table. He followed with two cornstalks. "Charmaine will be gone by then," she said lightly.

"Maybe I'll keep you on anyway," he answered in the same tone.

That would be fun, she thought wryly, *working together after Charmaine had returned to Hawaii.* The forced intimacy would no longer be necessary, but what would they do about the curious electricity between them that grew stronger every moment?

They'd talked about movies while they'd eaten Bismarks at a little round table in the bakery. They hadn't mentioned their kisses in the park, or their argument last night, and the subjects hadn't arisen since he'd helped her decorate the lobby.

"Great," she said. "I'd love to handpick the tree for the vaulted ceiling in here."

"The job is yours," he said.

She used a platter of gourds and corn for the table, and placed a tall pumpkin filled with sunflowers in the center. Stalks of barley made it seem busy and added interest. She placed colorful leaves over the rest of the table with that artless precision.

"Beautiful," Eli Gifford said from behind Shane. He turned to see that they'd collected an audience of staff and guests alike.

Gifford was a salesman, already on his third stay, though the hotel had been opened only six weeks. He came to clap Shane on the shoulder. "I hope you've been inoculated," he said.

Shane laughed. "Against what, Eli?"

The salesman indicated Sonny, compulsively moving the leaves into a more random pattern. "The cozy flu." Eli shook his head as though Shane were already terminal. "I saw the look on your face while you watched her. A man finds a woman who can create such a cozy atmosphere and he may as well cash it in, know what I mean? Things'll never look the same after that."

Shane nodded dutifully. "Thanks for the advice, Eli. Everything okay? You comfortable?"

"Always. Wish you'd been here for the past twenty years when I had to stay at the Cranberry Cabins. Floors were so wet, cranberries grew *inside*." Eli glanced at his watch. "Need some lunch before I make the rest of my calls. You got a great chef, but what I wouldn't do for some good down-home cooking! See ya."

It was almost three before Shane was able to force Sonny to stop. They'd done the second and third floor elevator areas and an employee lounge on the fourth floor.

"I never stop for lunch," she argued. "And I'm on a roll. I'd sell my soul for a mocha, though. I don't suppose you'd consider going down to the res—"

"No," he replied flatly, pushing her cart into a storage closet and locking the door. Then he took her hand and pulled her with him to the elevators. "If you want a mocha, you can call room service for one while I make meat loaf sandwiches. I've been thinking about that ever since Eli mentioned it."

"Who?"

"Never mind. Just come along quietly."

"Quiet," she said as he ushered her onto the empty freight elevator, "isn't my style."

"Try." He pushed the button for the top floor, and the car immediately obeyed his command. Then it jolted to a halt, inched up several bumpy feet and stopped.

Shane groaned and reached for the emergency phone. "This damn thing. We've had the elevator company out here I don't know how many..."

He turned toward her while waiting for maintenance to pick up and found her right beside him, eyes wide.

Touched by that little glimpse of vulnerability in her, he put his arm around her and asked gently, "Claustrophobic?"

She leaned against him with no apparent reluctance. "No. I have that fear of falling in an elevator and arriving in the lobby in a hundred pieces. What do you call that?"

He laughed softly and kissed her forehead. "Good sense," he said, then held the phone away when the car began to move smoothly upward. "Ah, here we go."

The comfortable hum usually associated with the smooth operation of the car filled the small space. They eased to a stop and the doors parted on the sixth floor. Shane hung up the emergency phone and followed Sonny out.

He called room service for Sonny's mocha, then called the elevator company.

Very grateful his tone was not directed at her, Sonny made sandwiches while Shane talked.

"No, it is not used by our guests," Shane replied, his voice lowering a decibel, a change she guessed was not for the better. "It is used by my staff, each and every one of whom is important to me personally and to the smooth operation of this hotel. I want the car repaired today." He listened a moment. "Yes, I would appreciate that. Thank you."

He replaced the receiver and went to answer the door. It was room service with her mocha.

He carried it to the coffee table and she met him there with a plate of sandwiches.

"So, there's a temper under that professional cool," she observed, kicking her shoes off and curling into a corner of the sofa.

He sat at the other end, propping his feet on the table.

"Where the safety of my family, my staff or my guests is concerned. I don't usually lose it over *things.*"

"Good policy," she approved. "My father's a retired army colonel. He has no concept of an even disposition."

Shane shrugged a shoulder. "I imagine handling large numbers of young men is harder on the nerves than dealing with hotel guests—even the difficult ones."

Sonny made a face at him as she peeled her sandwich apart and nibbled on the meat. "My brother's a lot like him. I'm trying hard not to be."

Half of Shane's sandwich was already gone and he reached for the second half. "Every family needs a commandant, but one's enough. I imagine your decision to become an adventuress would worry your father a lot."

She had to agree. "He thinks in terms of winning and losing, not learning."

"The man deals in combat situations, Sonny. If he cares about the men under his command, I'm sure he'd rather see them come out dull and alive than personally enriched and dead."

She turned to him, the smallest trace of resentment inside her. She'd thought that, of course, but her father's impatience with her curiosity and her eagerness to explore had always been so personal. She'd resented that he'd treated his family like just another platoon.

Her mother, who'd grown up an army brat, had been no help. She'd conformed for so long that she moved cheerfully all over the globe and expected her children to be happy little soldiers.

Sonny put the subject away. It had been a great, if unsettling, day so far, and she wanted nothing to spoil it.

She turned to Shane to tell him so, and found his eyes on her. Then she heard the silence of the suite, the ticking of the clock, the hum of the refrigerator, the subtle ding of the elevator somewhere down the hall and realized that they were alone.

Usually Dusty was here, or Charmaine. They'd never been alone in the suite they pretended to occupy as lovers. And suddenly the afternoon took on a completely different quality.

Shane saw the change take place in her eyes. She went from relaxed and open, to sharply aware. He knew what had alerted her to the change in atmosphere. After the kisses they'd exchanged in the park that morning, and the subtly veiled admissions they'd made, even she had to admit there was a volatile chemistry at work here.

"No," she said calmly, evenly. But he noticed that she had to look away from him when she said it. "I am doing this on a lark, and you—" she glanced at him quickly, then looked away again toward the window "—aren't ready for anything meaningful."

He leaned back against the sofa with a sound of exasperation. "I like the way you analyze my life when I'm not even sure what's going on in it."

"Someone," she said primly, "has to think straight."

"I was going to kiss you, nothing else."

"I don't want you to kiss me."

"This morning," he reminded, "*you* kissed *me.*"

"To make a point!"

He turned his head to give her an even look. "You did. You're as wild about me as I am about you."

"But feeling wild and being in love are very different things."

He sat up and nodded with forbearance. "So you said last night. But how do we find out what we're feeling without showing each other?"

"When I fall in love with you," she said, "I'll tell you."

He rolled his eyes. "How romantic. When I fall in love with you, I'll send a memo."

She raised an eyebrow in affront. "There's no need to be snide."

"I beg to differ," he said angrily, "but there is. I think you want to make love with me, you're just afraid you're not up to the adventure. Despite all your claims about yearning for new horizons, you're still pedantically analyzing and organizing everything to death. And I think it's all an excuse to prevent you from ever having to take a chance." He shook his head at her. "Some adventuress. I think you should give it more thought before you decide to embrace the life-style. Come on. I'll help you take the rest of the cornstalks down to floor three."

She placed a hand on his arm to hold him in place, her usually dormant temper sparking to life. "I'll do it myself, thank you very much," she said coolly, "and before you go criticizing *my* ability to handle my life, you might recall that it's in chaos because *you* apparently don't handle your own very well, or Charmaine would understand that you don't love her. You wouldn't have to use me to put on an entire theatrical production to convince her!"

She stood, intending to make a dramatic exit, but he caught her arm and yanked her down again—into his lap. His arm across her knees held her still, while the other hand closed gently, but inescapably, on the nape of her neck.

"We went through this at the park this morning," he said quietly, but with a grave note that caught her attention. "And you decided it was all my fault. But who walked into my bathroom when I was just out of the shower and wearing only a towel? Who charmed my son into believing he and I need you for the future of our family? Who turned out to be so good at the seductive looks and the playful banter that I have no other choice but to believe that you're no longer acting any more than I am?"

Then he drew her upper body down into the crook of his arm, closed a hand over her thigh to prevent the kick he sensed was coming, and kissed her senseless.

She was angry and frustrated and wanted more than anything to lie lifeless in his arms. But her body had a will of its own, and he was so damned good at this.

With a touch that combined an insidious tenderness with a competent confidence, he shaped every curve of her possessively, traced every subtle indentation, kissed her eyes, her lips, her throat, and the ribs he bared with an upward thrust of her sweatshirt. His lips there caused her knees to tremble and gooseflesh to rise all over her body.

She felt feverish when he finally put her on her feet.

"You're not without responsibility here, Sonny," he said. "So don't pretend that you're just a victim of circumstance. You're not. You're a victim of cowardice."

She turned to face him, both hands on her hips, as he stood beside her.

For a moment she was too exasperated to speak. Then she settled inanely for, "Oh, yeah?"

He leaned down to within an inch of her face. "Yeah," he retorted, his patience thinned to a thread. "So go back to your produce where you feel comfortable, and I'll bring the cornstalks down. Then you can spend the rest of the afternoon with dry and dead things that don't require you to take any risks."

She grabbed his arm as he would have walked past her to the bathroom and the cornstalks. He allowed her to stop him and looked down at her belligerently.

"What you don't see," she said, her voice tight with anger, "when you're blinded by *testosterone*—" she gave the word insulting emphasis "—is that it might require more courage for me to resist your winning ways than to go to bed with you." Then she punched him in the arm, surprised to discover there was more of a soldier in her than she'd thought. "So watch out who you call a coward. And leave the damn stalks. I'll get them myself."

"I said," he enunciated with exaggerated patience, "that I would bring them down to you. If you don't want to be bundled up with them, I suggest you leave now."

She did, but not without a backward glare over her shoulder.

Chapter Eight

Shane carried the cornstalks down to the third floor and propped them up against her cart. She was engaged in conversation with Rojelia from Housekeeping and he took the opportunity to escape without having to speak to her. What he wanted to say would not benefit either of them.

He took a long walk. He followed the bay-front path all along Jones Point where Lewis and Clark were supposed to have spent several days before wintering across the bay. He wandered along the docks at the marina, then crossed the highway and walked up and down the hills that rippled like a cloak along the waterfront.

He walked down the far side of the hill through Merriwether's busy little shopping area, picked up a bright red fire truck Dusty had admired the evening they'd come to town for groceries, then headed back to the hotel. The bright blue sky was darkening to dusk, and stars began to appear when Regis opened the hotel's big glass doors for him.

SONNY KNEW WHEN he was back in the building. She wasn't sure how, but some unrecognized radar caused a little shudder in the pit of her stomach. It combined anticipation with excitement, a composition she found difficult to reconcile with the annoyance she still felt over their conversation.

The fact that he was at least partially correct about her using every excuse to keep her distance from him didn't help. She was already a little bit in love. She knew that. And what he felt for her went beyond lust. She knew that, too, even if he didn't. But that simply cleared the path for deep, true feelings and that was where all the dangers lay.

She put the finishing touches on the lobby display on five, then stood back to admire her work. It was beautiful, pumpkins, gourds and leaves atumble in a deep wicker basket she'd retrieved from the shop, along with a length of ragged-edged vanilla linen she wound through for effect.

She dusted her hands off, pleased that she'd managed to do her job despite her bad mood. In fact, when Charmaine returned from her excursion with Dusty, she just might take her aside, explain the situation, and let Shane get out of it as best he could.

Call her a coward, would he?

She sighed, knowing she wouldn't do that to him. She'd promised to see this through and she would. But she wouldn't make it easy for him.

Sonny glanced at her watch. It was after six and she still had one more floor to tackle. She pushed the passenger elevator button, hoping Shane had gotten a call to replace the night manager. Not that she had anything against Ken Dimaggio, but if he'd relapsed with the flu, it would be so much easier with Shane absent during the evening.

No such luck. The elevator doors parted and there he stood, looking fresh and smelling like the outdoors. He tucked a brown paper bag under one arm and held the door open for her with the other hand. He didn't smile.

"Thank you," she said, stiffly polite as she pushed her cart onto the car.

She looked tired, he thought. Everyone in the lobby had stopped him to tell him how beautiful it looked. He would have liked to tell her that, but she appeared testy. He searched his mind for a neutral topic of conversation.

"Did the elevator repair crew come?" he asked as the doors snicked closed, enclosing them in the small space. She'd been careful to place the now almost empty cart between them.

"I wouldn't know," she said without looking at him. "I was working all afternoon with my *dead* things. If a flesh-and-blood man happened by, I missed it." She turned to him with a bland smile. "Why don't you try the freight elevator? If you're two inches high when you reach the lobby, we'll know they haven't made it."

Shane closed his eyes to summon patience, sorry he'd asked.

They heard the screams the moment the elevator doors parted on the sixth floor. Shane took off for his suite at a run. Sonny followed, recognizing Charmaine's voice.

"You stupid, moronic Neanderthal!" the high-pitched voice shouted in extreme agitation. "If you don't put me down this instant, I'll—"

Sonny reached the partially open door just as Shane stepped inside. She followed, prepared to back him up with her meager knowledge of self-defense, then stopped in openmouthed disbelief.

Shane allowed himself one moment of grim pleasure at the sight of his sister-in-law suspended in the right arm of a burly giant in a military uniform. Her arms and legs flailed the air as she struggled helplessly, threatening the man's ugly demise at the top of her lungs.

Then two thoughts struck him simultaneously. He didn't see Dusty, and he had no idea how the marine had gotten into his suite. It was easy to deduce that Charmaine hadn't let him in.

He reached for the man's shirt collar and pulled back his right fist, assessing absently that the man had a good thirty pounds on him, but he had him in height by a good two inches.

"No!" Sonny caught his arm in both of hers and hung her weight from it when he tried to shake her off.

"Sis?" the marine bellowed in a voice that matched his size. He looked first relieved, then righteously displeased. "You have a lot of explaining to do, young lady."

"Brad, what are you doing here?" she demanded.

"I got leave after coming home from Somalia," he said, "and I thought you might want to come to Mexico with me to visit Mom and Dad. I didn't know I was going to have to scour the town to find you! What are you doing here?"

Sonny groaned and looked up at Shane, a mixture of apology and pleading in her eyes. "Shane," she said, gesturing toward the intruder. "I'd like you to meet my brother, Major Bradley Winslow. Brad, this is Shane Archer, the manager of this hotel and..." She gave him another quick pleading glance before she wrapped her arms around his waist and added lightly, "the love of my life."

Winslow looked confused. Shane couldn't blame him, so he extended his hand as Sonny dug her nails into his ribs. "Winslow," he said, "welcome to the Coast Convention Center."

His expression reluctant, the major shook his hand, Charmaine still suspended from his other arm.

"Ah . . ." Shane pointed to her. "That's my sister-in-law, Charmaine Prelotsky."

If he'd thought an introduction would make Winslow put her down, he was mistaken. He continued to hold her. "I found her in the bedroom," he said, his square jaw firm with purpose, "going through my sister's things." He turned to Sonny. "She was shaking out that yellow scarf I sent you from Thailand. She had your stuff spread all over the bed."

Sonny turned to the dangling woman in surprise. "Why?"

Charmaine spread both arms out, her face growing more purple by the moment. "I wanted to borrow something, all right? Is that a crime?"

The major chuckled. "We know that isn't true, darlin'. You got a little too much detailin' to fit into Sonny's clothes."

Charmaine's scream of indignation was primal and desperate. She curled her fingers into claws, and tried to strike at him, but her position made her efforts futile.

Winslow shook his head at Shane. "Maybe you should call hotel security."

Shane called to bear every ounce of self-control he possessed to hold back the laugh.

"Shane Archer," Charmaine said, her voice dangerously low and breathless, her breathing probably compromised by the burly arm around her waist. "If you don't make this cretin put me down this minute, I—"

"Brad, put her down," Sonny said, taking her brother's arm to try to force the action.

Shane pulled her back and shook his head at Charmaine's captor. He tipped his head sideways to look into her face. "Where's Dusty?" he asked.

She pointed toward the door, giving another futile kick to free herself. Brad held firm. "Asleep in my suite," she said angrily. "He was worn out from our trip."

"I see. And what are you doing in *my* suite, going through Sonny's things?"

"I told you, I—"

"Tell me the truth this time," Shane interrupted, "or we'll see just how long the major can hold you like that."

"Forever," Brad replied in a congenial tone. "I once carried an unconscious private all the way back from a twenty-mile hike, and she's not quite as big as he was."

Charmaine doubled her fist and punched Brad on the thigh.

"Hey, now." Brad pretended to lose his grip, Charmaine screamed as she dipped a few inches, then he held her firmly in place. His quick grin at Shane was filled with self-satisfaction. "Hate to drop you on your head, darlin'."

"Yeah, well somebody must have already dropped you on yours, Major Moose!"

"Your manners are sadly lacking, Miss Prelotsky. I believe Mr. Archer asked you a question."

Charmaine groaned painfully and raised her head, her hair hanging in her face. She looked exhausted, Sonny thought, and just a little over the edge. Charmaine parted her hair with her fingertips and focused a glare on Sonny.

"I was looking for proof that she's a fraud. That you're not really living together. All right? Now will you make him put me down?"

Brad's expression turned from interest to displeasure. He put Charmaine down without being asked, all his attention focused on Sonny. "You're *living* with him?" He looked Shane over once, then a second time, as though looking for something with which to take exception and not finding anything. Then he refocused on Sonny with a frown. "Do Mom and Dad know this?"

Before Sonny could reply, Charmaine rolled her eyes heavenward, combed her mussed hair back with her fingers and yanked at the hem of the sweater hiked up by his manhandling.

"What planet are you from, anyway?" she demanded, facing him with both hands on her hips. "She's over twenty-one. Certainly she doesn't have to fill Mom and Dad in on the details of her liaisons."

Shane saw the major turn a loftily judicious gaze on Charmaine. "Winslow women do not have liaisons," he said calmly, repeating her word with scornful emphasis, "because Winslow men don't allow it. We love and cherish our women and if a man fancies one of them, he can damn well marry her."

Charmaine made a sound of disgust and folded her arms. "After he's asked your permission, of course. And offered the requisite four horses and stud bull."

"He would ask my *father's* permission," Brad replied politely, "and there would be no horses required, but should there be bull involved, I'm sure you'd do nicely."

As Charmaine sputtered, mute and purple with indignation, he turned his full attention on Shane. "But since my father isn't here, I believe I'd like to know your intentions toward my sister."

Shane liked him. But before he could answer the question, Sonny moved to stand between him and her brother. She looked just a little panicky, he thought. He gathered from what the man had said already, the notion of her living with him would not please her family. Though deep down, he believed in an individual's need to please himself, he certainly loved and respected his family enough to share her concern about upsetting them. "Brad, you have no right to come into a man's home, throw his relatives around and ask personal, intimate—"

"Excuse me." Shane placed a hand over her mouth and drew her back to his side. "I believe the question was directed at me."

"But..." she mumbled beneath his fingers while gesturing wildly toward her brother.

Shane shook his head at Brad. "She has an answer for everything," he said. "Unfortunately, it isn't always right."

Brad nodded knowingly. "That hasn't changed in the two years I've been away." He cast a glance at Charmaine. "And seems to be a general problem around here."

"You—!" Charmaine began. Shane caught her arm and pushed her gently, but purposefully, toward the door. "Why don't you check on Dusty and ask room service to send up dinner? Your choice."

"I'm not eating with him!" she said as Shane pushed her out the door.

"Fine. You can have yours delivered across the hall."

Certain Shane had ejected Charmaine so that he would have the opportunity to explain the deceit to

Brad, Sonny searched desperately for an immediate and credible solution. Brad would never believe that she'd moved in with Shane to deceive Charmaine, that she slept in his bed and that the situation remained innocent. He lived in marine bachelors' quarters, after all.

So she took the one half-formed solution that occurred to her, too short of time to think it through. "We're married, Bradley," she blurted. She reached for Shane as he stopped dead several paces from her and yanked him to her side. She wrapped both arms around his waist and smiled into his eyes with a threat in her own that promised slow and painful retribution if he contradicted her.

"I know we should have called or written," she babbled on, creating the scenario as she went, feeling very much as though she ran along the edge of a cliff that crumbled as she passed. "But we . . . we . . ."

Shane on the other hand, was used to dealing with dire problems that required clever and immediate solutions. And though he saw a hundred pitfalls to the path Sonny had taken, he saw many advantages for himself—and he wasn't averse to making the most of them.

"We just did it a couple of weeks ago," Shane said, remembering the few details Sonny had told him about her family, "and we didn't want your parents to cut short their trip, or ruin it by worrying about her."

Sonny squeezed him, surprise and relief in her eyes. "Right. And you were on that special mission thing. . . ."

Brad frowned. "You couldn't have waited a few weeks?"

Shane said with convincing lovesickness, "No. I couldn't have."

Sonny rewarded him with another squeeze.

Brad's frown deepened. "Why does the gorgeous cat burglar there—" he hooked a thumb toward the door through which Charmaine had left "—think you're a fraud?"

"She...um...she wanted Shane herself," Sonny replied. "And her parents own the hotel, so...they'd fire Shane if they knew he'd married me instead of her, so we're letting her think we're just living together."

She knew it was all going bad on her as the words tumbled out of her mouth, but she didn't know how or where to stop it. Each lie required another even more bizarre one, and she didn't seem to be able to stop creating them.

Shane thought there was a certain comfort in knowing that the woman he was falling in love with couldn't lie worth a damn. And he was sure one day he would reap the rewards. But right now, all he wanted to do was shut her up.

"It's not quite as bad as all that," he said, seeing that the major was having a little difficulty swallowing the story. He thought he'd seen something in him earlier he might be able to use to their advantage. "The truth is, Charmaine's been married twice, both times to royalty, thinking, I guess, that a man with a title will be able to provide the stability she needs. The last breakup was a little hard on her and she's rebounding in all directions."

Shane saw the major plant his feet and place his hands loosely on his hips. It appeared to be a sort of battle-ready stance for social situations. He pressed just a little harder.

"She's a fine woman, but a little out of control. Used to having her own way in everything. "

"Really."

"This time she wants me, and I think she just doesn't want to believe I'm already taken."

Brad nodded sagely. "You have to speak plainly to a woman like that."

Sonny watched what transpired with horrified fascination. It was saving her hide, but she couldn't quite believe it. Her six-foot-two-inch, two-hundred-pound brother was falling hook, line and sinker for the suggestion that all Charmaine needed was a third man with a title—that of "major."

All Sonny wanted to do was put this evening behind her.

"So, you're on your way to Mexico?" she asked brightly.

She wasn't sure Brad heard her. She was about to repeat the question when he stopped staring at the door and turned to her, as though her words had just registered.

"Maybe I'll stick around for a few days," he said with a sudden smile. "I didn't tell the folks I was coming, so if you're not in the position to travel with me, maybe I'll just spend some time with you instead."

"Oh, good." The words came out flatly. Sonny tried to give them some buoyancy with a bright but belated smile.

Shane gave her a warning glance and went to the phone. "I'll get a room for you, Brad," he said.

Sonny began to feel extremely nauseous. While Brad followed her to the sofa and carried on with uncharacteristic ebullience about their parents' construction of a retirement home in Mexico City, and how anxious he'd been to visit, she did her best to appear as though she wasn't sinking deeper and deeper into a hole. She smiled and nodded and even exclaimed, while wishing

desperately that Shane would return so that she would
have something to hold on to.

He returned, but she guessed by the warning look he
gave her yet again, that he did not have good news.

"I'm afraid we're full up tonight," he said.

"Not a problem. He can stay at my place," Sonny
said, congratulating herself that for once in the last few
minutes her brain had thought quickly and clearly.

"*Your* place?" Brad asked with a frown just as
Shane, standing behind him, put a hand over his eyes.
"Don't you live here? I thought—"

"I mean . . . my *old* place," Sonny amended quickly,
heat filling her cheeks and the pit of her stomach. "My
rent isn't up yet. We just got married three weeks ago,
like I said."

This time Shane rolled his eyes and held up two fingers.

"Two," Sonny corrected. "Two weeks ago. We got
married...two weeks ago." She ended lamely and closed
her eyes, sure Brad was about to demand an explanation for her psychotic behavior.

But she opened her eyes to discover that her brother
seemed to have other things on his mind. His eyes had
lost focus. "I think," he said absently, "that I'd like to
stick around. You know. So I can tell the folks how
you're doing when I see them. Take a few pictures."

Sonny darted Shane a panicky glance.

"You could stay with us tonight," Shane suggested
calmly. "A suite on the floor below will be free tomorrow afternoon."

This time Sonny's glance was murderous, but Shane
stared it down. She smiled suddenly when Brad focused on her.

"You wouldn't mind that, sis?" her brother asked.

She clenched the fingers in her lap. "Of course not."

"Good. I can sleep on the sofa. I promise I'll be practically invisible." He patted her hand. "You two are probably still honeymooning."

Chapter Nine

The evening went from bad to worse—at least as far as Sonny was concerned. Charmaine joined them for dinner after all, claiming Dusty had awakened and demanded that he be instantly returned to his father.

She stared down Dusty's attempt to clarify the story. "But I only..."

Then Dusty noticed Brad and said, eyes wide with wonder, "It's Butler Shaw!"

Sonny turned to Shane in confusion. "The blockade runner," he said under his voice, "who supplies Eos with horses."

"Hey!" Brad said, leaning down to swing the child up into the air. "And who are you? Don't tell me. Burn Starby?"

Dusty saluted him. "Guess who Dad is?"

Brad glanced Shane's way and grinned. "Piece of cake. The Mission Master, right?"

"Right!" Dusty was beside himself with glee. "And Sonny?"

Brad gave that a moment's thought, then replied uncertainly, "Not the Sun Queen?"

"Right!" Dusty shrieked. "And Aunt Charmaine?"

Brad focused on her with an innocent expression Sonny mistrusted immediately. She'd been the victim of that look one too many times when they were children. "Oh, let's see," he thought. "The Devil Duchess?"

"No."

"The Ruler of the Meanoids?"

"No."

"I know. The Dragon Dame!"

"Right!"

Charmaine, about to take her place at the table, turned a fulsome glare on Brad. But Sonny had seen the hurt feelings in her eyes before Charmaine allowed the anger to take over.

So, apparently, had Shane. He blocked her way to the door and said placatingly, "The Dame is a very powerful element in our planetary government. The dragon in her name suggests the fire of her zeal as our equivalent to a secretary of defense."

Charmaine studied him doubtfully.

"It's true, Aunt Char," Dusty said, coming to take her hand. "Calling you the Dragon Dame is a *good* thing."

She looked from Shane to Dusty, her eyes softening on the boy. She put a hand to his hair and ruffled it gently. "Well, if you say so."

Dusty tugged her toward the table and Brad stood to follow. He took the chair beside hers. She gave him a look that breathed fire. He smiled back.

"And how do you know so much about Dusty's favorite cartoon? I guess we know what you're doing on Saturday mornings while the taxpayer thinks complacently that you're keeping the world safe for democracy."

Sonny knew the answer to that and was happy to explain. She ignored the surreptitious shake of Brad's head.

"One of his friends was killed by a sniper in Mogadishu." Shane held a chair out for her and she sat, thinking what a curious little drama this had become, filled with lies and truths becoming so entangled it was difficult to remember which was which. "He had five children under nine. His buddies alternate sitting with them while their mother works. Brad's shift is every other Saturday morning."

Charmaine stared at him for a moment while he looked charmingly modest. Her opinion of the man who'd manhandled her had obviously been shaken. Then she unfolded her napkin and squared her shoulders.

"Well," she said after a moment, "I guess that qualifies as keeping the world safe for democracy." She turned to pinch Dusty's cheek. "We all know what little tyrants children are."

Then she picked up the basket of rolls and passed it to Brad. He accepted it, their eyes met and Sonny got the horrible feeling that the little drama was going to grow even more complicated.

"THERE. GOT EVERYTHING you need?" Sonny put an extra blanket on the foot of the sofa where Brad was already stretched out.

"Everything." He held up the TV remote. "I promise to keep it low, I'm just too wound up to sleep. It's been quite a day. I expected to be making plans with you to fly to Mexico in the morning. And here I am—in a high-rollin' hotel in Podunk, Oregon." He frowned. "Does this all strike you as weird?"

He had no idea. She leaned down to kiss his cheek. "This is Merriwether, Oregon, and just because you're used to living on bases that are bigger than this town, don't get uppity."

Brad pulled her down onto the edge of the sofa and folded his hands behind his head. "So, you love this guy?"

That was one of the truths about which she was no longer confused. "Yes, I do."

"He seems all right. Seems to love you."

"He does?" she asked with pleased surprise, then realized how that must have sounded to him. She changed her tone. "Of course he does. He also has a wife who can get him flowers at any time."

Brad smiled fondly. "It's more than that. He looks at you like he thinks you really are the Sun Queen. Like you've got all the answers to his questions in that flighty little brain."

"It might be small, but it's not flighty."

He laughed and pulled her down to him for a bear hug. "Your heart's always been the biggest thing about you. I just want to know he's somebody who'll give you as much as you give him."

She rolled her eyes and pulled his blankets up. "My happiness is no longer your responsibility. Besides, I saw how you looked at Charmaine when she left tonight."

He raised an eyebrow and turned his attention to the ceiling. "It's hard to be in the same room with a tush like that and look away."

"I thought you were a leg man?"

He drew in a deep breath that swelled his considerable chest, then let it out slowly. "Sis," he said, frowning, "she's got everything. Not bad in hand-to-hand either. A little more weight on her and I might have been in trouble. I can't believe she's vice president of a hotel chain. It's hard to imagine all the fire in that lady tied up in a three-piece suit."

"She's a modern woman." Sonny got to her feet and turned down the light just above his head. "You've got to stop thinking like a military chauvinist if you want to get her attention."

"Who says I want her attention?"

"I do. Good night, Brad."

"Good night, sis."

Sonny walked purposefully toward the bedroom, hoping to create the impression that she did this every night, and that she was eager to join the man who awaited her there. If Brad suspected for a moment that this was all a hoax, her parents would be here so fast even Burn Starby couldn't track them.

She stepped into the dimly lit bedroom, closed the door behind her, and leaned against it for a moment, her eyes closed in relief. Relief that lasted until she remembered that now she had to cope with life on *this* side of the door. And that meant Shane. After the beautiful morning, the stormy afternoon and the fabricated evening they'd shared, she couldn't begin to imagine what lay in store for her now.

She turned toward the bed and found him lying on his side, an elbow propped up on his pillows, his chest bare. His dark gaze seemed composed of equal parts of sympathy and amusement and a considerable element of desire. Oh, God.

Her own passion sparked a little fire inside her at the sight of his. She'd thought of nothing all evening but the fact that they'd have to share this bed tonight. The memory of how volatile and unpredictable the day had been made it difficult to plan a strategy. But the possibility of letting fate determine what happened was entirely too enticing—and therefore dangerous under the circumstances.

She decided to take a practical approach. A thank-you was in order.

She walked toward the bed and stopped halfway between it and the door. "Thanks," she said, "for going along with my story."

He shrugged a bare shoulder. It was large and golden in the lamplight, and looked like just the place to rest her weary head after a difficult day. But she fought the impulse.

She felt her cheeks grow warm, though everything else about her seemed chilled.

"I owed you that one." He held a hand out toward her. "You did the same for me once, remember?"

His understanding reply softened her resistance. She'd expected him to be angry or at least critical of her impetuous lie. It had saved them for the moment, but—and she'd had all evening to think about this as Brad sparred with Charmaine and traded service stories with Shane—she'd made a complete quagmire of their little ruse.

Now Brad thought they were married, and though she and Shane had pressed upon him the importance of keeping that secret from Charmaine, the very real threat existed that the lie would be revealed at any time.

She went toward him, all those concerns piling up as weariness overtook her.

"I don't know why I did it," she said, taking his hand and sitting on the edge of the bed beside his waist. "Except that it seemed like a good idea at the time."

He smiled gently. "The explanation for many a mis- deed."

"Oh, God." Sonny put a hand to her eyes. They felt as though they'd been sanded. "This is all going to blow up in our faces. I should have just told him the truth. I mean, it's really so simple when you think about it. 'Bradley,' I should have said, 'we're pretending to be lovers so that Charmaine will go back home and leave Shane alone.' That would have worked, wouldn't it?"

Shane frowned at the genuine dismay in her face and ran a hand gently up and down her arm.

"But, no!" she went on. "All I could think about was that he'd never believe I hadn't slept with you, and he'd call my parents, and my father would be here be- fore breakfast tomorrow and I'd have to explain my- self." Unconsciously, she leaned against Shane's body, resting her elbow on his upper arm. "I used to hate having to explain myself. I'm a perfectly competent and capable woman, but I don't always have a good reason for what I do, you know? Sometimes it just seems like a good idea to take a chance. How do you explain that to a man who plans his every move, and includes a plan B and C?"

He would have offered a suggestion if she'd given him a moment, but she continued. "So I had to go and dig us into a catacomb of lies and . . . and—"

"Sonny," Shane interrupted. "You're getting a little crazy about this. It's not that bad. All we have to do is keep our heads and handle one crisis at a time."

Her smile was rueful and weary. "I was thinking of taking the night train to Singapore."

He stroked her hair. "You've found one that's am- phibious?"

She sighed. "From Victoria Station. After I fly there from Portland. No one would think to look for me there."

"You once jumped all over me for calling you a coward." As her head slipped sleepily to his shoulder, it occurred to him that he'd do anything to have her jump all over him for *any* reason. He turned slightly to make her more comfortable.

She settled in without complaint. He guessed she was too tired to feel threatened. "Oh, I wouldn't do it," she said in self-deprecation. "I just like to think about it. Incidentally, I didn't know there were horses in space."

She lost him on that one. He looked down at her, wondering if she'd drifted off and was talking in her sleep. But, no. She lay against him, heavy-lidded but still awake, waiting for his answer.

"Give me a clue," he asked, unfastening the sweatshirt still cinched at her throat, "what we're talking about."

She turned onto her back so she could look up at him. Her drowsy eyes, her pink cheeks, her full-lipped little mouth in a scolding moue were almost more than he could bear.

"You said Butler Shaw brought horses to our planet through the stockade."

"Ah. *Block*ade," he corrected. "He brought them from Earth. They function better on our planet's sandy interior than machinery that collects grains of sand that wear away its parts."

"Oh." She shook her head and said fatalistically, "Even our fantasy lives are complicated, aren't they?"

Shane laughed softly. "That's my son's fantasy life, not mine."

"Really." She turned onto her side toward him, nuzzled her nose into his shoulder and closed her eyes. "What's yours?"

"It involves you and me and a little sailing yacht," he replied, "and miles of open sea. No phones, no hotel, no relatives."

She smiled, her eyes still closed. "No Dusty?"

"Dusty is with Charmaine for a couple of weeks. Or with your brother and his Saturday morning cartoon contingent."

The smile settled on her lips as she fell asleep. Shane pulled the blanket up to her shoulder, then reached past her to turn off the light. He settled her back against him, enjoyed her soft burrowing motions while she snuggled into just the right spot and finally wrapped both arms around her.

This was not going to be an easy night, he knew, but he'd thought about it for hours while sitting at the dinner table. He'd fantasized a different outcome to the scenario, of course. And he guessed he'd just have to imagine it again.

SONNY LAY in the captain's arms. The moon was high, the night balmy, and a gentle, fragrant wind caught the mainsail and pushed the little yacht gently on its course.

"I love you," she whispered over and over. "I've loved you all the time I've been waiting for you. I've loved you for years."

It was such a relief to say the words. They rose out of the depths of her heart like daisies pushing through the sidewalk, unable to be held back.

"And I love you," the captain said. "But I didn't know I needed you. Now I'm taking you to Eos."

She pointed to the sky. "But that's ... up there."

"It doesn't matter," he replied. "I can take us any-where." And the little yacht caught the wind and rose right out of the water, caught an air current, and dis-appeared beyond the moon.

Sonny held fast to the captain, and smiled into his eyes as they sailed over the moon's crescent tip. The moonlight lit his face. Shane smiled back at her.

"Shane!" Sonny gasped, caught somewhere in the misty world between sleep and wakefulness. Surprise and pleasure turned in her voice and need swelled in her as she sat up, reaching for him.

"Shane!" she said again, finally coming awake, dis-appointed and vaguely sad to find that she sat alone in the bed.

Shane, sitting on the window seat, heard the curious quality in her voice and crossed quickly to the bed.

"Right here," he said, putting a hand to her tum-bled hair. "What's wrong? Bad dream?"

Sonny caught his hand as it skimmed down to her cheek and held it there, leaning into it, searching for balance and the *real* reality. "No," she said breath-lessly. "It was a good dream. A beautiful dream."

Shane had left the bed because she was more of a cuddler than he'd bargained for, and because he wasn't strong enough to remain as distant as the situation re-quired. He tried to remember that she was probably still half asleep. He tugged at his hand. She held firm, then turned her lips into it.

Everything inside him rioted. "Sonny..." He began a vague, unstructured warning. Moonlight from the window highlighted the gold in her hair, the gentle planes of her cheeks and chin. The delicate slope of her breasts pressed against the sweatshirt she'd worn to bed. His heartbeat began to pick up speed.

She brought his hand down to hold it in both of hers and looked up at him—eyes wide and limpid in the darkness, filled with moonlight from the window, and the memory of her dream.

"We were on a beautiful yacht," she whispered, "and you sailed us past the moon."

"I sailed," he asked with a questioning smile, "across the sky?"

She nodded. "You assured me you could take me anywhere. We were going to Eos."

"Clever me."

"You said you loved me," she whispered.

Shane felt something inside himself close. It wasn't a conscious action; it simply happened, even though he wanted it otherwise—or thought he did.

Love bloomed in Sonny at the memory of her dream, but she saw caution invade Shane's eyes. The rosy dream dissolved into their strangely unique reality filled with love that grew around them but never quite between them.

Shane felt her withdraw and closed his free hand over hers, preventing her from pulling away.

"And what did *you* say?" he asked softly.

She sighed and lowered her eyes, as though reluctant to reply. "Actually," she said finally, "you were responding to me. I was the one to say that I loved you first."

"Ah," he teased gently. "So, in this dream, you were a serious adventuress and no longer willing to resist me."

She shrugged a shoulder. "You talked about love. That's hard to resist—asleep or awake. I know, I know..." She pulled her hands away from him and turned to plump her pillow. "You don't like to talk about love, but the dream was all your fault."

He rolled his eyes but couldn't help but smile. The combative nature this exchange was taking was more familiar, and therefore more comfortable, than discussions of love.

"Of course, it was," he said amiably, stretching out beside her as she fell back against her pillow. He leaned up on an elbow. "But *how* was it my fault?"

She huffed a displeased sigh. "You planted the suggestion with your talk about 'you and me and a little yacht.'" She mimicked the deep timbre of his voice, then sighed again. "That's how. So just keep your fantasies the hell out of my dreams, okay?" She turned onto her side, facing away from him.

Shane hooked an arm around her waist and pulled her back against him. The night still stretched interminably ahead of them, but holding her in dire frustration was better than aching for her nearness.

"You," he said, putting his lips to her head and whispering softly, "can invade *my* dreams anytime. What's your fantasy?"

"You," she said on a yawn, "tied to the mast of this little yacht."

"Oh..." He held her tighter. "I like it. Go on. What are you doing to me while I'm tied up?"

She burrowed into her pillow. "Go to sleep, Shane," she grumped.

Shane smiled into her fragrant hair and closed his eyes, prepared to flesh out the fantasy on his own.

BURN STARBY WALKED the perimeter of Hearth Base I, alone in the darkness with his vision of a powerful planet at peace in its galaxy.

There'd been times when he'd doubted his own dream, but at the moment, it looked as though he would see it realized.

He inspected the communications center and found Butler Shaw renewing himself with sleep. That was good. Soon, when it was time for the Interplanetary Conference, they would need more horses and more supplies. Shaw would have to run the blockade again. He needed his rest.

Satisfied that Communications was secure, Starby checked the gate. Also secure. The Dragon Dame was somewhere out there, watching for the enemy. She did her job well. He knew he could trust her.

Quiet murmurs came from the officers' quarters. Starby approached the door and listened. The discussion inside was indiscernible, but he knew the Mission Master and the Sun Queen discussed strategy. He could hear the MM's deep voice and the Queen's soft tones.

Starby drew a deep breath and headed for his own quarters. For the moment Eos was secure.

Chapter Ten

Caffeine. He needed coffee. Shane slipped out of bed, pulled on a pair of jeans and a blue woolen shirt and dug an old pair of Reeboks out of the back of the closet.

He stopped in the middle of the room as his gaze fell on Sonny still fast asleep in the middle of the bed. Her hair was a tousled stroke of pale color in the room darkened by a rainy morning. He was exhausted from *not* making love to her.

He tiptoed out of the room and closed the door quietly behind him.

He needed time alone to analyze what he felt—to think about her without her distracting softness in his arms.

Was it love? It felt like love. He remembered the absolute, deep-down rightness of what he'd shared with Allie and thought how like that this was.

But could it be? What were the chances that a profound grief could be supplanted by love in such a short time? Was it just that he missed having a loving woman in his life and wanted that again? That he would never be the classic bachelor and that he longed for a mate to warm his bed?

He didn't think so. But it would be safer for everyone involved if he was sure.

Dusty sat at the table with a bowl of cereal, watching a diet infomercial on television. The sofa was empty, blankets and pillow folded neatly on one end.

"Good morning," Shane said, kissing the top of Dusty's head. "Desperate for culture, huh? Where's Brad?"

"He left a note," Dusty said, stuffing a heaping spoon of Monster Munchies into his mouth. "Ifincde!"

"Excuse me?"

Dusty waved a small slip of paper at him, mouth still full, and enunciated as carefully as he was able. "Ifs—in—code!"

"Ah." Shane accepted the note and sat across from his son. In Dusty's world of fantasy and reality coexisting side by side, words too big for his rudimentary reading skills were considered messages in code.

"Gone exploring." Shane read the note aloud. It was written in a bold, square hand. "Insist on taking everyone to dinner tonight. Back by five. BW."

"I think he went exploring with Aunt Char," Dusty said. "I heard him whistling in the bathroom, then when Aunt Char's door closed, he ran and got his jacket and went out."

"I think he likes her," Shane said, folding the note aside as he waggled his eyebrows. He went to the kitchen to put on a pot of coffee.

"I think so, too," Dusty shouted above the TV.

Shane shushed him and pointed to the bedroom door. "Sonny's still asleep."

Dusty muted the TV and whispered loudly, "I think so, too. They're always yelling at each other. That means you're in love."

Shane looked up from his fight with the tight cluster of paper coffee filters. Dusty's assessments of life and living were sometimes very on-target, and interestingly skewed.

"Really?" he asked. "Your mom and I didn't fight very much."

Dusty tilted his head. The action usually preceded a revelation of some kind. "You screamed at her that time she almost drownded when the surfboard hit her in the head."

It amazed him that Dusty remembered that. He'd been barely four at the time. "That was because I didn't want her to get hurt."

"Because you loved her. She told me." Dusty went back to his cereal. "You and Sonny yell sometimes."

Shane spooned coffee into the brewing basket. "That's because . . . we have different opinions on things."

Dusty nodded. "Mrs. Potter says fighting can be healthy."

Shane looked up again, concealing a smile. "Really?"

"As long as you don't yell or hit. Are you gonna get married?"

Shane remained calm. It was always imperative when dealing with Dusty.

"Brad thinks you *are* married," Dusty went on. "But we didn't have a wedding."

Shane nodded, pushing the brewing basket into place and pouring water into the machine. "I explained that to you, remember? Sonny was afraid he'd be angry because she was living here, so she just *told* him we were married."

Dusty nodded knowledgeably. "'Cause only moms and dads are supposed to live together. But we're sure lying a lot. 'Cause Aunt Char's supposed to think Sonny just *lives* here, and everybody in the hotel says it's just a matter of time."

Shane turned from a perusal of the slim contents of the refrigerator and raised an eyebrow. "What's a matter of time?"

"Before you get married."

Shane grabbed a bowl out of the cupboard and went to join Dusty at the table. He poured cereal, then milk, not surprised the hotel staff was speculating on the status of his love life. This was a very cozy group.

"Would you like it if I got married?" Shane asked.

Dusty nodded. "Grandma wants you to marry Aunt Char. I guess 'cause that way you'd still be her outlaw son, 'cause Aunt Char's her daughter. Like Mom was."

"Her son-in-law," Shane corrected. "I like Aunt Char, but I don't think either one of us would enjoy being married to each other."

"'Cause she's bossy."

"'Cause she has to have things her way."

"But you'd like being married to Sonny, wouldn'cha? I heard you guys last night." Dusty stuffed another spoonful of cereal into his mouth.

Shane frowned at him over the milk carton. "What...did you hear?"

Dusty shrugged a bony shoulder. "Talking." He smiled, a curiously retrospective smile for a six-year-old with a relatively short supply of memories.

"It was like when we still had Mom, and I heard you talking when I was in bed. I liked that." Then he became suddenly serious. "You know, if you and Sonny are gonna have babies, I think you have to get married."

Shane put the milk down. "Who says we're going to have babies?"

"That's the only way to save Eos."

Right. Eos. Shane wasn't sure whether to be frustrated or relieved that Dusty's real and fantasy worlds remained confused.

"And anyway, that's what happens when moms and dads sleep in the same bed. When you're together, the sex bird knows where to find you."

Shane let a heartbeat pass. "The sex bird?"

Dusty nodded, leaning toward him, apparently eager to share what he knew. "Everybody thinks the stork brings babies, but he doesn't. Sex brings babies. Frankie Kendrick told me when we were playing with clay. He made boobs. His mom's in Housekeeping."

Shane nodded, trying to decide how to straighten out the misconception that sex had wings and feathers. He had no idea what to do about the boy who copied the female anatomy in clay.

Dusty studied him in concern. "Don't you know about the sex bird?"

"Y—well... I didn't understand it in quite that way."

Dusty shook his head at him with tolerant sympathy. "Then how did you get me?"

For a moment, Shane put aside his parental responsibilities and simply enjoyed the moment. He reached across the table for Dusty and pulled him into his lap.

He hugged him fiercely, wondering how he'd have survived the last few years without him.

"We got you," he said, settling him into the crook of his arm, "because your mom and I had so much love we had to make a third person just to have a place to put it.''

Dusty considered that a moment, apparently pleased with the notion. Then he glanced up at him, reminding him that the next fifteen or so years were not going to be easy.

"But you had sex deliver me, right?"

It seemed safe enough to agree to that. "Yes."

Dusty sighed, apparently satisfied.

The quiet sounds of movement came from the bedroom. Dusty leapt off Shane's lap. "I'll call room service for Sonny's breakfast."

"Maybe you should ask her what she wants first."

Dusty dragged a chair to the phone, stood on it, and picked up the receiver. "No," he said matter-of-factly. "She said she could have scones for breakfast for the rest of her life. Hi, Celia. This is Dusty. May I have the kitchen, please?"

Satisfied that his son's telephone manners remained impeccable, Shane turned his attention toward the hallway at the quiet sound of the bedroom door opening.

He was both eager and reluctant to see Sonny's face. How would she feel this morning? Uncomfortable because they'd had to share the bed? Angry because she'd awakened during the night with thoughts of love and found him less ready to admit to being in love than she was?

She wore purple, a soft amethyst shade of wool that rose high on her throat and fell to midthigh, richly textured and bulky. Under the sweater she wore tights in the same shade.

Her eyes were wide, their blue interestingly altered by the color she wore. He stood, and she smiled warmly at him and came to kiss him on the cheek.

He felt all his senses go on alert. He wasn't sure what she was up to. She never reacted to anything the way he expected, or responded to him in a way he considered logical. Was he to believe he'd endured ninety minutes of sleep and six and a half hours of frustration and she remained unaffected by last night?

"Good morning," she said, combing his hair back with her fingers.

Sonny was pleased to see the uncertainty in Shane's eyes. She'd presumed he'd be expecting petulance, or at least a dignified silent treatment after she'd invited him into her dream last night and he'd retreated.

He didn't know she'd carefully planned her strategy as she showered this morning. She loved him, and felt fairly sure he loved her. And if he thought she'd pout over being rebuffed rather than fight back, he didn't know as much about the nineties' adventuress as he thought he did.

He needed her until Charmaine left, and she intended to do all in her power to make him forget that deceit even entered into their relationship. If her plan worked, she would have more than any woman had the right to hope for. If it didn't, she'd learned a lot about adventuring and she'd be . . .

She aborted the heroic thought and faced the fact that if it didn't work out, she had no idea what she'd do.

But for now, she was willing to be a risk-taker. She gave him a blandly innocent smile. "Sleep well?"

Shane was both annoyed and exhilarated. It confounded him that she could confuse him like that. He pinched her chin punitively. "No, I didn't. Did you?"

"Yes." She sighed and gave him a taunting glance as he pulled out a chair for her at the table. "Yes. I just went back to my dream."

He stopped her from sitting by turning her toward him. "Really. How did it end?"

She smiled intimately and wrapped her arms loosely around his neck. "It was *your* fantasy," she said. "Don't you know?"

He splayed a hand between her shoulder blades and pulled her against him. "I'm hoping you've embellished it with your personal touches."

She felt the solid, muscular length of him against her and leaned into him, indulging herself, torturing him. "I wouldn't want to jinx it," she said, giving him that look she usually reserved for when Charmaine was around, "just in case my dream comes true, and your fantasy becomes reality."

He leaned over her, his eyes dark with warning, his lips a millimeter from hers. "You're flirting with retribution," he warned. "You know that."

THE SUN QUEEN and the Mission Master were locked in the Stellar Embrace, Starby noted, as he put aside the communicator. He smiled, pleased that his efforts to save the planet were finally taking hold.

He glanced overhead, watching for some sign of feathered flight. The sex bird must be close.

The communicator buzzed. He answered. It was the Federation President!

"Hi, Grandpa!" Dusty said excitedly.

"What are you doing this morning?" the loud voice on the other end of the line asked. He always sounded, Dusty thought, like the voices at church—deep and just a little scary.

"Just eating my Monster Munchies. Dad and Sonny are kissing, though."

Shane heard the one-sided conversation and pulled Sonny reluctantly out of his arms. She asked, her eyes wide with concern, "Your father-in-law?"

He laughed softly. "Sounds like it. Have some coffee. Dusty ordered your breakfast so it should be up in a minute."

He pushed her gently toward the kitchen and went to the bedroom to take the phone so Dusty could remain on the line.

"Good morning, Josh," he said, leaning back against the headboard. Sonny's fragrance lingered among the sheets and wafted around him. He let himself slip into it, touching his bottom lip where her kiss remained imprinted.

"Shane." Josh said. "How are you? Charmaine tells me the CCC is running like a clock."

"Don't you want to know who Sonny is?" Shane asked candidly. He enjoyed a comfortable relationship with the Bedford chain's CEO. Shane had been banquet manager of the Kauai Bedford when Allie had still been away at school, so he'd known Joshua long before he'd met his daughter.

"I know who Sonny is," Josh replied. "Charmaine's been keeping us posted. Listen. I need you here for a board meeting Tuesday. I know it's short notice."

Shane was accustomed to crossing the globe with little warning. But he thought the present circumstances made the sudden meeting a little suspicious. "And I suppose you want me to bring Sonny," he said.

There was just a moment's pause. "By all means."

"She has a flower shop!" Dusty interrupted with enthusiasm. "And she fixed up the hotel for Halloween!

We had a hundred pumpkins in Dad's bedroom, and corn things in the bathroom!"

"Cornstalks," Shane provided.

"Charmaine insists she's done wonderful work," Josh said. "Mother wants to meet her. She might be just the person we're looking for to replace our floral designer on the west coast. And, of course, we miss Dusty a great deal. So we'd like the three of you to spend a few days. We'll do a little business, a little socializing, and Char will keep an eye on things there while you're gone. What do you say?"

Shane knew precisely what was happening here. When he'd been a young man alone in the world all those years ago, the Bedfords had taken him under their wing. And when he'd married their daughter, he'd been treated like their own offspring rather than an in-law.

And Allie's passing hadn't diminished their love for him. This trip amounted to a very simple matter of bringing the woman in his life home to meet his family. Undoubtedly Charmaine had explained their situation as she saw it.

He considered the dangers for one brief moment, then dismissed them. "Sure," he said. "We'll be there."

He heard Dusty go ballistic and hang up the phone. Through the bedroom door, he heard him shout, "Sonny! Guess where *we're* going!"

Shane secured a few details with Josh, then hung up the phone, wondering what Sonny's reaction would be.

"Hawaii?" SHE ASKED, breathless with surprise. Dusty sat in her lap, helping himself to her treasure kabob. "But I don't think...I mean, I can't leave. I have to make the centerpieces for the dining room, and finish our costumes and...my brother just arrived!"

Shane nodded. "We'll only be gone a couple of days, and the centerpieces can't be started too far ahead. I hate to tear you from your brother, but he can stay until we come back for the Halloween ball, and longer if he likes." He picked up the note Brad had left and handed it to her. "He wants to take us all to dinner tonight. If he's upset at the idea of you leaving for a few days, I'll go without you. It's not a problem.

"Seems Charmaine's been singing your praises to my in-laws." He poured himself another cup of coffee.

Sonny frowned in confusion. "You're kidding, right?"

He grinned. "Well, your professional praises, anyway. Nina—my mother-in-law—thinks you might be the one to replace our West Coast floral designer, who quit when she heard she was expecting twins."

"Floral designer? I thought hotels just used local flower shops?"

"Not the Bedfords. They want someone who works for them full-time. It's easier to control quality."

Her jaw dropped. He reached across the table to pull a chunk of pineapple off the kabob Dusty held. He popped it in his mouth and chewed while her eyes widened and she considered the possibilities.

"Me?" she asked, her voice high, obviously afraid she'd misunderstood. "A floral designer for Bedford's?"

"You," he replied.

Sonny sighed wistfully. "It would be nice to get out from under the various deceptions we have going here."

He nodded. "Good point."

She turned to him with a frown. "Of course, if they've been talking to Charmaine, they think we're..." She stopped short of saying the word "lovers." She didn't think Dusty knew what that meant, but she wouldn't be entirely surprised to discover that he did.

Shane nodded again. "That's about to become reality, anyway," he said, making it clear he'd "heard" the word. His eyes were the warm dark velvet that defined the way she felt when he held her.

She raised a challenging eyebrow. "Really. What makes you think so?"

Shane studied her bright eyes and pink cheeks, absorbed the delicious memory of having her in his arms, remembered the monochrome of his life before she'd walked into it and admitted with grinning fatalism, "Because I'm falling."

"Falling?"

"In love."

She was certain she'd misunderstood. She'd hoped to make him capitulate, but expected it to be a long and difficult struggle.

"With . . . me?" she asked.

He closed his eyes, shook his head, then gave her a dry look. "No. With Charmaine, the Dragon Dame. Of course, with you."

She laughed softly, and reached across the table for his hand. "Well, maybe I *can* fit in a trip to Hawaii."

Chapter Eleven

Burn Starby pointed out the runway to his copilot and lowered his landing gear. This was an antiquated craft borrowed from the Terrans, but he was finding it adequate. He wouldn't want to travel to the far reaches of the Crab Nebula with it, but for planetary hops it seemed to do the job.

"I CAN'T BELIEVE," Sonny said, her voice sounding wounded in the lush interior of the Bedford Hotel's executive jet, "that Brad's reaction to my going away for a few days was, 'Of course I don't mind. Stay as long as you like. I'll be fine!' "

"Don't take it personally," Shane replied, cooperating with Dusty's instructions from the copilot's seat to fasten their safety belts. "He's a victim of love—big time."

"He didn't even look at me when he said it!" Sonny complained, failing to hear Dusty's instructions in her agitation. Shane reached over to fasten the belt for her. "He just kept staring at *her*."

Shane grinned. "You're overreacting."

Sonny was distracted for a moment by the aerial view of tall buildings interspersed with lush green, and thought how foreign it looked to her. She'd lived in many places as a child, but her father had never had a tropical assignment. And this was as different from Merriwether as it was possible to be.

She turned to Shane with a frown, resisting the exciting tug of the Islands. "What if Charmaine becomes my sister-in-law?"

"Big deal," he replied. "She's already *my* sister-in-law and you don't see me making a scene."

"Hah!" she said scornfully. "Don't try to sound heroic. You just changed the courses of both our lives to discourage her attentions!"

Shane laughed softly and pulled her close to plant a kiss on her temple. "Don't you like the way it's going so far?"

"Oh, of course. So far we've lied to Charmaine, my brother, your in-laws, and have involved the entire staff in a parlor farce. We even have *different* lies going." Her indignation was swamped an instant later by the absolute absurdity of the situation—and the fact that she did like the way it was going.

She leaned into him as much as her seat belt would allow. "I guess as a first adventure, it's been pretty remarkable."

He kissed her again, this time on the lips. "It's going to become even more remarkable," he promised, a smoky quality in his eyes pinning hers.

"Really?" she breathed. "How?"

"I don't want to jinx it," he said, repeating her words to her, "on the chance that my fantasy becomes reality and your dream comes true."

THE TROPICAL HEAT warmed her the moment she stepped out of the plane onto the steps. She stopped a moment to absorb it, fascinated by the sensation of summerlike air at the end of October. Dusty raced past her into the arms of a couple waiting on the asphalt.

Sonny took a deep breath of the perfumed breeze and let it settle inside her, thinking how different it was from the woodsy, herbal air of the north coast of Oregon. This smelled of exotic flowers, the trade winds and sun-baked earth.

It took hold of her in a way she hadn't expected.

Shane tugged her down the few steps and was immediately wrapped in Nina Bedford's ample embrace. Every time her arms closed around him, Shane experienced the maternal care and concern he'd felt the first time she'd ever hugged him when Josh had brought him home to a party. His parents had been killed in an automobile accident the month before, and though he'd been away from home since college, he'd missed their support and the knowledge that they were there when he needed them.

Nina had given him a firm embrace and told him she was very good at mothering, and would happily provide her services anytime. She'd begun by introducing him to her younger daughter.

Nina held Shane away and looked into his eyes. Her own were probing, assessing. Apparently seeing nothing to complain about, she nodded and smiled. "You're looking well. The rainy northwest doesn't seem to have dampened your spirits."

Josh enclosed him in a bear hug. "He's probably been moving too fast to get wet. Your figures for the first month were phenomenal for a hotel that size."

Shane spread his hands modestly. "Putting a Bedford there was your idea—all I did was open it. And I have a fine staff."

Joshua clapped him on the shoulder. "Good to see you. I haven't had a decent tennis match since you've been gone."

"We'll have to fit a game in if there's time." Shane reached a hand out for Sonny and drew her forward.

Before Shane could begin formal introductions, Nina took Sonny's hands and looked her over in the same way she'd studied Shane.

Sonny saw a woman of average height, who was comfortably plump and impeccably dressed in a beige cotton skirt and flatteringly cut top. She had short, loosely curled gray hair and the flawless complexion often seen in the northwest where there was more than average moisture.

Sonny tried not to flinch under the scrutiny—or to imagine how she compared with the elegant Allie and the outrageous Charmaine.

"Dusty tells us that you're royalty," Nina said.

Sonny blinked, then remembered her fantasy persona. "Oh, yes," she laughed. "The Sun Queen. I forget if I'm not wearing my crown."

"She's traveling incognito this trip," Shane said.

"Well, that's too bad." Josh gave her a platinum, bushy-browed frown that was alight with humor. He offered her his hand. "I'm president of the Archer Interplanetary Federation and I was anxious to introduce you around. You've met my Martian Mamma." He put a proprietary arm around his wife's shoulders. He was very tall and thickly built, and gave an impression of gentle power.

Nina rolled her eyes at him. "The Martian Marquesa, Josh. How many times do I have to tell you?" To Sonny she whispered loudly, "How he got to be president, I'll never know. I'll bet you could use a tall, cold drink, and a quiet place to lie down. We're not very far away—just the other side of Diamond Head.''

Sonny nodded, thinking that sounded heavenly.

Dusty took her hand and began to lead her toward a long silver limo that waited nearby. ''Grandma and Grandpa have a *pool*,'' he said excitedly, ''and a cat named Lava and a housekeeper who cooks as good as Fernando. I have my own room there with a...''

He went on during the drive through downtown, then along the coast and past hotels stacked together like Monopoly buildings, yet still managing to look beautiful. Hotels and restaurants claimed every cliff-top view, reinforcing everything Sonny had ever heard about Hawaii being shamelessly commercialized. But it was all so different from anything familiar, that she found it exciting all the same.

Beside her in the seat facing his in-laws, Shane pulled at his tie and unbuttoned his shirt collar. He felt the pressures of opening a new hotel—and being the one where the ''buck stopped''—fall away from him.

Josh and Nina liked Sonny. While Josh pointed out sights of interest, Nina studied her more closely. Her shrewd eyes focused on Sonny's face for a long time, then slipped over her casual white cotton dress, her stockinged legs, the thin-strapped sandals. Then they went over her once more to be sure.

Nina turned to Shane, unembarrassed at being caught scrutinizing his companion. She winked and smiled, and gave him a thumbs-up partially concealed by her straw bag.

THE BEDFORDS' HOME was a glass-and-pine structure perched atop an emerald cliff that led to a stretch of silver beach. Sonny stared at the view from the patio, experiencing a strange but not uncomfortable sense of dislocation—as though Burn Starby had been in control of their flight and taken them to some alien destination light years from earth.

"Josh, would you make them a drink, please," Nina said, "and I'll take them to their room. Dusty, Lani's in the kitchen if you'd like something to eat."

Dusty raced off into the house and Shane followed Nina and Sonny with their bags.

Sonny saw that there was a deep patio on all sides of the house. Three of the four sides were comfortably furnished with wicker. The poolside had vinyl woven chaise longues. And glass doors, most of them left open, separated the interior of the house from the patio, creating an atmosphere of living à la Robinson Crusoe.

Birds fluttered around the patio where there were many flowering plants and bushes, and Sonny found the cat Dusty had told her about, fast asleep in a wicker Queen's chair, unaware or uninterested in the prey circling within a paw's reach.

"*That's* Lava," Nina said, reaching down to ruffle the cat's fur as she passed his chair. He turned onto his back, front paws stretching up, back toes curling, never opening an eye. "The laziest cat God ever made. He thinks birds were created for his entertainment, rather than as his prey."

Sonny laughed, reaching down to pet him, too. He rewarded her with a loud purr, but still didn't open his eyes.

"I've always wanted a perfect Eden where everything lived in harmony with everything else. Maybe that's what you've got here."

Nina pinched her chin and grinned. "You wouldn't think so when Josh pays the monthly bills and takes me to task for my extravagance. Right through here."

Sonny followed her into the cool, shadowy interior of what appeared to be a kind of family room with books, a big screened television and needlework waiting on a crewel frame.

All the furnishings were paler than pastels—subtle pinks, blues and yellows that blended harmoniously. There were exotic flowers everywhere, green plants trailing, and island motifs on the white walls.

Their destination was a pale yellow bedroom filled with more wicker and filmy curtains tied back with dolphin-shaped clips. A sliding glass door was open to the patio beyond, and a perfumed breeze blew in, stirring a mobile made of shells.

Sonny went to the edge of the patio and looked out. This was the back of the house, beyond which green grass spread all the way to the road that had brought them here.

She turned to Nina, at a loss for words to express the beauty she saw, and found that Nina had gone and Shane stood right behind her. He opened his arms and she went into them.

"How could you have ever left here?" she asked. "It's like paradise."

"It was for a while," he said, kissing the lobe of her ear. "Then I discovered that . . . a man needs more than paradise."

She couldn't absorb the concept. "More than paradise?"

Before he could try to explain, Josh walked in with a tray bearing two tall, frosty glasses and a bowl of sliced fruit on a bed of ice. He placed the tray on the table on the patio.

"Nina will be back with more pillows," he said with a wry smile. "Whenever she isn't sure how to make someone comfortable she brings more pillows. As though goose down will accomplish what she can't."

"I heard that." Nina waltzed into the room, four pillows in her arms. She gave Josh a scolding look. "Well, you have to admit the situation is a little awkward. Sonny knows we've invited her to make sure firsthand that our 'son' is in good hands." She placed significant emphasis on the title bestowed upon Shane. "And now that I'm already sure he is, I don't want her to think we're just a couple of nosy old fogeys."

"We are," Josh said.

Nina nodded. "I know, but we could have kept it from her if you weren't so forthright."

For an instant, Sonny thought she'd gotten her deceptions confused. It *was* Charmaine who thought they were lovers, and Brad who thought they were married, wasn't it? So, why was Nina talking as though it were the other way around?

"Oh, I know, I know...." Nina read the confusion in her face and dismissed the issue by tossing the pillows onto the bed. "You probably haven't even decided to get married yet. I know you youngsters have a different approach to the whole man-woman thing today. Try it first and see if you like it, rather than take each other's hand and walk boldly into it, fearless and determined to be happy." She closed her eyes and shook her head, placing a hand over her broad bosom as she went on with an airy wave of her hand. "Doesn't make sense to me, and certainly takes the adventure out of loving, but, of course, that's your business."

She opened her eyes and smiled at each of them in turn. Josh folded his arms and stared at his shoes, wincing in embarrassment.

"I'm just thinking ahead," Nina said. "But don't mind me. No one usually does."

She caught Josh's hand and tugged him after her toward the door. "Now, you two have a nice rest, because we're going to ask you to barbecue for us tonight, Shane. And you, Sonny, will need energy to answer all our questions about Shane and Dusty. Josh is going to take Dusty golfing with him this afternoon, and I'm catching up on Women's League paperwork in my study. So, why don't you two have a swim, or just—" her glance bounced off the bed and she added airily "—whatever. If you need anything, just holler and Lani or I will come running."

Shane looked from one to the other, his expression blandly innocent. "When's the urgent board meeting?"

"Oh, uh . . . maybe tomorrow," Josh replied.

"Maybe?"

"Maybe," Josh repeated, daring him with a look to challenge his reply. "I have some figures to get together for it that I'm having trouble compiling."

"Really? With linked computers, faxes and . . . ?"

Nina and Josh walked out on him, arm in arm. Shane closed the door behind them, grinning. "Just as I thought. I'll bet you there's no board meeting at all."

"But they sent a jet for us." Sonny watched him cross to the patio, pull the door closed, then drop the raffia shades that covered them. "Something else must be urgent, besides the need to look me over."

He accepted that with a nod as he flipped the switch that sent the Casablanca fan in a slow, silent circle.

"Something is. They missed their grandchild. They wanted to see for themselves that I'm adjusting to that alien environment and getting on with my life. So how about it? Want to lie out in the sun?"

"Ah . . . yes." Tension crackled as they faced each other across the bed. She delved into her bag for the bikini she'd bought two years ago for a Fourth of July weekend in Bend.

Shane's eyes fell on the small scraps of fabric, then went to her eyes with clear masculine interest. She grabbed the matching cover-up and disappeared into the bathroom.

Studying her reflection in the mirror a few moments later, she thought twice about the cover-up and decided to be a risk-taker.

When she came out, Shane was waiting for her at the French doors in a Bedford Hotels T-shirt. His long legs, still tan from the years he'd lived in the Islands, were braced slightly apart, his taut hips neatly encased in dark blue swimming trunks. The sight of him reminded her sharply of that fateful afternoon she'd delivered the pumpkin to his suite.

Shane turned when he heard her and felt all the air in his lungs rush out. She hadn't put on her cover-up, but hooked it over her shoulder with her index finger, leaving everything it would have concealed open to his perusal.

The tops of small but artfully rounded breasts rose from the white-and-lavender top and moved enticingly when she drew a breath. Smooth ivory skin covered the jut of her ribs, followed the neat indentation of her waist, flared out in slender hips and led his eyes to the elegance of long, beautifully-shaped legs and the surprise of lavender-painted toenails.

His eyes went to hers and saw a warm challenge there. And that look, more than her considerable charms and the desperate state of his lust for her, swelled the emotion in his chest he now understood was love.

He'd wanted so much to be cautious before admitting that this was the same thing he'd felt for Allie. Yet here it was, warming every shadowy corner of his being, and it seemed foolish and wasteful to treat it with suspicion.

He smiled and extended a hand to Sonny. "I took our drinks out to the pool," he said, "and found a mermaid with your name on it."

She blinked at him while placing her hand in his. "I thought mermaids only lived in the ocean."

He drew her out into the sunshine. "But this is a paradise full of wonderful surprises."

The mermaid was an inflated latex raft shaped like a chair, the smiling face and flowing blond hair forming the back, the green tail making the seat. The mermaid's arms served as armrests, one of which held Sonny's icy glass.

She loved it and momentarily forgot everything but the pleasure of sunshine, scented breezes and the whimsically wonderful comfort of her raft. Shane lay beside her on his stomach on an ordinary air mattress, his face pillowed on his arms, his eyes closed.

They floated for an hour slathered in sunscreen, talking cozily and absorbing the perfection of the afternoon.

Then Shane decided it was time.

"Had enough?" he asked, bracing himself on his elbows, water lapping around him.

Sonny sighed without opening her eyes. "I don't think I could ever get enough of this," she replied. "You go ahead."

Sonny, lost in the warm, tranquil quiet, screamed in shock when a hand closed around her ankle and yanked her into the warm water. She submerged with a splash, but only as far as her waist.

Shane's strong arm caught her and held her to him as their crafts bobbed drunkenly away. The water was deep, and only the lazy movement of his legs kept them afloat.

She hooked an arm around his neck and blinked into his eyes. They were dark with mischief—and a passion that stole her breath.

"I take it that wasn't the answer you wanted," she said breathlessly.

"No," he answered, the mischief dissolving and giving full reign to passion. "Because I'm not going anywhere without you—ever again."

Joy rushed up inside her, but she struggled to remain in control. He was always saying things that meant one thing to her and another to him.

"I only meant 'go ahead' into the house," she said, being deliberately obtuse.

He gave her a brief nod, dipped sideways and began to sidestroke them to the edge of the pool. "You're coming with me into the house."

"But I like it out here," she protested mildly, though she helped their progress with smaller strokes of her left arm.

They reached the side of the pool and he lifted her to a sitting position on its rim. His eyes were now fathomless.

"But I can't make love to you out here," he said softly, holding on to the tile on either side of her and planting a kiss on her left knee. She felt as though she were melting. "At least not in daylight."

She whispered his name, unable to form another coherent thought.

"I love you," he said with all the conviction a woman could ever hope to hear. "I think I just didn't believe it could happen to me again. But it has. And I won't question it any longer."

Sonny's burst of joy bubbled over. She took his face in her hands and looked deeply into his eyes.

"I love you, Shane," she said earnestly. "I know how much you loved Allie, and that she'll be with you forever. I just want to help fill the rest of your life."

He climbed out of the pool, pulled her to her feet and simply held her . . . the admission of love finally binding them together, and freeing them—as paradoxical as everything else about their relationship.

Shane snatched a towel from the end of the bar near the chaise, wrapped her in it and took her inside. He slid the French doors closed behind them and drew the bamboo shades.

When he turned back to her, she held the towel open in invitation—her eyes deep with love and desire. He went weak with tenderness. She dried his back with the ends of the generous towel. Damp breasts to wet chest, they shared a long, intoxicating kiss.

Then he tugged the towel from her and let it fall. He unhooked the simple catch on her bikini top and dropped it, too. He placed gentle, reverent hands where the fabric had been and felt his pulse leap as she gasped softly, closed her eyes and leaned into him. Her breasts beaded against his palm, and he closed his fingers as her hands reached for his shoulders.

She reached up for his lips and he closed his mouth over hers again, lifting her into his arms and placing her in the middle of the bed.

He traced every curve and indentation with adoring fingertips.

She remained docile under his touch, but finally pushed gently against him until he lay back into the pillows. She laced her fingers in his and spread their arms wide so that she could press her upper body against his, murmuring a little groan when her breasts touched the hair-roughened muscled hardness of his chest.

Sensation rippled through her at the sound of his low, elemental gasp of pleasure.

She rubbed against him mercilessly, the pearled tips of her breasts teasing across his chest in one direction, then the other. He needed desperately to slow her down.

"Sonny." He pushed her gently upright, intent on turning her onto the pillows beside him so that he could return the attention she lavished on him.

But the action succeeded only in sitting her astride him, precisely where he needed no more encouragement.

"Sonny..." he gasped, wanting to caution her to stop before he could no longer take control of the situation. But that seemed unnecessary when she took bold control herself.

Trying to prop himself up on his elbows to pull her down beside him, he lost his strength when he felt her fingertips in the waistband of his trunks. He fell back to the pillows, resigned to his fate.

He thought that the gentle scrape of her fingernails down the outside of his thighs, then his calves, as she pulled the garment from him, was a sensation that would live with him for days.

Sonny began planting kisses at his ankles and was halfway to his knees when steely hands took hold of her upper arms and snatched her from the end of the bed to the blankets beside him.

He kissed her protest into silence and peeled the bikini bottoms from her. Then he closed his hands over her breasts until the pulsing pressure became one with the beat of her heart and the flow of her blood.

She arched into his hands, running her fingers over his shoulders, down his sides, around his back to the lean tapering of his waist.

He braced himself on his hands and trailed kisses down the middle of her body, stopping at the juncture of torso and thigh to pull her knee up and touch his lips to the sensitive skin on the underside.

She stirred restlessly, the heart of her femininity pulsing for his touch, waiting, tensing.

He moved his lips to the other knee and made his way slowly back to the top of her thigh, then onto her lower stomach and up.

She stirred again, turning toward him, yearning for him. Then she stopped still when he closed a hand over that hot pulse and reached inside her.

She heard her own gasp, felt a relief curiously allied with tension, and the immediate, rippled explosion of sensation that drove every thought from her head.

She was his now, helpless in his arms, willing victim of the effects of their love. Pleasure rode over and over her until her body finally quieted.

Smiling, she stroked the muscled thighs bracketing her waist, intent on returning the pleasure he'd given her. But he tipped her hips up and entered her, eliciting another gasp. She experienced several seconds of amazement that it could all begin again so quickly, and that two bodies could feel so much like one. She drew in his breath, her heart beat for his, and her body enfolded him like a part of itself.

And she realized that at that moment she was a new entity. Not just Sonnet Winslow, but someone else—a woman inextricably connected to Shane Archer.

Then pleasure exploded and time seemed to telescope into forever. Despite the brightness of the afternoon around her, she had the impression of sailing through a starlit universe high in the sky, and crossing over the tip of a crescent moon.

MEMBERS OF THE Federation met around the fire, eating shrimp from the Water Planet and rice with bits of fruit in it. Starby kept a wary eye on the platter that contained the Green Menace and other contributions brought to the table by a source he had yet to identify. He was sure they represented a serious danger to all present and had probably been sent to the banquet by the Cave Conqueror as a way to undermine their unity.

He tried to explain the danger to the Sun Queen.

While the Mission Master prepared the food over the fire, and the Federation President went back onto the ship for more supplies, Starby cornered the queen in her chair under the pink bougainvillea.

She held a piece of the Green Menace in her fingers. He stopped her just in time.

"That's poison," he told her urgently. "It looks like food, but it isn't."

"It isn't?" She studied the piece she held.

He shook his head. "It's junk from another planet, painted green to look like a vegetable. The taste can kill you."

Sonny examined the piece of broccoli one more moment, then dipped it in the dressing on her plate and popped it into her mouth.

Dusty placed a hand over his eyes and groaned.

"I can eat this and live," Sonny assured him quickly, putting her plate aside and lifting him into her lap. "You know why?"

"You're going to die," he insisted worriedly.

"No, I'll survive. Because I'm going to take the antidote before I finish dinner."

He frowned at her and shifted to place an arm around her neck. He'd become her confidant in the last several days. "Auntie who?"

"Anti*dote.*" She reached out to her plate, took a small piece of broccoli, dipped it in the dressing and offered it to him. "Now you can enjoy the Green Menace, too, and live to tell about it when I share the secret."

He shrank back against her arm. "Enjoy it?"

She raised an eyebrow. "Didn't you know? We eat the Green Menace all the time on the Flower Planet, and the Orange Stick and the Brain Vegetable. Know why?"

Starby was sure she was already dying. "Why?"

"Because they give us special powers that make us smart and strong. And if you're going to be my champion, you'll have to be smarter and stronger than my enemies."

"But, they *taste* like poison."

"That's what the enemy thinks, too, so if they don't eat them and you do, you'll defeat them every time."

Starby took the Green Menace from her. He wasn't convinced that she hadn't been tricked, but he ate it to save her from it.

It tasted like poison to him.

"What," he asked urgently, "is the Auntie Dote?"

She squeezed him to her and kissed his cheek. He preferred her to be less demonstrative in front of the other Federation members, but he found the gesture comforting all the same. Particularly if he was about to die.

"Sugar," she replied. "If you eat dessert after dinner, the sugar kills all the poison in it and leaves only the vitamins and minerals that make us strong. And tonight we're having macadamia fudge cake with ice cream."

He leaned against her with a deep sigh. "If I die anyway, you can have my piece."

Dusty fell asleep in Sonny's lap even before the main course—shrimp skewered with vegetables and served over rice—was on the table.

Shane took him from her. "I'll go put him to bed. Don't nibble off my plate. I have those shrimp counted." A glance at her worried expression made him laugh lightly. "I was teasing. You can pick off my plate if you want to."

She shook her head to deny that was the problem. "That isn't it. I convinced him to have a bite of broccoli by telling him that dessert was the antidote."

Shane smiled down at the burden in his arms. "I heard the whole thing. You're almost as good at fantasy as he is."

"But if he wakes up in the middle of the night and remembers that he hasn't had dessert . . ."

"Don't worry. He never wakes up in the middle of the night." Shane sauntered off with him.

Sonny doubted she would ever forget that evening. They ate for hours in the balmy darkness, exchanged stories of hotel life and Sonny's experiences on army bases and decided that—given the transient population, the last-minute crises and the loneliness of adjustment—the life-styles weren't so different after all.

The macadamia fudge cake tasted like something prepared in heaven. Sonny was pleased to see that more than half of it remained after the men had had seconds, so there would be a piece for Dusty.

It was almost midnight when Shane and Josh checked to make sure the coals were cooling and moved the barbecue aside. Sonny helped Nina carry plates and leftovers into the house.

The kitchen was large and open and painted a subtle sandlike color. The brightly patterned cushions on the rattan dining room chairs stood out in sunny contrast, matched by a ruffled valance over the wall of windows.

Sonny went to the refrigerator to put away the butter and saw a magnetic picture frame attached to the door. The photo had been taken on the patio where she'd just enjoyed the long, leisurely dinner. It was of Shane and Dusty and a smiling young woman with dark hair. Allie.

There were photos of the family on the piano and on a credenza in the hallway, but Sonny had been deliberately careful not to study them. It wasn't that she didn't want to know about Allie, but being found studying her likeness might concern or upset the Bedfords.

"That's Allie," Nina said, coming to look over Sonny's shoulder. There was pride and grief in her voice. "They lived just down the road from us and had stopped by one Sunday afternoon. Josh had just loaded the camera and... I guess that's my favorite photo of the three of them because it was so impromptu, and so... full of love."

She studied the photo a moment longer, then added with a sigh, "Had my disposition and her father's intellect. She was invincible." Her voice caught and she swallowed. "Well, against things that fought fair, anyway."

Sonny had developed a deep affection for the Bedfords in the past few days. She turned to Nina with deep sincerity. "I'm sorry you lost her. I'm sorry for all of you."

Nina's eyes filled, then she sighed again and her smile returned. "Thank you. But we were all sorry enough for ourselves for a while. Now we've learned to go on with the love she left us." Nina placed an arm around her shoulders and squeezed. "I hope it doesn't upset you that I talk about her. Josh and I had decided not to bring her up unless you did, afraid you'd think we were comparing you, or something."

Sonny put the butter inside the refrigerator and smiled at Nina over the door, feeling guilty about the deception. Then she realized she and Shane had become precisely what they were pretending to be—lovers. She felt off-balance for a moment, startled that a lie, a dream and a fantasy had all become truth.

She closed the door and smiled down at the obviously happy, loving little group in the photo. Knowing that they'd lost the unity that glowed out of the picture made her feel sad, even though it was the only reason she now found herself in the lives of the man and the little boy.

She smiled at Nina. "I know you both love Shane and Dusty so much. And you know better than anyone how good she was for them. Even I know, and I've never met her."

Nina gave her a small frown of concern and drew her to the dining room table and pulled out a chair.

She sat opposite her, her eyes probing. "Are you suggesting that you shouldn't have a place in their lives because they were a happy family?"

Sonny tried to analyze the complex emotion that combined love and need with guilt and something that could only be defined as jealousy.

"I'm a simple army brat," she said, knowing she was skirting the edges of the issue, "who grew up to crave adventure. When I finally found it, I discovered that I still want things secure and in order after all."

Nina made a face. "Order is so dull."

"I guess what I mean is, I'd like to know I can give them everything she gave them."

Nina blinked. "Well, of course you can't." Then realizing how that sounded, she reached out to cover Sonny's hand and explain quickly, "Allie gave them all that she had to give, and that's what made them happy. You will give what you have to share and that will make them happy again."

The men barged in with an armload of dirty linen and a small folding table they'd borrowed from the family room. The delicate discussion was brought quickly to a close.

Joshua stopped in the middle of the room, studied their intimate expressions, and turned worriedly to Shane. "Oh, I know that look. We're going shopping at the Ala Moana Center tomorrow, and it's going to cost us a bundle."

Nina rolled her eyes at Sonny. "Men. They think shopping is the only thing we can get serious about." She paused a moment, then asked gravely, "So how many diamonds do you think you'll need?"

SHANE CAME QUICKLY AWAKE when his eyelid was lifted up to his hairline. He had a one-eyed view of another eye a mere inch away from his in the darkness. There was a squirming weight across his middle.

"Dad?" Dusty demanded in a loud whisper. Shane's face was taken in two small hands and shaken. He thought the experience could be likened to being caught in the jaws of some playful predator. "Dad, are you awake?"

He pulled the small hand away from his eye. "Dusty, Rip van Winkle couldn't have slept through that. What?"

"I need Antie Dote!"

"Who?"

"You know. The lady made of sugar that kills poisons so that you get big and strong!"

Shane knew he was losing it. There was too much on his mind. First the sex bird, now a sugar woman named Auntie Dote. His brain was going fast. He didn't want to consider what part of him could be next.

Then something about that came together and he groaned and closed his eyes as Sonny's whimsical efforts to get Dusty to eat his vegetables at dinner came back to him.

Shane reached out to turn on the bedside lamp and studied his son in its small ray of light.

"Do you really think the broccoli poisoned you?" he asked.

He watched the little face he knew so well and saw for the first time since Dusty had begun talking about Martian probes and a place called Eos, a distinction between reality and fantasy. The bright brown eyes told Shane he knew he hadn't been poisoned, but that a piece of cake in the middle of the night could be an antidote for many other things—loneliness, confusion, the heavy burden of learning to live without one's mother at six years of age.

Dusty put a hand to his throat and said in a strangled voice, "I think it's starting to work!"

Sonny sat up beside Shane and threw off the blankets. She pulled on a light cotton robe. "I'll cut the antidote," she said to Shane, "while you make the cocoa." To Dusty, she added, "Race you to the kitchen."

With a squeal of laughter Shane hoped didn't wake his in-laws, Dusty followed Sonny's figure as she disappeared down the hall, flowered cotton billowing after her.

Shane watched them, happiness filling his being along with a gut-wrenching sense of possession.

When he reached the kitchen, Sonny had already sliced two pieces and held the knife poised over the cake as she raised a questioning eyebrow at him.

He stopped behind Dusty, who was already forking into his cake as though it truly were an antidote to something that had poisoned him. "I'm still full from dinner," Shane said rubbing the bony little shoulders before him. "How do you have room? You ate as much as I did."

Sonny leveled the knife in his direction and made a threatening little circle in the air with it. "Very unchivalrous of you to point that out. And I'm having another piece because I'll probably have to work it off before I go to sleep." Her eyebrow arched a little higher as she waited for him to grasp the significance of her reply.

It took about a nanosecond. "Actually, I'm starving," he said, going to the coffeepot and opening the cupboard in search of filters and coffee. "I'd like a big piece. I did have a lot of broccoli."

Dusty gave him a sympathetic look, his mouth ringed in chocolate icing. "I tried to tell you, Dad. But you believed Sonny instead."

Shane took exception to the criticism. "Well, so did you."

Dusty acknowledged that fact with a very adult nod. "Grandpa says women are all the same, and if we want to get their babies, we have to do what they say."

Shane was startled only long enough to realize his son meant that "getting their babies" remark in the purely political sense of populating Eos.

Sonny kissed Dusty's cheek as she handed Shane his plate across the table. "You could *not* eat the cake and take the chance that the broccoli won't kill you," she suggested.

Dusty looked up at her and smiled winningly. "I'd rather be sure."

She nodded her agreement. "Good move."

They ate several bites in silence, then Dusty frowned across the table at his father. "Dad? Do you suppose the sex bird is a girl?"

"THE SEX BIRD?" Sonny whispered in the darkness an hour later when Dusty was settled into bed again. She and Shane stood with the door open to the patio, breathing in the fresh air.

Shane had already removed her robe and now slipped the thin gown off her shoulders.

"A fairly logical misconception," he said, holding her hand as she stepped out of the gown. "He has the stork confused with the undefined theory of a buddy of his from day care that sex brings babies."

"Ah." Sonny laughed softly as she parted the snap that fastened Shane's pajama bottoms. "And they think sex has wings and delivers babies in a diaper caught in its bill."

He kicked the pile of cotton aside, already losing his grip on the world around him. "Something like that." He looked into her eyes and found them smiling at him.

Sonny turned to draw him toward the bed, but he resisted her, pulling her instead toward the pool where the air cushion on which he'd sunned himself that afternoon still bumped against the edge of the pool.

"Shane!" she whispered on a giggle. "We'll drown."

"Trust me."

"Hah. Show me flippers and a snorkel and I'll trust you!"

As Shane drew her after him down onto the edge of the pool then over the side, he was satisfied to see that she followed despite her protest.

Sonny felt the cool water of the pool embrace her, the warm night air drift around her shoulders and her face. The sensations were primal, deep-reaching, and the melting warmth that occurred inside her every time Shane touched her, ignited and roared to life when he lay back on the mattress.

He reached one hand to the railing to hold them steady, then helped settle Sonny atop him with the other. She reached for the side of the pool with a little scream when they pitched dangerously. He closed a wet hand that smelled of chlorine over her mouth and laughed softly.

She took him inside her and watched the smile melt away into a contentment so deep, it almost hurt her. He let go of the railing, and they drifted across the pool like the Mission Master and the Sun Queen on the sailboat to Eos.

Love and passion flowed between them, energized by their inability to propel it for fear of swamping the mattress. Their stillness somehow intensified their physical release, and they clung together, bodies wet but warm, water lapping around their little craft as it sailed across the moon.

Chapter Twelve

"Grandma and Grandpa are coming back to Merriwether with us," Dusty told Sonny as they wandered hand in hand down the road that fronted the Bedford property. "'Cause we're going to have a big Halloween party."

"Right." Sonny smiled down at the boy as he swung their hands between them, even more lighthearted than usual this afternoon. Shane and the Bedfords were discussing hotel business in Josh's study, and Sonny had decided to take Dusty for a walk.

She felt torn between hating to leave this island paradise and wanting to return home to make sure every decorating detail was in place for the hotel's party.

She was so in love, she knew it didn't matter where she was, as long as Shane and Dusty were with her.

"You're gonna marry Dad, aren'cha?" Dusty asked as he took a turn in the road. It was a quiet little street lined with eucalypti, and Sonny followed his lead, breathing in the trade winds and the perfumed flowers.

Sonny squeezed Dusty's hand. "Your father hasn't asked me yet, Dusty."

"He's going to. He talked to me about it last night."

"Did he?" Happiness and excitement swelled inside her. "And what do you think?" She waited expectantly for his enthusiastic endorsement.

"I..." When he hesitated, Sonny looked down at him, vaguely disappointed that he wasn't gushing.

His little face looked troubled, and the hand that held hers suddenly tightened its grip. His eyes were focused on a home set back in a forest of imported pines. It reminded Sonny of the Bedfords' home, though its shape was more octagonal, and it had a second floor. But it had the glass and surrounding patio details seen all over the islands.

Sonny wondered what it could be about the house that had caused his mood to pall. She knelt down beside him in the middle of the road and looped her arms loosely around him.

"Do you know who lives there?" she asked gently.

His eyes grew wider as he stared at it, and Sonny got the impression he was remembering something. She didn't know if it was simply good instincts, or the rapport she'd developed with the boy since she'd moved in with his father, but she knew the answer before he said the words.

"I . . . lived there."

Sonny felt real fear rise up inside her. Something traumatic was happening to this little boy and his father wasn't here.

"My mom..." he said, his voice breathy and choked, "used to make sandwiches, and we had picnics under that tree." He pointed to a spreading poinciana, heavy with flame-colored flowers at the edge of the property. "She was very pretty."

Sonny found herself speechless, her throat aching painfully.

"She went to the hospital," he said sadly, a tear spilling over and another following in rapid succession.

"I know." Sonny rubbed his back and kissed his cheek.

"She said she loved me." He sniffed and leaned sideways against Sonny, still watching the house. "Then she got on an elevator." He heaved a ragged sigh as tears now fell rapidly. "Then she died."

Sonny tightened her grip on him as tears spilled down her own cheeks. She racked her brain for words of comfort, and settled desperately for, "She's with God now, Dusty. He makes everyone with Him happy." Then wondered if his child's mind could even comprehend the concept of heaven and life eternal.

"I know," he said simply. Then pointed again to the big flame tree. "But she used to be right there."

He began to sob. Sonny had no idea what to do for him except get him back to his father. She lifted him in her arms and he wrapped himself around her, holding fast as she made her way back to the Bedfords, weeping as hard as he did.

Shane and the Bedfords were on the front patio when she started up the walk, her strength waning under Dusty's weight.

Shane caught sight of them when they were halfway up the flagstone and raised a hand to wave, ready to tease them about almost missing the final round of macadamia fudge cake, when he noticed Sonny's tears and heard the sound of his child's.

"What is it?" He was only vaguely aware of Nina's question as he ran down the steps and met Sonny at the bottom.

"What?" he demanded, taking Dusty from her. "What happened?"

Dusty clung to his neck, sobbing. He pulled Sonny into his arm.

"I'm sorry," she said, swiping at her eyes, putting a comforting hand to Dusty's back. "I...brought him out for a walk because the three of you were busy. He was leading the way and turned up the road...some instinct leading him, I guess." She pointed in the direction they'd taken. "And...there was...your house. I didn't know. I'm sorry."

Dusty leaned up off his shoulder, his tear-filled eyes wide with distress and confusion. "Mom used to be there," he said, the same amazement in his tone Shane felt when the doctor had come to the waiting room to tell him she was gone.

"I know," he said gently, kissing his cheek. "But she isn't there anymore. She still watches over you, she still loves you, she just can't be with you anymore."

Dusty shook his head. "That's not fair," he declared angrily. "'Member how we used to eat under the tree? And how Mom used to sing in the kitchen...?"

Emotion stuck like a sharp-cornered block in Shane's throat as he saw the memory play in his mind's eye. Grief grabbed him and shook him. He pulled Dusty back against him as the boy screamed with an anguish for which there was no other release. Shane's own tears fell on the shoulder of Dusty's cotton shirt. A pain no one else quite understood imprisoned them together, shutting out everyone else.

Sonny had been forgotten. She understood, of course, but she watched father and son torn by a grief with which they thought they'd made their peace and faced the truth.

Old love could be stronger than new love. Grief could be tougher than fantasies and dreams.

Nina appeared to take Sonny's arm. "Come inside," she said quietly. "Josh will make you a cold drink and you can lie down before dinner. Please don't blame yourself," she added. "You didn't know about the house. There's a new family in it now, but I'm sure that's hard for a six-year-old to understand."

She sent Sonny up the steps to Josh, who waited at the top to take her hand. Then she turned to Shane. "What can I get you?" she asked, her own eyes brimming with tears. "What can I do?"

Shane shook his head as he sank to the bottom step with Dusty. "Nothing," he said thickly. "Maybe we'll just sit down here for a little while."

Nina nodded. "Call me if you need me."

SHANE CLOSED Dusty's door behind him and leaned back against it, feeling himself begin to come alive again after that startling immersion into the past. It was almost nine. Dusty was asleep after having eaten a big dinner, and Shane felt reasonably sure that his son was himself again.

"I didn't think I was going to cry about Mom anymore," Dusty had confided when Shane tucked him in. "I thought I wasn't a baby anymore."

"I'm not a baby," Shane said, fluffing his pillow, "and I cried, too. We cry because the love we felt for Mom was important, and it hurts when that's gone. Even a long time after it happens."

Dusty stiffened his feet under the blanket and watched the arch they made when he moved his feet from side to side. "Sonny cried," he said. "And it wasn't even *her* mom."

"That's because," Shane said, "she loves you, and it made her feel bad that you were sad."

He remembered guiltily that he'd had an arm around her one moment, then grief had overtaken him and he'd unconsciously pushed her away. He hated to think what complexion she'd put on that in view of her reluctance to believe he was ready to fall in love again.

Dusty frowned. "How come you didn't ask her to get married yet?"

Shane turned on the night-light, and turned off the bedside lamp. "How do you know I haven't asked her?"

"I asked her if you did. She said no."

Shane groaned and sat on the edge of the bed in the eerie glow of a light in the shape of Aladdin's Genie.

"I bet she'd say yes," Dusty predicted. "She looked happy when I told her you told me you were gonna ask her."

So much for suave and dramatic planning, Shane thought. Then he braced a hand on the other side of his son's little body and asked easily, "So are you still okay with that? Getting Sonny as a mom?"

Dusty nodded quickly and, Shane was sure, honestly. He even seemed surprised that he'd had to ask. "I think she'll be a great mom."

SHANE FOUND HER SWIMMING laps like a demon. She moved through the water with more strength than style, as though trying to outdistance something. He knew with absolute certainty that he wanted her with him for the rest of his life—and that she intended to fight him on it because of what had happened this afternoon.

Curiously, in spite of—or maybe because of—Dusty's emotional scene and his own response, he felt a freshness of spirit he hadn't known since Allie's death. It was as though it had pulled up the last of the pain and left only the parts of their love that had strengthened and renewed him.

Shane snatched a towel from the pile always waiting at the end of the wet bar and went to stand at the edge of the pool. He waited until Sonny noticed him, then opened it and held it out.

She came to the edge of the pool and leapt gracefully out. He wrapped her in the towel and looked down into her carefully composed face. . . .

That is, he thought it looked serene. But he'd come to know that wide eyes focused on him, mouth set in a firm line and chin at a regal angle meant she felt anything but calm. She was impassioned about something. And he was a step ahead of her this time.

"I want to talk to you," she said, curling her hands inside the towel to hold it closed at her breasts.

"That's good," he said, swinging her up into his arms, "because I want to talk to you."

Helpless in her cocoon, she looked him in the eye. "I said *talk*."

He nodded. "I heard you," and strode to the cushioned, redwood double chaise longue that allowed him to lie on it and tuck her in beside him. "You want to go first?"

She didn't want to go at all. She felt confused and concerned and downright desperate. But if she let him go first, she might lose her nerve. And there were things that had to be said.

"I think we should stop seeing each other," she blurted. She waited, expecting an outburst. He would push her away, sit up, shout. Her heart sank at the realization that he, too, thought it a good idea. So, it must be. It wasn't simply her anguish, her hysteria.

"You and Dusty aren't ready for me." She went on with all the rational arguments she'd compiled while pretending to nap through dinner. "We've had this great thing going, but you were lonely and I happened along at an opportune moment and that's maybe... all it is." She faltered, knowing that it wasn't—at least on her part. But he'd probably just been carried along on the tide of companionship and physical compatibility while still in love with Allie. And his son's grief had reminded him of that. She'd seen it in his face. "I," she said with a breath for courage, "need to set off on a new adventure. Nina told me yesterday that she'd like me to look over the Kauai Bedford, so as soon as I've finished the centerpieces for the Halloween ball, I'm leaving Merriwether."

She began to grow concerned when he remained silent. Passiveness wasn't usually his style. Unless her speculation had been right on target and he wanted out of the relationship.

She braced herself and asked bravely, "You had something to say to me?"

He turned to her, his expression still completely calm, his wonderful mouth even smiling. He pulled her even closer to him. "Will you marry me?" he asked.

She pushed him away and bolted upright. Then she shouted, "Haven't you heard anything I've said?"

He, too, sat up to look sternly into her exasperated face. "Keep your voice down. Yes, I did, but it was all bull, so I ignored it. *Will* you marry me?"

"No!" she whispered loudly, trying to get to her feet. He pulled her down again. "Dusty was truly upset today, Shane. And so were you. You're not ready for another woman to move into your lives.''

''Yes, we are,'' Shane insisted quietly. ''Dusty just isn't ready to forget the old one. And I'm trying to help him understand that he doesn't have to.''

''Of course he doesn't have to, but he's still in so much pain.''

They spoke in more normal tones now, her indignation deflated, his calm slightly diminished. ''He has to grieve, Sonny,'' Shane said. ''Even if it's uncomfortable for you.''

She turned hurt blue eyes on him. ''That isn't what I mean, Shane,'' she said gently, ''what about you? Your grief was deep.... I...'' Her mouth quivered dangerously. ''I saw Allie in your eyes.''

Shane reached out to catch her hand. ''You saw *love* in my eyes, Sonny. I loved Allie deeply, just as I love you. I pushed it down, cast it away, so I could cope, so I could help Dusty adjust. I chose to go to Merriwether because I thought it would help distract him, give him new things to think about. I found it hard to watch him grieve, too.'' Shane leaned his elbows on his knees and looked out at the moonlight on the pool. ''It worked. He was distracted. But he wasn't healed. No matter how hard it is for all of us, that's what healing is—screaming and crying and carrying on.''

Sonny's tears spilled over. Shane brushed them aside with his thumbs.

''And this is what love looks like,'' he said, leaning forward to place a kiss where the tear had been. ''Someone else's tears on your face. You love Dusty.''

''Of course I do.'' More tears spilled over than he could brush away. So he pulled her into his arms.

''And you love me.''

She wrapped her arms around his middle, and he felt deep strength in them as she clutched at him. "Yes."

"The next step is getting a license. Nina and Josh are coming home with us to look over the hotel. So, we'll call your parents—"

"Shane—"

"Before Halloween."

"That's five days away."

"Then, the first of November."

"We'll think about it," she mumbled.

"We'll do it," he said.

STARBY AIMED the terran craft back toward Eos. With the Federation President and the Martian Marquesa aboard, he took special pains to make it a smooth flight.

They were edgy, he noticed, laughing about things that didn't seem funny and smiling as though nothing were wrong.

They thought he was simply a freight jockey, that he wasn't aware the alliance between the Mission Master and the Sun Queen was in jeopardy. He wasn't sure what had happened. But he knew they were both unhappy.

Sadness tried to envelop him, but he shrugged it off, remembering that he'd always had faith in the Mission Master—and he'd never let him down.

SHANE SENT DUSTY up to their suite with Josh and Nina while he got a bellman for their bags and had a word with the desk clerk. Sonny tried to follow the Bedfords, but Shane kept a firm grip on her arm.

"Just stop this," he said a moment later after he saw the bellman onto one elevator and ushered Sonny onto another.

"What?" she asked innocently.

"Trying to pull away."

"Well, your thumb was drilling a hole in my arm."

"I mean stop trying to pull away emotionally," he said, putting a finger to the Stop button. The elevator glided to a halt. "I won't let you."

Sonny gave him an even stare. "I'm moving out of the suite." She folded her arms and squared her shoulders, prepared to do battle. "You cannot make me do something I don't think is wise, no matter how much you want it. We need time apart to think."

He imprisoned her with his body, one hand against the wall behind her head, the other still on the Hold button.

"That sounds like a colonel talking, and not an adventuress. You're staying with me."

"I'm not."

"How would you explain moving out to your brother, who thinks we're married?"

She shrugged a careless shoulder. "I'll tell him the truth."

"That you've been living with me? That you just spent four days with me in Hawaii and made love with me in a swimming pool? Won't he have to report that to your father?"

"My father's in Mexico," she replied firmly. "And Brad's so besotted with Charmaine, he probably doesn't even remember we left for Hawaii. I'm going home."

Sonny dared him to challenge her further. She fixed him with determined blue eyes in which she tried to focus all her conviction in the belief that she, Shane and Dusty needed more time.

Shane, to whom every moment of the last year and a half had been a challenge, dropped his hand from the Hold button and told her with calm authority, "You *are* home."

Sonny sailed off the elevator, resolved that words, no matter how beautifully spoken, were not going to stop her. Shane followed her, knowing if she persisted in this line of thinking, he would lock her in a closet before he would let her leave him.

Sonny stopped before the threshold of his suite as shouts, screams and several other, calmer voices filtered out the half-opened door.

"Great," Shane grumbled as the bellman hurried out, pushing the luggage cart, appearing anxious to be on his way. "Does *everyone* have a keycard to my suite?"

Sonny pushed the door open silently and had two of the truths critical to her present peace of mind shattered.

Firstly, her brother no longer seemed besotted. Brad and Charmaine stood toe-to-toe in the middle of the living room, screaming at each other at the top of their lungs.

"I did *not* get an MBA to live on a military base!" Charmaine shrieked at him.

"And I will *not*," Brad shouted back, "quit the army three years from retirement to satisfy your spoiled little butt!"

Secondly, her father was no longer in Mexico. Colonel Robert Winslow stood behind his son, as though prepared to take up arms in his support—or his defense, as seemed more likely at the moment. Beside him,

Joyce Winslow, Sonny's mother, studied the tense tableau with a hand to her mouth in a thoughtful pose.

Ranged behind Charmaine were Josh and Nina, apparently enjoying the fracas. Dusty, peeling a banana, observed from the safety of the sofa.

"Fine!" Charmaine said, straining up on tiptoe to place her nose half an inch from Brad's. "Then my spoiled little butt is out of here!"

"Fine!" Brad replied.

She ran past Sonny and Shane without seeing them. Her suite door slammed. Brad grabbed a jacket off the sofa and marched off. Shane moved Sonny aside just in time to prevent her from being marched over.

Then Robert Winslow's gaze focused on the doorway and he said in a voice that belonged on a parade ground, "Sonnet Roberta Winslow. What in the hell have you been up to?"

Sonny went to wrap him in a hug, determined not to behave like his inadequate daughter. "Hi, Dad," she said, forcing a cheerful tone while her brain frantically considered her options. She reached an arm out to embrace her mother. "Hi, Mom."

Joyce, a small but athletic woman in jeans and a denim jacket, was as weathered and muscled as any service veteran. She made cynical teenagers fall in love with Shakespeare, and gardens grow in deserts. She could make any bland base housing look like home within twenty-four hours of their arrival, and Brad had always teased that she probably knew more about geography than Rand McNally.

But there were a few more lines around her eyes, Sonny noticed, though the wattage of her smile hadn't diminished. In an odd sort of sudden revelation, Sonny saw that smile as genuine courage rather than as the rah-

rah propaganda heroism she used to think it was when she'd been in her teens and it was time to move *again*.

She studied her mother for a moment, wondering why she should realize that now. Because she now understood that loving did require courage, perhaps, and she found herself just a little short?

"And *you?*" Winslow made his way between the women to confront Shane. "Are you the man who made off with my daughter?"

Shane took his measure. It wasn't difficult. It was there for anyone to see—retired or not, Robert Winslow was still soldier through and through.

Then he analyzed the question and decided he could safely answer in the affirmative, and the Winslows would think he'd married Sonny, and Josh and Nina would think only that they were lovers. And Charmaine and Brad, with their respective thoughts on their marital status, were mercifully absent.

Shane offered his hand, careful not to lie directly. "Shane Archer. Pleased to meet you, sir. Mrs. Winslow."

The colonel studied his hand a moment, then glanced at his daughter with disapproval that melted after a long moment into a stiff and reluctant smile. He shook Shane's hand.

"She's a little bit of a loose cannon," he said with another glance at Sonny. She was amazed to see a small sparkle of approval in it.

Shane introduced Dusty and the Bedfords while Sonny, on the verge of a nervous collapse, went to the kitchen to telephone room service. It occurred to her, while she waited for someone on Fernando's staff to pick up, that she was beginning to act like she actually lived in the suite.

"Well." Joyce perched on a stool in the corner of the kitchen, wrapping her legs comfortably around the rungs. "He's really something. I was always sure you were going to end up with an accountant or an insurance agent."

"Mother," Sonny scolded, putting her hand over the receiver. "If you're implying that they're dull, that's a bigoted generalization."

Joyce smiled shamelessly. "I was military most of my life, dear. That's what we do."

Sonny's eyes widened, then saw the humor in her mother's. She swatted at her arm. "You should go back to the men before they start posturing for each other and a fight breaks out."

Joyce dismissed that possibility with a roll of her eyes. "Something worse has already happened. They've already discovered they've all served at Fort Benning at one time or another. Your father won't miss me for days."

"I thought you were in Mexico."

"We knew Brad was due home and when we couldn't find him and couldn't find you, we got worried and came to see for ourselves. Denise Potter told us where to find you. We just arrived before you did."

The kitchen picked up the phone and Sonny shushed her mother with a wave of her hand while she ordered coffee, tea and scones, then hung up.

"Anyway," Sonny said, leaning a hip against the counter. "I've become an adventuress in the last few weeks."

Joyce nodded, appearing impressed. "I would say so. Marriage, a child, purveyor of flowers for a major hotel." Her gaze narrowed and her voice quieted. "But you're not married, are you?"

Sonny's jaw dropped in surprise, then she rolled her eyes and focused on her mother with an expression that combined admiration with exasperation. "I hate that you can still do that—now that I'm twenty-seven!"

Joyce shrugged. "It's something you learn the first time your baby calls you 'Mama.'"

Sonny heaved a sigh, feeling as though she no longer controlled anything, particularly her own life. "First we pretended to be lovers because Charmaine was after Shane and she came all the way from Hawaii to seduce him."

Sonny paused to relate the pumpkin and blow-dryer incident.

Joyce nodded gravely. Sonny went on. "Then Brad appeared out of nowhere and Charmaine blurted that Shane and I were living together, and Brad got all indignant and I had visions of him calling you and Daddy in Mexico—"

Joyce interrupted with a nod. "So you told him you were married. Who is Charmaine, by the way?"

Sonny explained, then related the interesting details of Brad and Charmaine's first meeting.

Joyce laughed as though pleased. "Well, doesn't that beat all? Both of my children brought to life at the same point in time." Then she frowned as Sonny folded her arms and wandered across the narrow corridor kitchen. "Or are you waiting in the wings, as usual?"

Sonny turned on her, annoyed. "What do you mean, 'as usual'?" She repeated her mother's words scornfully. "I've taken a big chance falling in love with Shane Archer and his son."

"Something's gone wrong?" Joyce guessed.

Sonny explained about Allie. "She was wonderful," she said, "and they both still love her very much. I don't think they're ready to put another woman in her place."

"Shane didn't look hesitant to me when he told your father he was the man who'd made off with you."

Sonny rolled her eyes. "He's been a manager most of his life. He thinks that because he wants something he should have it."

Joyce winced, obviously perplexed. "Well, if he thinks he should have you, doesn't that suggest that he's ready to move on with his life?"

Sonny told her about Dusty and their impromptu walk by the house. And the obvious grief in the child and his father.

"Wasn't that just honest emotion?" Joyce asked.

Sonny shrugged. "If they're still grieving, are they ready for someone to replace Allie?"

Joyce studied her shrewdly, then uncurled her legs and slid off the stool. "I imagine they're ready for someone to take up where she left off. But I'm sure they're *not* ready for a woman who isn't ready for *them.*" Sonny opened her mouth to rebut, but Joyce stopped her with a very maternal look. "The trouble you've always had, Sonnet, is that you're always second-guessing yourself. How you were born into this military family, I'll never know, but I've been trying most of your life to straighten you out."

"Daddy doesn't think it can be done," Sonny said in the same aggressive tone she remembered using as a child. "Didn't you hear him call me a loose cannon?"

Joyce sighed patiently. "Sonny, I've been telling you for years, and I'll tell you again, that your father's problem with you isn't that he doesn't think you're good enough, it's that it irritates the hell out of him that *you* don't think you're good enough. His being a stickler for rules, we can't help. I know you've found that hard to live with, but that's his life, so it was ours, too. But apart from that, you seem to think you have to fill every hole, answer every question, find every solution. You don't. All you have to do is show up for the battle.''

Sonny listened, eyes defiant.

"And on that subject," Joyce added, looking straight into her daughter's rebellious gaze, "if you think you took a big chance falling in love with Shane Archer and his son, you ain't seen nothin' yet. Wait till you try to *live* in love."

Chapter Thirteen

"We have a problem," Sonny said as she and Shane lagged behind the penthouse contingent on their way to dinner in the hotel's dining room. The Bedfords and Brad led the way across the busy lobby while the Winslows followed with Charmaine and Dusty.

"We certainly have," Shane replied, returning a greeting from the reception desk. "Which one in particular?"

Sonny also waved in response to the greeting. "The one concerning our relationship."

"That one will no longer be a problem when you marry me."

Sonny stopped in her tracks, finally driven to distraction by their various deceits, and the certainty that they were in imminent danger of being found out around the dinner table. Shane had cleverly skirted the issue with her father, and the men had spent all afternoon talking fishing while Nina and Joyce discovered they had a mutual friend at Hickham Field. Charmaine had remained pouting in her suite.

But that was over. This was dinner—the time for family talk. Her father would want to know about her wedding, the Bedfords would wonder what on earth she was talking about. Her father would declare martial law before the evening was out.

"The problem of what everyone *thinks* our relationship is," she corrected with a calmness she didn't feel.

Shane spread his hands in a gesture of simplicity. "We'll come clean. I don't see any other way."

She gasped in disbelief. "Are you crazy? My father will stroke out on us."

Shane drew a breath for patience. "You know, this may come as a surprise to you, but I'm not afraid of your father. However, I'm beginning to lose track of all the things *you're* afraid of—Dusty, me, your father, your brother, the fact that Charmaine could become your sister-in-law. Have I missed anything?"

She grabbed the front of his jacket in a fist. "It isn't fear! It's—"

Shane glanced over her head to where their families waited for them at the entrance to the dining room. "Go ahead and slug me. That'll convince them we're married." Then his gaze moved to her eyes with a quiet threat. "But take your best shot, and be prepared to find yourself in the bay among your precious ducks."

Sonny gathered every shred of self-control she possessed and replied quietly, "I am not afraid of anyone. I simply do not want a scene over dinner."

"Then when *do* you want it? I think we've played out our line here and we're about to be reeled in."

Sonny looked heavenward in supplication. "You've obviously talked too much fishing today."

Shane caught her arm and pulled her toward their families. "Come on," he said. "I'll take care of everything."

"How?" she asked warily.

But they reached the group before he could answer.

They were seated—one half of each couple across from the other, Dusty on an end beside Shane—at a banquet table in a corner of the smaller dining room where the hostess promised they would enjoy more privacy. Shane ordered champagne and appetizers, and Nina offered the first toast to "the happy couple."

Sonny cast Shane a nervous glance and took a large sip of the bubbly in response to the safely innocuous toast. Dusty raised his glass of apple juice.

Sonny toasted Brad's safe return from Somalia, hoping to turn conversation in a safe direction. Shane asked him several questions about the United States's mission there and led the discussion through the canapés and the ordering of dinner.

Then Sonny's father cleared his throat and she felt her spine stiffen even further.

"Where do you two intend to live?" he asked, focusing his attention on Shane.

Shane prepared to reply, but Sonny, certain he intended to "come clean," put in quickly, "Wherever there's a Bedford Hotel, I guess." Then she tacked on just as quickly, "So how's the house in Mexico coming? Last I heard you were having trouble with . . . what was it?"

"The water pressure," Robert replied. "But that was in the spring. That's solved and now we have the spare rooms finished and we're ready for company. I know you've just been to Hawaii, but if you'd like to seriously honeymoon in Mexico . . ."

Sonny felt the champagne bubbles choke her at the same moment that Nina said with obvious delight, "Oh! You've finally set a date?"

Sonny's world of cards collapsed. But she tried to make herself think, to consider damage control. Before she could take action, her father said, "Set a date?" He looked from her to Nina in perplexity. "They were married weeks ago."

Charmaine frowned across the table. "No, they weren't," she said, leaning back as their waiter placed a plate of seafood fettucini before her. "They're just living together."

Brad gave Charmaine a superior look. "A lot you know. They're married."

"No, they're not," Charmaine said seriously.

Brad looked at Sonny in genuine puzzlement. "You're not? You told me you *were.*"

Sonny saw the entire scene as though she watched it on a monitor like some video game—only there was no control command to stop the play.

Aromatic dishes were placed around the table, wafting steam into the air. Sonny considered it prophetic of the eruption she felt sure was about to take place. There was a long moment of tense silence.

"You told *me,*" Charmaine said to Sonny, "that you were lovers."

Sonny leaned against the back of her chair with a defeated sigh, and opened her mouth to explain.

But Shane interrupted. "The truth is," he said with a quick, level glance around the table, "we're lovers who are about to be married."

"No," Sonny corrected quietly, "we're not. And would you stick to the issue."

Shane gave her a quelling glance. "Our marital status is the issue."

"So," Robert said, pushing his prime rib aside and focusing a laserlike stare on Shane, "you are not married to my daughter?"

"No," Shane replied.

Robert slapped his linen napkin on the table and prepared to stand, but Joyce caught his arm and held him in place. "Do you love her?" she asked Shane.

He didn't hesitate a moment. "Very much."

"Then why *aren't* you married to her?" Brad demanded.

Charmaine leaned across the table toward him, her jaw firm. "Because she's old enough to plan her own future. Maybe with you as an example of what the current male generation is like, she doesn't want to get married!"

Brad leaned toward her and Sonny swore they were going to exchange blows.

"The state of the current male generation didn't stop you from doing it twice," he said. "And all wrong, apparently."

Charmaine went crimson with indignation.

Josh pushed away from the table, "Now see here..."

Nina put a hand on his arm and a finger to her lips, asking for silence as Sonny began to explain.

"It began very innocently, really," she said, "and was supposed to be very temporary." She explained about their meeting in the market, the pumpkin she'd made for Dusty and her intrusion into their suite just before Charmaine arrived.

"Shane wanted Charmaine to think..." Sonny hesitated, wanting to put it diplomatically, wanting desperately not to hurt her now that she understood what it was like to love a man who belonged to Allie.

Shane came to her aid. "I wanted Charmaine to understand once and for all that I love her dearly—but not romantically." He gave his sister-in-law a gently apologetic glance. "I'm sorry. But you were so insistent, so

I thought maybe seeing me with another woman would discourage you. But you persisted, so I asked her to stay with me until you left, hoping that would convince you that I was involved in a relationship.''

"Winslow women," Robert said stiffly, "don't have *relationships*." He emphasized the word with disapproval. "They get married."

"She will," Shane assured him.

Sonny opened her mouth to refute Shane's statement, but her father ignored her.

"So to authenticate this performance for Mrs. Prelotsky's sake," Robert asked, "you compromised my daughter?"

"He slept on the sofa." Sonny pushed away her Oysters Rockefeller, the aroma beginning to nauseate her. She avoided Shane's eyes. "But I fell in love with him and Dusty anyway. Nina and Josh invited us to Hawaii...." An artless shrug of her shoulder made it clear to everyone that that was where the situation changed.

"Then why," Brad asked with big-brother candor, "don't you want to get married?"

Robert turned the issue on Shane. "What did you do to her? Why is she afraid to marry you?"

"She's not afraid of him," Brad said reasonably.

At the same moment Charmaine shouted, "Shane wouldn't hurt a fly!"

Shane acknowledged their support with an appreciative glance, then turned to Robert with a calm, controlled expression. "I appreciate how much you care for her," he said, "because I love her as much as you do. And I apologize for lying to Brad about being married, and letting you believe we were husband and wife, too.

It was thoughtless, and self-serving, but we'd backed ourselves into a corner."

Robert subsided and grumbled his agreement.

"But the reason she's resisting marriage," Shane went on, "is between us."

Robert bristled. "Is that so?"

"Yes, it is," Shane replied. "I can only assure you that it has nothing to do with my hurting her, and that I'll make her change her mind about it soon enough." His gaze narrowed to Sonny, daring her to contradict him. Then he returned his attention to Robert. "In the meantime, I consider her mine, and would appreciate it if you'll accept our relationship..." Then, remembering how Robert felt about that word, amended "...our love for each other."

Sonny had to admire Shane's style. The need to protest his high-handedness was overridden by appreciation for his competent, self-assured handling of the situation.

Her father stared at him for a long moment, then turned to her. "Is that the way *you* want it?"

There were four more days until the ball, and everyone was staying in the two penthouse suites. Harmony was critical to their survival.

At least, that was why she told herself she answered with a firm "Yes."

She dared Shane with a look to take advantage of her compliance.

Robert nodded grudgingly. "Very well." He picked up his utensils and pulled his plate closer.

Dusty stretched up to whisper in his father's ear. "What happened? Is the colonel gonna take Sonny away from us?"

Shane shook his head. "No one's going to take Sonny away from us. Eat your dinner."

EVERYONE WAS still asleep when Shane got up to shower at 6:15. He dressed, except for his jacket, then walked softly into the kitchen to kick start his system with a cup of French press. He was surprised to find the colonel standing there in a hotel robe, sipping a cup of conventional coffee.

The Bedfords had shared Charmaine's suite, Robert and Joyce had slept in his room, Brad on a cot in Dusty's room, and he and Sonny had shared the sofa bed—though he didn't consider sleeping on opposite sides of it sharing.

To his surprise, the colonel handed him a cup, then glanced beyond him to where his daughter still slept, her arm curled around his pillow. She didn't stir.

"You know anything about military history?" Winslow asked very quietly.

Shane was surprised by the question, and hoped he wasn't going to have to start his day being quizzed.

"Ah—no," he said, taking a sip from the hot cup. The coffee was strong enough to fuel a tank. He liked it. He toasted the colonel with his cup. "Good brew."

Robert accepted the praise with a nod. But that obviously wasn't what he wanted to talk about. "Falling back is an acceptable military tactic, you know."

A small sound came from the living room as Sonny turned and resettled. Robert moved to the inside of the corridor kitchen, beckoning Shane to follow. Robert leaned against the counter, Shane against the refrigerator.

Shane repeated Robert's statement to himself, trying to make sense of it. He took another sip of coffee, hoping it would help.

"It can confuse the enemy, make them wonder what you're up to."

"Really."

"Best of all..." Robert considered him long and hard, then smiled sincerely. And that was when Shane got the message. "It can lure the enemy onto your ground. All you have to do is lie back and wait to spring your trap."

Shane swirled the coffee in his cup, then looked up at Robert.

"Understand?" Robert asked.

"I'm not sure," Shane admitted.

"She thinks she can live without you," Robert explained softly, "because she hasn't had to. So—fall back. Let her see what her life would be like without everything you've brought into it. Joyce is convinced it'll bring Sonny to you." Robert downed the rest of his coffee and placed the cup on the counter behind him.

Shane frowned at him in confusion. "I thought you disapproved of me."

Robert studied him evenly. "So did I," he said finally. "But Joyce likes you. The woman has good instincts. And she explained to me why Sonny's having second thoughts. I want you to win this one." He clapped Shane on the shoulder. "Good luck, son," he said, then walked into the living room, pulled the blankets up over Sonny's still sleeping form, and headed for the bedroom.

Shane left the suite, planning tactics.

"I CAN'T BELIEVE," Robert said, scooping a spoonful of slimy string and seed onto newspaper, "that we track down our children all over God's green earth and end up gutting pumpkins in the back room of a restaurant."

Josh sat across the table from him in the Coast Convention Center's banquet room, closed off from the restaurant by a sliding wooden door. He waved his spoon in the air. "How do you think I feel? I'm CEO of this operation and I'm wearing an apron."

Nina and Joyce, seated beside their husbands and across from each other, shared a dry look. "You might recall that you volunteered," Nina pointed out.

"Somehow," Charmaine grumbled from the other end of the table, "Sonny saying, 'I could use a little help with dining room centerpieces,' didn't give me a clue that I'd be up to my elbows in squash giblets."

"And eighty-five pumpkins!" Robert complained. "You could decorate the mess hall at Hickham with less than this."

Sonny ignored their complaints, knowing it was just good-natured teasing.

The vaguely alarming truth was that her family and Shane's were getting along famously—as though they expected this to be a lifetime happening. The problem of their relationship's status hadn't been brought up after that first evening. Even her father seemed to be developing a sense of humor and a relaxed air that astounded her.

The only problems were Brad and Charmaine. He sat at another table, claiming to need more elbow room, and hadn't looked at or spoken to Charmaine in the past three days.

Sonny was worried about them. While in Hawaii, she'd begun to accept the notion that her brother was in love with Shane's sister-in-law. When she'd considered herself near the brink of marriage, it had all seemed like a warm and cozy turn of events.

Now it was all falling apart. Her situation couldn't be helped, of course, but she wished she could do something for Brad. She had a feeling he and Charmaine would be good for each other if they could find a way to merge their very different life-styles.

The door to the banquet room slid open, and Shane walked in, pushing a dessert cart. Cheers rose as he approached the table.

Everyone attacked the cheesecakes and tortes like starving refugees from some gourmand society, and moved to clean tables to eat. Shane took a soda and pulled up a chair beside Sonny. She felt her heart begin to beat out of control. They hadn't talked seriously since that first night on the sofa. And in the intervening two days, he'd worked long hours and kept carefully to his side of the sofa bed.

That was what she wanted, Sonny told herself. This emotional distance would make things easier later, when the families were finally gone and she was free to leave. But right now, she wanted to know that it was hard for him, that it hurt him to be emotionally removed as much as it pained her.

But Shane didn't seem to be suffering. Since their last discussion, it was almost as though he finally saw things her way. She resented that—especially since her heart was breaking.

He seemed to be conducting the formative stages of this breakup like he did everything else—with the calm competence that was Shane Archer.

He looked over the table covered with hollowed-out pumpkins and nodded his approval. "You must be about half finished," he said.

When his gaze finally did settle on her, they were interested but remote. She found that hard to take when she was accustomed to always finding lust in his eyes, smoldering passion.

She stiffened a little and returned his neutral smile. "It's going very well. They're all grumbling, but helping a lot."

He grinned. "I guess this means you'll be too busy to finish our costumes by tomorrow night." That smile was the first sign she'd seen of their old connection. But when she looked into his eyes and tried to tap into it, it was gone. She felt as though she had fallen three stories to concrete.

"No such luck," she said briskly. "Denise, who works for me, is finishing them up with some help from her daughter, Dusty's teacher."

"The folks," he said seriously, "will feel out of place if we're in costume and they're not."

Sonny couldn't help a superior, and just as serious, tilt of her chin. "Since we're all going in our Eos dress, she's making simple Archer Federation robes for everyone."

Shane looked into her eyes and saw loneliness, despite the crowd of family surrounding her and the very female reaction of hurt feelings. He was pleased to see that his "retreat" was getting to her. He couldn't resist the urge to push it just a little harder.

"Are they all going to have the Archer Federation symbol?"

She looked perplexed. "What symbol?"

"The one in your sketch," he replied. "The rose crossed with the crescent moon." He took a sip of his soda.

"Oh." Sonny felt a light flush of color rush up her throat. She'd forgotten she'd done that. At the time it had been a whimsical personal commentary on Dusty's fantasy alliance of the Mission Master and the Sun Queen.

Now it was no longer whimsical. She remembered clearly drifting across the water, her body united with Shane's in the midnight waltz.

She looked into his eyes and thought she saw the same memory there—or maybe she simply wanted to. Because the next moment, he pushed away from the table, kissed her forehead with a very platonic "Gotta go," and left.

THE FEDERATION was in chaos. The Sun Queen had a tendency to burst into tears, the Mission Master spent most of his time preparing for the assembly and Butler Shaw and the Dragon Dame had declared war.

The Federation President and the Martian Marquesa spent most of their time preparing the squash bombs the Sun Queen had ordered as their last line of defense should negotiations fail. They were lined up in the cryogenic room, waiting.

Starby was concerned. If the assembly didn't insist on the alliance of the Sun Queen and the Mission Master, Eos would be weakened and the entire Federation put at risk.

Starby discussed the situation with the Federation President, who suggested he take it up with the MM.

SHANE STUDIED THE rose-and-crescent-moon doodles
he'd made on his desk blotter and thought he really
should go back to the suite. It was late, and he was tired.
But he was afraid that the sight of Sonny already in bed,
or warm and sleepy-eyed as she'd been last night when
he'd come home, would shake his resolve to stick to
tactics.

It had taken every ounce of willpower he had to ignore her baleful glances and park himself in front of the
television until she fell asleep on the sofa bed.

He'd never be able to do that a second time. He
glanced at the clock and decided to wait another hour.

At the sound of a knock on his door, he slid a file
folder over the doodles and called, "Come in!"

Josh's face peered around the door and way down
near Josh's waist, Dusty's face appeared.

"Hey." Shane smiled and held an arm out to his son.
Dusty ran into it and he hauled him into his lap. "What
are you doing up? It's almost eleven o'clock."

Josh remained in the doorway. "He really wanted to
talk to you. You don't mind?"

Shane shook his head. "Of course not. Everything all
right?"

Josh shrugged. "Well . . . you know."

He did. Everyone was aware that things were taut
between him and Sonny despite their attempts to pretend otherwise. He felt angry at her and at himself that
it was bothering Dusty.

"Yeah, I know."

"Want me to wait and take him back?" Josh asked.
"Or are you coming?"

"I'm coming. Thanks, Josh."

His father-in-law closed the door behind him, and Shane turned his attention to his son. He looked very grave.

"Federation business?" Shane guessed.

Dusty shook his head. "Real-life stuff."

Shane's concern deepened. This really was urgent. "Okay. Tell me."

"Did Sonny say no when you asked her to get married?"

Shane accepted his son's brutal thrust to the heart of the matter. "Yes, she did," he replied, but added quickly, "but, she didn't mean it."

Dusty's eyes questioned skeptically. "How do you know? Maybe she doesn't like me."

Shane laughed that off, confident he'd instilled enough self-esteem in his son that the question had been asked merely for the purpose of hearing him refute the suggestion.

"You know she loves you," Shane replied. "And I know she loves me."

"Then why doesn't she want to get married?"

That he had to put carefully. "Because... she thinks you and I are so used to being happy together, that it'll be hard for us to fit her in."

Dusty didn't get it. He couldn't blame him; he didn't either.

Dusty hooked an arm around his neck and gave him a man-to-man look. "I noticed something."

He almost hated to ask. "What?"

"You don't hug her and kiss her anymore like you always used to do. Maybe she thinks *you* don't love *her.*"

That was going to take some explaining. Shane leaned back in his chair, propped his feet up on his desk and settled Dusty against his chest.

"That's what's called a tactic," he explained. "It's like a plan."

"You're planning," Dusty asked in confusion, "to make her think you don't love her?"

"No. I just want to make her miss getting hugs and kisses so that she'll realize she does want to get married."

"What if it doesn't work?"

"It will."

"What if it doesn't?"

"Then I'm going to lock her in a closet and keep her with us anyway."

Dusty giggled, thinking he was kidding. "No, really. What if she still doesn't want to get married?"

There was that possibility, but he'd refused to think about it. Still, he had to prepare Dusty for that eventuality.

"Then, it'll just be you and me, and we do all right, don't we?"

"Yeah," Dusty said with enough reluctance to jab at Shane's self-confidence. "But with Sonny, we do really great." Dusty raised his head to look into Shane's face with smiling candor. "You like it better with her, too, don'cha?"

"I like it with her a lot," he said, then hugged the boy to him. "But I'd still think I was the luckiest dude in the whole world if all I had was you."

Dusty patted his shoulder like a comrade assuring him of his support should the worst occur.

SHANE LOOKED AT HIMSELF in the closet mirror. High-collared khaki shirt, jodhpur-style pants in the same color, knee-high boots borrowed from Regis, the door-man, and a cape of some red fabric that flowed behind him like something out of a Maxfield Parrish painting. He closed his eyes and wondered how far away he could get in ten minutes.

"Dad! You look cool!" Dusty's image appeared be-side his in the mirror, in a khaki jumpsuit and a jacket the same color as his cape. Each had the crossed rose and crescent moon embroidered on his sleeve.

"Shane! Whoa!" Charmaine walked into the suite and appeared on his other side in a flowing red gown trimmed in a shinier version of the khaki, the crest em-broidered at the base of a small V at the neck of her garment. She rested a hand on his shoulder. "It's not too late for us to run away together, you know."

He smiled at her reflection. "I am considering run-ning away, but I'd make better time by myself. I don't think I can bring myself to do this."

She swatted his shoulder. "Nonsense. Guests start arriving in ten minutes and you're supposed to be part of the welcome committee."

Dusty smiled at his aunt. "Nice gown, Aunt Char."

She held the skirt out and did a turn. "It's not a gown," she corrected imperiously, "it's a robe of of-fice."

Shane turned to her hopefully. "You could tell them I've been called to Tanzania for a hotel conference."

"Oh, that'll be convincing." Josh appeared behind him, wandering in through the door Charmaine had left open. He pushed Shane aside and surveyed himself in the mirror.

He wore the same robe of office as Charmaine. Nina trooped in behind him along with Robert and Joyce, all identically garbed, all marked with the signature crossed rose and crescent moon. Only Brad had the shirt, jodhpurs and cape that Shane wore.

Robert frowned at his son. "How come *you* get pants?"

Brad did a turn in front of the mirror. "Tighter butt, Pop." He gave Charmaine a challenging stare, then moved aside.

Robert took one look at his own reflection and turned away in disgust. "Well, *I'm* out of here."

Joyce caught his arm. "Not so fast, Abdul. You promised to do this for Sonny, Dusty and the hospital."

"I did *not* agree to wear a dress. And if you call me Abdul one more time..."

"It's not a dress," Dusty corrected, smiling up at him. "It's a robe of office. Come on, I'll show you where to go."

Robert and Dusty, hand in hand, led the way from the room. Shane watched his in-laws follow the three Winslows. Charmaine hung back.

"Where's Sonny?" she asked.

"Last-minute details in the dining room," he replied. "Aren't you going down?" He gave her a knowing look. "Or are you afraid to admit to Brad that you're changing your mind about living on a base?"

Charmaine wandered out to the living room. "Daddy would give him a good job."

"He has a job," Shane pointed out. "One that he likes and is good at."

"Well, I'm good at mine. And I couldn't do it at a military base."

"Maybe it's time for a career change." He followed her doggedly to the door, and put a restraining hand to it when she would have escaped him. "All you've ever wanted was a man you could love."

She gave him a look from confused green eyes that told him some little part of her would always love him. "That man's in love with Little Mary Sunshine."

"Brad's better for you than I would be," Shane said. "Tell him you love him, Char. The admission is very liberating."

She gave him a quick hug, and reached for the doorknob. Then she turned back to him in concern. "Are you and Sunshine going to be okay?"

He wished he had the answer to that one. "Eventually."

She frowned. "That's not very reassuring."

"At the moment," he said, "it's the best I've got." He covered her hand to pull the door open. "I have to go."

"Right," she said. "See you in a bit. I want to check my makeup."

SONNY PULLED ON the lamé gown, studiously avoiding her reflection. She didn't want to see the Sun Queen. She didn't even want to think her name. All she wanted to do was get this evening over with, take her family to the airport and move back to her quiet, comfortable little place on the bay.

She ignored the lonely prospect that presented and told herself bracingly that it was the best solution. Shane seemed to think so, too. He'd been more and more remote from her since they'd come home, and she guessed he was finally realizing she'd been right. He and Dusty weren't ready for a new woman in their lives.

Even if the woman was beginning to believe she was ready to be there.

Sonny attached a gauzy, gold-speckled cape over the dress, thinking Denise and Terri had gone a little wild in finishing her costume. She probably looked like a lightning rod from a Hobbit book.

She groaned when she found a little gold crown in the bottom of the bag, and was forced to look in the mirror to put it on.

What she saw horrified her. She *did* look like some poor little victim of unrequited love—eyes large and sad, face pale, mouth vulnerable. Her eyes fell on the crossed rose and crescent moon appliquéd at the base of the gown's V-neck and they quickly filled with tears.

She covered the crest with one hand, went to get a tissue, freshened her makeup without looking in the mirror, then saw the time and ran out of the suite. She met Charmaine in the hallway.

Charmaine gave her a quick once-over and Sonny braced herself for a sophisticated jab at her appearance. Instead, Charmaine smiled reluctantly. "You look beautiful," she said.

As Sonny stared at her in shock, Charmaine took her arm. "Come on. We'd better hurry. They're backed up at the passenger elevators. A lot of the guests are staying the night. We'll make better time on the service elevator."

The doors parted the instant they pressed the Down button. They stepped on and Charmaine pushed the main floor button, then settled into the corner. Sonny leaned back against the railing.

"I think you'd be happy with my brother," Sonny said without preamble. "You should think twice be-

fore you decide you can't live on a base." Another
thought occurred to her and she added it, almost sur-
prising herself. "I remember a lot of happy times, a
strong sense of mutual support among the families
there."

Charmaine smiled in self-deprecation. "But they
wouldn't let me be queen. And I'm pretty used to that."

Sonny blinked. "You mean you'd pass up happiness
because you can't be in charge?"

Charmaine considered that a moment and finally
nodded without apology. "Yes." Her gaze focused
challengingly on Sonny. "Why are you passing it up?"

Sonny had just a moment to be shocked by the question before the elevator jerked to a stop and the lights
went out.

"Damn it!" Charmaine said. "They're supposed to
have fixed this thing."

Sonny concentrated on remaining calm. She didn't
like elevators. She particularly didn't like ones that got
stuck.

She breathed a quick prayer. "Please. Don't let the
drama of my relationship with Shane end with my broken body on the elevator floor."

She reached to the panel for the phone. A cheerful
voice picked up. "Mr. Busby," she said. "This is Sonny
Winslow. Mrs. Prelotsky and I are stuck in the service
elevator."

There was a round oath on the other end of the line.
"Hold tight. I'll be right there."

"Mr. Busby will be right here," Sonny reported to
Charmaine while replacing the phone. She screamed
when the car dropped another foot. She heard a thud
and a sharp cry from her companion.

"Charmaine?" she asked, groping in the dark.

"Down here." Charmaine's voice came wryly from the murky shadows. "I think I sprained my ankle."

Sonny bumped into her, then felt her way down beside her. Charmaine laughed as Sonny touched her already swelling ankle. "If you were Brad," she said, "this could have been fun."

Sonny tried to remember her first-aid class. Ice. Ace bandage. Elevation. One out of three wasn't bad. She moved to sit in front of Charmaine and gently lifted her foot onto her own lap. "There," she said, as though taking that small action had put her back in control of the situation. "Mr. Busby should be here any time. He's very efficient. He once got Dusty out of a fishbowl."

Sonny heard the pause and closed her eyes.

"Are you babbling?" Charmaine asked. "Or was my nephew truly in a fishbowl?"

"It's a long story," Sonny replied, leaning backward on her elbows, trying to stretch suddenly tight muscles. If the elevator wouldn't slip anymore, she was sure she could deal with this.

"We might be here a while," Charmaine said. "Go ahead and tell me."

Sonny did.

Charmaine laughed. "Little devil. He's going to be really crushed if you and Shane don't work it out."

Sonny opened her mouth to reply, but didn't begin to know how to explain. Then, to her utter and complete surprise, Charmaine said gently, "It's Allie, isn't it?"

Silence rang again, then Sonny replied candidly, "Yes, it is. Well, at least partly." She related the story of Dusty and the walk that led them to the house in which he'd spent the first few years of his life. "He was very upset, then Shane became upset. I was just beginning to think I could fit in, then I saw how strong a force Allie still is in their lives, and then I wasn't so sure anymore.''

Charmaine sighed. ''Join the club, Sunshine. I was always in Allie's shadow—not because she tried to put me there, but because she *was* wonderful. And she got a lot of the things I wanted.''

''Shane?''

''Well, first Jason Goodman, then Nathan Andover, then Javier Delgado. Then Shane.''

''Delgado was your first husband?''

''Yes. And the first man who'd ever come to our home who paid attention to me before he noticed Allie.'' Her voice took on a tone of acceptance. ''I didn't realize at the time that it was because I had already come into my trust fund at twenty-five. Apparently he wanted to restore his Castillian castle with my bucks.'' She sighed. ''Prelotsky wanted my money, too, but he, at least, was honest about it. I married him because I thought I could make him love me for me.'' She laughed scornfully. ''That was silly.''

Sonny patted Charmaine's good foot consolingly. ''Don't be like that. I think you're pretty remarkable. I wish I had your courage. That's part of what appealed to Brad.''

''Really?'' Her voice was ingenuously breathy in the darkness.

''That and your body. He told me he thought you had everything.''

''You're just saying that.''

''I'm not. I promise.''

There was silence for another moment, then Charmaine said thoughtfully, ''The worst thing about Allie was that you couldn't hate her because she truly was one of the world's good people. I had a hard time adjusting to that."

"But you did?"

"As best I could. Ah!" There were eerie creaks and groans outside the car. Sonny tried not to think about cables fraying and snapping.

"I wish Brad was here," Charmaine said, her tone grudging but wistful. "The big bully makes me feel safe."

Sonny nodded understanding in the darkness, resisting the urge to shout for Shane at the top of her lungs.

Chapter Fourteen

"So, where are they?" Brad asked Shane as the costume parade began.

Shane had just called the suite and gotten no answer. He frowned, uncertain. It might be like Charmaine to stay away from the festivities in a pout because she was angry with Brad, but it wasn't like Sonny to do that. Particularly since she knew how eager Dusty was to march with her.

"Did you find her, Dad?" Dusty ran up to ask anxiously. "We're supposed to walk together."

Shane ruffled his hair. "Why don't you go with Grandma and Grandpa and the Winslows? Brad and I are going to get her and Aunt—"

Shane's beeper interrupted him. He reached for his jacket pocket and was frustrated to find his hand entangled in his cape. He said something he usually didn't say in front of Dusty and reached around to his hip pocket for his portable phone.

"It's Busby, boss," the maintenance man's voice said. "Service elevator's stuck, and your lady's on it with Mrs. Prelotsky. I've got a call into the elevator company, but he's coming from Portland. The ladies are safe, but do we want to leave them in there for two hours if we can get them out with a ladder?''

Shane looked into Brad's eyes and saw the same concern he felt. ''Is the emergency brake engaged?''

''Yep. First thing I checked.''

''Where are you?''

''On three.''

''I'll be right there.''

Shane looked around for Josh, and waved a hand when he spotted him. Josh worked his way across the room, smiling, then frowned when he saw the expression on Shane's face. Shane explained about Charmaine and Sonny. ''They're fine,'' he assured him quickly. ''And the emergency brake's in place. Will you keep an eye on Dusty? Brad and I are going to get them out.''

''Of course. But won't you need help?''

''Busby has a few men with him.''

''But, Dad. I want to—''

Shane silenced Dusty's protest with a quick hug. ''The less time I argue with you, the sooner I can get her out, okay?''

''No!'' Dusty said, his mouth quivering as Shane and Brad left at a run.

They found the doors open on three, and directed two members of his crew in the placement of a ladder atop the car, which was stopped a good eight feet below the floor. They'd hung an emergency light from one of the cables.

Busby frowned at him. ''Just an electrical failure, I think.'' Then his eyes went over their costumes and he looked blandly into Shane's face. ''Came dressed for rescue work, did you?''

"Funny, Buzz," Shane said. The men had removed the ceiling panel and one knelt to look through the opening.

"You ladies okay?" he called down.

"I'm fine." Shane recognized Sonny's voice. "But Charmaine has a sprained ankle."

"The problem is going to be getting them up through the opening." Busby picked up the coil of rope he'd placed on the floor beside him. "Particularly if Mrs. Prelotsky has a bad foot."

"You won't need the rope," Shane said, pulling off the cape and tossing it aside. He grinned at Brad. "This can't be that different from the obstacle course."

Brad tore his cape off and rolled up his sleeves. "You're leaner," he said. "You go in and send them up to me."

"Right." Busby's crew overheard their intentions and held the ladder steady. Disregarding the dark, depthless space between the car and the wall of the building, Shane took a leap to the ladder and landed squarely several steps from the top.

"There's no foot room at the bottom, Mr. Archer," one of the coveralled men said. "Step to the side of the ladder."

Shane did as the man suggested and landed nimbly on top of the car. It felt gritty and tacky to the soles of his boots—or, rather, Regis's boots.

"Shane?" Sonny's voice came with flattering hopefulness from inside the hole. "Is that you?"

The crew had dropped another light into the car, and she shined it up into his face. He squinted against it and got down on one knee to look in on them.

"Sorry," she said, quickly lowering the beam of light to the floor.

"It's all right. Brad's here. The elevator company's on the way, but they might be a while, so we're going to pull you out."

"If Brad's up there," Charmaine said, "I'd just as soon stay here."

Brad landed lightly beside Shane. "Fine," he said loudly enough to be heard inside the car. "We'll bring Sonny up, then seal the car closed with Charmaine inside and cancel the service call."

"Rat!" Charmaine shouted up at him.

"Brat!" Brad shouted down.

"Good Lord!" Sonny exclaimed, holding the light away from the hole and looking up at her brother. "Just a few minutes ago she was wishing you were here because you make her feel safe. This perversity is just for show."

"Traitor," Charmaine whispered. Then she called up to Shane, "And Sunshine told me she doesn't want to face her life without you." She made a face at Sonny. "So there."

Shane and Brad looked at each other across the hole. Then Shane glanced up at Busby now lying on his stomach and hanging over the edge.

"You're sure this car isn't going anywhere?"

"Positive. Emergency brake's in place."

Shane and Brad exchanged a smile, then sat down as though prepared to proceed at their leisure.

Sonny frowned up at him. "What's happening?"

"Well..." Shane spoke slowly, as though completely relaxed. "It occurs to us that we could use this to our advantage."

She peered up at him warily. "How?"

"Will you marry me?" he asked.

She groaned frustratedly. "Shane..."

"Sonny. I'm not coming in for you until I have an answer."

"I gave you an answer."

"It wasn't the one I want."

Sonny pointed a threatening finger. "Archer, if you don't get us out of this black box this minute, I'll—"

"You know." Charmaine stopped her tirade with a contemplative tone of voice. "Our conversation was interrupted when the maintenance crew arrived. I didn't tell you that I finally came to the conclusion that whatever I can or can't do has nothing to do with anyone else. I don't have to measure up to anyone or anything, except what I want of myself. So think about it. Do you want to be without Shane—" she raised her head to shout through the hole "—creep that he is!" then lowered it again to go on. "Or do you want to just do the best you can and know that that's all anybody can ask of you?"

Sonny turned on Charmaine. "What's with you? I thought we were in this together?"

"My ankle hurts like hell," Charmaine replied, "and I'm having a personal spiritual awakening. You can't plan these things."

"Does that mean you're willing to live on a base after all?" Brad asked.

"Can I decorate from Bloomingdale's?"

"Who's that?"

Charmaine put a hand over her eyes and groaned. Then she rested her head against the elevator wall and shouted up to him, "Yes, I will marry you. Yes, I will live on a base. But I can't promise that I'll ever be any different."

"I don't recall asking that," Brad said, then leaned over the hole and blew her a kiss. "Go get her, Shane."

Sonny stepped to the opposite side of the car as Shane's lower body dropped through the hole, long legs in shiny boots and neat hips in jodhpurs hanging suspended for one moment before he dropped to the carpeted floor.

His dark eyes met Sonny's for one brief, censorious moment, then he turned to Charmaine. He knelt beside her and put a comforting hand to her cheek. "How you doing, Char?"

She smiled. "Great. This has been fun, but I'm ready to get out of here. How are we going to do this?"

"You're going to climb onto my shoulders," he said, "and Brad's going to pull you through."

She looked doubtful. "I think I'm a little too Rubenesque for that to work."

Shane shook his head at her and grinned. "You've got to stop thinking of the men in your life as people to play with, and realize that they have talents they can share with you—and I know this is an alien idea—even a few things they can teach you."

Charmaine looked indignant for a moment, then she sighed and admitted with a trace of embarrassment, "I just don't want to hurt you."

"That won't happen." He beckoned to Sonny to help him get Charmaine onto his shoulders. "Brad's a martial arts instructor, and I delivered heavy appliances part-time in college."

"Heavy ap—! Shane Archer, you're...ah!" Charmaine swatted the top of Shane's head as he first balanced her on his shoulders and then, with the elevator railing to steady him, stood easily.

Sonny trailed behind, ready to help, as Shane moved carefully to stand under the hole. "Raise your hands, Char," he said. "And see if Brad can reach you."

Charmaine raised one hand, clutching Shane's hair with the other. Brad caught her wrist easily.

"Got her," Brad said triumphantly. "Give me your other hand, darlin'."

Sonny watched with a mixture of astonishment, pride and simple pleasure as her brother pulled and Charmaine disappeared through the elevator's ceiling, smiling.

"All *right!*" She applauded.

There was a brief moment of squeals, groans and kisses, then the sounds of Charmaine being helped up the ladder and onto the floor. Sonny thought she heard her father's voice and Joshua's.

"She's all right," Brad shouted down. "You get the answer you want Shane, or shall I pull *you* up and seal the car?"

Shane turned to Sonny, hands lightly on his hips, his eyes grave and unyielding. "What's it to be?"

Sonny folded her arms and studied her shoes. "Maybe you'd better seal the car. You've been behaving as though you wouldn't mind being rid of me."

Shane smiled at the top of her head and shifted his weight. "That must be why I asked you to marry me."

He quickly dropped the smile when she looked up at him.

"You've been very distant," she accused quietly. "As though you might be having second thoughts."

"You told me we were breaking up," he said with all innocence. "That you were moving out as soon as—"

"Just a few days ago," she interrupted in an injured tone, "you were telling me you'd never let me go."

He couldn't withhold the grin any longer. "I haven't, have I?"

"No, but you—" She stopped midsentence, seeing the self-congratulatory look in his eyes. "You mean," she asked ominously, stepping to within an inch of him, her attitude lethal, "that you made me feel this way deliberately?"

He stood his ground. "How *do* you feel?"

"Adrift!" she replied in obvious distress. "Abandoned. Alone!" She punctuated the last with a punch to his arm. "And you did it on purpose!"

He accepted her accusation with an unrepentant nod. "To illustrate a point. You need me. You love me."

"Then, how could you be so—?"

"I need *you.*" He jabbed an index finger into her shoulder. She felt as though it had been hit with a quarter-inch drill bit. "I love *you.* And it wasn't easy, believe me. My libido is less stable at the moment than nitroglycerine, so will you give me a 'yes' on the marriage question so we can get the hell out of here?"

"I love you more than anything," she admitted. "And I know you love me. I'd just like to know for certain that it'll be all right for Dusty."

Shane spread his arms in a gesture of helplessness. "If you love me and I love you, I don't see how it couldn't be. But I can't make promises I can't personally deliver. All I can guarantee is that whatever happens, you won't have to face it alone."

Sonny wrapped her arms around him, knowing that was as airtight a warranty as life had to offer.

"Yes," she whispered. "I'll marry you."

Through the hole they heard various voices. "What was that?" "What'd she say?"

"I said yes!" she shouted, bursting into laughter as Shane lifted her into his arms and kissed the base of her throat.

"Could you do that later?" Brad asked. "I'm hanging here like Tarzan without the vine."

Shane took firm hold of the backs of Sonny's thighs and pushed her upward. She raised both hands and felt her brother swing her smoothly up onto the top of the car.

There were laughter and cheers from above her head where her father, Josh, Busby and Charmaine waited. She made a quick trip up the ladder, then it was a simple but long step into her father's arms.

As he reached for her, Josh leaning out to lend him support, she had a sudden flash of memory. She saw herself as a child, riding her father's shoulders, of hanging upside down and laughing giddily while he held her ankles, of having gone too high on the monkey bars and being plucked down by strong, sure hands. She remembered that he hadn't dropped her once. She leapt into his arms.

He held her tightly to him for a moment, then put her on her feet. He kissed her forehead and held her to him while they waited for Brad to pull Shane up.

In a moment everyone was safe in the hallway, and Busby was posting caution tape across the doors.

"I want to talk to the elevator serviceman when he gets here," Shane said, his eyes dark with purpose.

"Right." Busby rounded up his crew and ladder and headed for the stairs.

Brad swung Charmaine into his arms and looked deeply into her eyes. "I'm going to make you happy," he said, his tone just a shade defensive.

Charmaine looped her arms around his neck and leaned her head on his shoulder with a contented sigh. "I don't doubt it for a minute."

"There's a doctor waiting in her suite to look at that ankle," Josh said. He turned to Shane and Sonny with a frown. "And maybe we'd better hurry back. Nina and Joyce took Dusty to your suite. He was pretty hysterical about Sonny."

"Oh, no." Sonny took off at a run.

Dusty flew into her arms the moment she opened the door. Nina, who'd been sitting on the sofa with him, reached over the child to put a hand to Sonny's face.

"Thank God!" she said. "We told him over and over that you were safe. I let him talk to Mr. Busby on his cell phone. But he wouldn't believe anyone until he saw you himself."

Sonny lifted him onto her hip and carried him back to the sofa. He clung to her still sobbing.

"I thought...you would die," he said between gulps for air.

"Hey." Shane sat beside Sonny and stroked his son's hair. "I told you I was going to get her."

Dusty raised his head from Sonny's shoulder, his eyes still wide with fear, his mouth curved downward and trembling. "Even you can't fix everything," he said tearfully. "'Member?"

Shane understood suddenly where this was going, and what had caused this almost hysterical distress. Before he could explain to Dusty that this situation had been very different from his mother's, Sonny said brightly, trying to cheer him, "It was just a stuck elevator, Dusty."

"Mom went on an elevator," Dusty said, his voice small and grave, "and she never came back. And Dad couldn't do anything about it because sometimes ... he just can't. The things God does are bigger than him," Dusty added as though quoting a truism he'd been forced to accept. "And that's the way it is. Sometimes God takes really great people early 'cause He likes to have them with Him." He leaned against her again and held her tightly. "I thought He wanted you, too."

Something scraped at Sonny right in the center of her heart. She held him to her as tears streamed down her face. Shane wrapped his arms around both of them.

"But that was a hospital, Dusty," she said after a moment, pulling the child away from her and smiling into his face, "and your mom was sick. I'm fine, and all that happened this time was that an elevator got stuck. Your father and Brad rescued me and Aunt Char."

Dusty sniffed, fear and old memories receding in the light of new fascination. "They did? How?"

Sonny related the tale as dramatically as possible.

"And guess what she promised before I pulled her out?" Shane asked.

"What?" Dusty asked.

"That she'll marry me."

"Cool!" Dusty said with such sincerity Sonny couldn't doubt that he was pleased. The fear she saw in his eyes this evening surfaced because of the way he'd lost his mother, but the concern had been all for her, Sonny.

"Tomorrow," Sonny said, kissing his cheek, "we'll go somewhere, just you and me and your dad, and plan the wedding, okay?"

"Okay." She was happy to see he was clear-eyed again and smiling.

Shane, Sonny and Dusty looked up to see that the Bedfords and the Winslows still hovered, watching them anxiously. Nina and Joyce crumpled tissues to their noses, and Josh and Robert appeared stoic.

"The Federation Assembly!" Dusty said suddenly, leaping to the floor. Then he turned to his father and said, "I mean...the Halloween party. We have to hurry!"

"Right!" The two older couples turned toward the door, collided, then walked around one another, looking, in their matching robes, a little like a dance troupe that needed more rehearsal. Robert held the door for the ladies.

"Josh, wait," Shane called.

Josh stopped at the door and turned. "Yes?"

Shane took Dusty's hand and pulled him between his knees, arms looped loosely around him.

"The Federation stuff," he said to Dusty. "You know it isn't really real, don't you?"

Dusty leaned trustingly against him and nodded without hesitation. "Yeah. But sometimes it's more fun to make believe it's real, 'cause then I can make stuff happen the way I want instead of having to have it the way it is. You know?"

Shane hugged him, thinking he couldn't offer a better or more sane reason for indulging in a fantasy life. "Yes. I know."

Dusty grinned at Sonny. "Only now, the real stuff's okay. Can we go? We're gonna miss *all* the party."

Shane walked Dusty to Josh. "You go down with Grandpa, so I can talk to Sonny for a few minutes, okay? Do you mind, Josh?"

Josh took the boy's hand. "Of course not. But don't be too long. Word's out the mayor's expecting to see *you* in costume before he makes his donation."

Shane nodded fatalistically. "I'll be there. Give us ten minutes."

"You got it."

When they were gone, Shane turned to Sonny and held out his hand. "Come on."

"Where?" she asked, going to him. "You're not stalling, are you, just because you look a little like a military superhero?" She glanced at the back of him with a seductive little growl. "You can wear riding britches all the time when we're alone. You have the cutest—"

He stopped her in the doorway with a hard, firm kiss. When he raised his head his eyes were filled with happiness and laughter. The sight warmed her to the soles of her feet. He reached to the chair for the red cape someone had retrieved for him.

"And you," he said, his gaze traveling over the gold outfit that had suffered remarkably little considering her experience, "look like very cleverly shaped gold bullion."

She stood on tiptoe to nip at his lip. "Thank you for not saying chicken bouillon."

He laughed, caught her hand, and ran with her to the doorway that led to the roof.

"The last time we did this," she said, her voice and their footsteps echoing hollowly, "you were trying to prove to me that you're romantic. What is it this time?"

The autumn wind had a suggestion of winter in it as he led her across the dark rooftop to the railing with its globular lights. There were no freighters tonight, just one lone fishing boat, running lights bright in the darkness, as it glided across the water it illuminated.

Shane turned her to him, wrapped her in his cape, and looked earnestly into her eyes. "I'm going to take a lifetime to prove it," he said, "but I wanted a private place to tell you how much I love you, because this is probably the last intimate moment we'll have together for some time. Between our son, our families and our staff, we'll hardly have a thought to call our own."

"They care," Sonny said, curling her arms between them and leaning into him. She felt the most delicious, deep-down sense of well-being.

"They snoop," he said, wrapping his arms around her.

She laughed softly. "I think that's dear. Even my father thinks you're special. He even seems to like me. I think retirement has mellowed him."

"And maybe you've learned a few things."

She looked up into his eyes, sure hers reflected the adoration she felt for him. "Thanks for not giving up on me."

"I had no choice," he replied. "I couldn't imagine life without you." His glance went up and beyond her, and he smiled suddenly. "Did you notice the moon?"

She didn't even turn. "When I can look at you?" she asked.

He rewarded her with a kiss, then physically turned her, wrapping his arms around her and holding her tightly against him. Sonny looked up and gasped. It was crescent-shaped and tilted slightly backward.

"That's our 'sailing to Eos' moon," he whispered as he kissed her temple.

She leaned back against him and sighed, deliriously happy. "We're home."

STARBY WATCHED the dancing with Butler Shaw and the Dragon Dame. They were confined to the chairs along the side because of the injury the Dame had acquired during her daring escape from the Cave Conqueror.

The lights were low and the music soft, and he was pleased to observe the fruits of the assembly's labors.

Not only had the Sun Queen and the Dame been rescued, but peace had been securely established among the Federation's warring factions.

Everywhere he turned, interplanetary representatives embraced one another. The Federation President and the Martian Marquesa looked into each other's eyes and laughed, and the other representatives from the Flowership stopped dancing to talk with them.

But it was the Sun Queen and the Mission Master who claimed his attention. They held each other tightly, she wrapped in his cape, he gazing into her eyes with an expression Starby had begun to recognize as love. It was different from the look the MM gave him because they were men and comrades, but it had the same quality of devotion that always made him believe that all was well.

Starby went to the window and looked out, watching for the sex bird. He could use an assistant, now that the Federation staff had grown. He'd speak to the MM about it in the morning.

Once in a while, there's a story so special, a story so unusual, that your pulse races, your blood rushes. We call this

Borrowed Time is one such book.

Kathleen Welles receives a most unusual offer: to sell one past day in her life for a million dollars! What she didn't realize was that she'd be transported back in time, to the very day she'd sold—the day she lost her true love, Zachary Forest. Can she right her wrongs and reclaim the man she loves in a mere twenty-four hours?

#574 BORROWED TIME
by
Cassie Miles

Available in March, wherever Harlequin books are sold.
Watch for more Heartbeat stories, coming your way soon!

HEART5

Take 4 bestselling love stories FREE

Plus get a FREE surprise gift!

Special Limited-time Offer

Mail to Harlequin Reader Service®

3010 Walden Avenue
P.O. Box 1867
Buffalo, N.Y. 14269-1867

YES! Please send me 4 free Harlequin American Romance® novels and my free surprise gift. Then send me 4 brand-new novels every month, which I will receive months before they appear in bookstores. Bill me at the low price of $2.89 each plus 25¢ delivery and applicable sales tax, if any.* That's the complete price and a savings of over 10% off the cover prices—quite a bargain! I understand that accepting the books and gift places me under no obligation ever to buy any books. I can always return a shipment and cancel at any time. Even if I never buy another book from Harlequin, the 4 free books and the surprise gift are mine to keep forever.

154 BPA ANRL

Name	(PLEASE PRINT)	
Address		Apt. No.
City	State	Zip

This offer is limited to one order per household and not valid to present Harlequin American Romance® subscribers. *Terms and prices are subject to change without notice. Sales tax applicable in N.Y.

UAM-295   ©1990 Harlequin Enterprises Limited

HARLEQUIN

AMERICAN ◆ ROMANCE®

He's at home in denim; she's bathed in diamonds...
Her tastes run to peanut butter; his to pâté...
They're bound to be together...

for Richer, for Poorer

We're delighted to bring you more of the kinds of stories you love,
in FOR RICHER, FOR POORER—a miniseries in which lovers
are drawn together by passion...but separated by price!

Next month, look for

#575 RYAN'S BRIDE
Julie Kistler

Don't miss any of the FOR RICHER, FOR POORER
books, coming to you in the months ahead—
only from American Romance!

RICHER-2

IS BRINGING
YOU A BABY BOOM!

NEW ARRIVALS

We're expecting! This spring, from March through May, three very special Harlequin American Romance authors invite you to read about three equally special heroines—all of whom are on a nine-month adventure! We expect each soon-to-be mom will find the man of her dreams—and a daddy in the bargain!

So don't miss the first of these titles:

#576 BABY MAKES NINE
by Vivian Leiber
March 1995

Look for the New Arrivals logo—and please help us welcome our new arrivals!

NA-G

On the most romantic day of the year—capture the thrill of falling in love all over again—with

Harlequin's

Bachelors

They're three sexy and *very single* men who run very special personal ads to find the women of their fantasies by Valentine's Day. These exciting, passion-filled stories are written by bestselling Harlequin authors.

Your Heart's Desire by Elise Title
Mr. Romance by Pamela Bauer
Sleepless in St. Louis by Tiffany White

Be sure not to miss Harlequin's Valentine Bachelors, available in February wherever Harlequin books are sold.

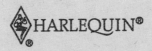

VB

Harlequin invites you to the most
romantic wedding of the season.

Rope the cowboy of your dreams in
Marry Me, Cowboy!

A collection of 4 brand-new stories,
celebrating weddings, written by:

New York Times bestselling author

JANET DAILEY

and favorite authors

Margaret Way
Anne McAllister
Susan Fox

Be sure not to miss Marry Me, Cowboy!
coming this April

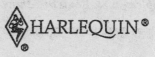 HARLEQUIN®

MMC

Bestselling Author

JoAnn Ross

Delivers a story so exciting, so thrilling, it'll have you begging for more....

Legacy of Lies

From the haute couture world of Parisian fashion to the glittering lights of Hollywood, Alexandra Lyons will find fame, fortune and love. But desire and scandal will shatter her life unless she can uncover her legacy of lies.

Look for it at your favorite retail outlet this February.

MIRA **The brightest star in women's fiction**   MJRLOL

HARLEQUIN®

Don't miss these Harlequin favorites by some of our most distinguished authors!
And now, you can receive a discount by ordering two or more titles!

HT#25577	WILD LIKE THE WIND by Janice Kaiser	$2.99	☐
HT#25589	THE RETURN OF CAINE O'HALLORAN by JoAnn Ross	$2.99	☐
HP#11626	THE SEDUCTION STAKES by Lindsay Armstrong	$2.99	☐
HP#11647	GIVE A MAN A BAD NAME by Roberta Leigh	$2.99	☐
HR#03293	THE MAN WHO CAME FOR CHRISTMAS by Bethany Campbell	$2.89	☐
HR#03308	RELATIVE VALUES by Jessica Steele	$2.89	☐
SR#70589	CANDY KISSES by Muriel Jensen	$3.50	☐
SR#70598	WEDDING INVITATION by Marisa Carroll	$3.50 U.S. $3.99 CAN.	☐
HI#22230	CACHE POOR by Margaret St. George	$2.99	☐
HAR#16515	NO ROOM AT THE INN by Linda Randall Wisdom	$3.50	☐
HAR#16520	THE ADVENTURESS by M.J. Rodgers	$3.50	☐
HS#28795	PIECES OF SKY by Marianne Willman	$3.99	☐
HS#28824	A WARRIOR'S WAY by Margaret Moore	$3.99 U.S. $4.50 CAN.	☐

(limited quantities available on certain titles)

	AMOUNT	$
DEDUCT:	**10% DISCOUNT FOR 2+ BOOKS**	$
ADD:	**POSTAGE & HANDLING** ($1.00 for one book, 50¢ for each additional)	$
	APPLICABLE TAXES*	$
	TOTAL PAYABLE	$
	(check or money order—please do not send cash)	

To order, complete this form and send it, along with a check or money order for the total above, payable to Harlequin Books, to: **In the U.S.:** 3010 Walden Avenue, P.O. Box 9047, Buffalo, NY 14269-9047; **In Canada:** P.O. Box 613, Fort Erie, Ontario, L2A 5X3.

Name:_____

Address: _____ City:_____

State/Prov.:_____ Zip/Postal Code: _____

*New York residents remit applicable sales taxes.
Canadian residents remit applicable GST and provincial taxes.

HBACK-JM2